The
Starr Baby
Case

The Starr Baby Case

A Simon Sol Dorsey Novel

Johnny Gunn

NEW PULP PRESS

Published by New Pulp Press, LLC, 926 Truman Avenue, Key West, Florida 33040, USA.

For information contact:
Publisher@NewPulpPress.com

ISBN-13: 978-1945734137 (New Pulp Press)
ISBN-10: 1945734132

Printed in the United States of America
Visit us on the web at www.newpulppress.com

The
Starr Baby
Case

1.

I' m in trouble, Sol. I got nowhere else to turn."
Simon Sol Dorsey listened to the recording again,
shaking his big, square head. *I know I've heard that
sweet little voice, but I'll be damned if I can put it to a
face or a pair of boobs.* Dorsey was one of the best PIs
on the west coast, hired by some police agencies to
help with high profile crimes, disdained by others,
well, because he was Simon Sol Dorsey. He was silly-
ass drunk when he stumbled into his Ocean View
Drive apartment half an hour ago, which made it
about nine in the morning. "I love Friday night," he
said for the third time, trying to rewind the answer
machine tape.

"Idiot, this is my new answer machine, all digital
or something. No tape to rewind, just play. Like that,
see?" and he giggled again. A six-foot-two, two
hundred thirty pounder giggling drunk was an
interesting sight that few have seen. Put blazing
emerald green eyes, a square jaw, and a nose that had
been splashed flat more than once, and you would be
looking at Sol Dorsey.

Dorsey would best be described as a throwback to
the twenties or thirties. The big man grew up on pulp
crime magazines, thought once about being a cop but
changed his mind as soon as he heard about things
like Miranda and perp's rights. "They got no rights.
Bang a head, get an answer," was a continuing
philosophy, which only became an issue when he
found himself working for the cops.

1

It would be easy to say the man didn't get along with the twenty-first century with one exception, the world of computers. He had a hard time making his cell phone work, but could write computer programs, Simple four-digit home alarm systems throw him curves, low and inside, yet Simon Sol Dorsey fully understood the most complicated computer soft-ware, either on the market, or self-written. Sol Dorsey was an enigma writ large.

He topped out at about six-two when he was still a teenager, and that depended on the boots he was in, and fought his weight with no enthusiasm. "Being in good physical condition is important," he said once. "I keep as svelte as I am by lifting weights," and he howled with laughter. His weights came in pint size glasses and were filled with cold beer. Dorsey wore his hair in a flat-top straight out of the fifties, felt more comfortable in jeans, T-shirt, and black leather jacket than suit and tie, and believed strongly that all women should be treated as ladies all the time, regardless of how they made their money.

The section of town that he either hated or loved, depending on whether he was making money from there or spending money because it was there, was Franklyn Street, just two blocks from the commercial docks. A street filled with saloons on both sides. The spaces between the booze palaces were either tattoo parlors or pawnshops, and all the upstairs rooms were rented by the half-hour.

There wasn't a working girl within fifty miles of the city that didn't love Simon Sol Dorsey, and he felt the same way about them. He was their favorite uncle, but one that came with special privileges.

~ ~ ~

He found the coffee pot, still had some in it from, when, two days ago? He put it on the stove anyway and plopped into a kitchen chair, pulled a big forty-five revolver out of his shoulder holster, pulled a neat little nine millimeter semi-auto from the inside of his left boot, slipped a knife with a seven inch fixed blade from the sheath on his left side, and punched the recorder again.

"Okay, lady," he said, "I give up." He poured the last of the acidic coffee, laced it with the last of the rotgut whiskey, and stared at the machine. "Oh, yeah," he mumbled, giggled a little bit, and hit the button that said, re-dial. "Damn, I'm one smart sumbitch today," and waited for someone to answer.

"Sol, Sol, thank you for calling. I'm so scared, please help." Before he could say anything he heard two quick gunshots, some heavy footsteps, and a gruff voice said, "Keep out of this Dorsey if you know what's good for you," and the line went dead.

"Sober-up time," Dorsey snarled, quickly made a pot of strong coffee and went to work to find out who the woman was. When he hit re-dial he hadn't looked for a number to be displayed, and this time he did, jotted it down quickly, and opened his computer, found his address book, and queried that number.

"Whatdya mean it ain't there?" he said. "She called me by name, knows me well enough to know I would respond to a call for help, but I have never called her or know her well enough to put her in my little black book?" Coffee boiled over and he poured some, turned the heat down, and sat back down. "A little reverse help here," he muttered, stroking some keys on the computer, watching the little wheel spin for a minute, and then the name Monica P. Fetterman splashed onto the screen.

Dorsey was known far and wide as one who spent more time talking to himself than he did to real people, and he was proving it this morning. "We sure got a long way there. Who the hell is Monica P. Fetterman, or maybe, who was ole Monica?" He called the name up on Google and there she was, Starr Baby, being arrested by the local dicks last year in a raid on a convention of men wearing animal horns on their hats.

"So that's your name," he muttered. A few more minutes on the computer, found the address where the telephone service was, and Dorsey made a quick phone call before heading out the door. "Stupid sumbitch," he snarled, went back in and shut off the stove. "I'll burn myself right out of here, someday," he halfway chuckled as he moved his monster '56 Caddy convertible through traffic, stopping at an apartment complex in one of the city's rougher neighborhoods.

"Glad I remembered the guns," he smiled, looking up and down the empty block in front of the complex. The gutters and sidewalks were filled with trash and garbage, paper products flew about in the wind, and the air was not filled with the warmth and love of a Pacific Ocean breeze. Of the cars parked on that block, most were without wheels, some without doors, and none had all their windows.

"Starr Baby shouldn't live in this kind of neighborhood," he muttered, kicking some trash aside. He watched a black Crown Vic squeal to a stop and Detective Captain Ulysses S. (Serious) Elmo stepped out. Two squad cars pulled in behind him. It was Saturday morning, three cop cars parked all crooked, no reds and blues flashing their warnings, and the passerby simply passed on by. "Must be the neighborhood," Dorsey snarled.

Elmo and Dorsey have worked together for years, sometimes on a friendly basis, sometimes not. They did have great respect for each other and between them weighed about a quarter of a ton. "Nobody called in a shots-fired, Sol. You sure that's what you heard?"

"Yeah, and then a growly man's voice saying something about me keeping out of whatever brought on the shooting. And this is Starr's address. How many times have I tried to keep that little beauty out of trouble? Damn." They walked toward the front of the building after Elmo sent two men around to the backside. "She's in three-twenty. I've never been here, so don't know if any of those windows up there would be hers or not."

"You stay down here, Flannery, and Smitty, you keep close watch on our six," Elmo said. "Let's take the stairs, Dorsey. Safer that way." There was no attempt at being quiet as the three lumbered up three flights marked for emergency use only. They had to plow through considerable refuse on the way, and Elmo muttered something about fire department regulations.

They moved out onto the main corridor of the third floor. The hallway was dark despite the lateness of the morning. One lonely light bulb burned near the elevator doors. The carpet was frayed and worn through in spots and what might have been wallpaper years ago was falling off in shreds. "Filthy," Dorsey muttered as they cautiously approached apartment Three-Twenty and found the door slightly ajar.

"There's a light on," Dorsey whispered, trying to see through the crack. "Damn," he said, spotting Starr's body splayed across the living room carpet. He stepped back, gave Elmo a nod and plunged through the door and into the apartment, Elmo and the uniform right behind him.

One bullet went through the lady's forehead and brain, splashing parts and pieces around the small living room. A second tore into the divan she was probably sitting on to answer the phone. The telephone was on the floor next to her body.

"Better get your people down here, Serious. Whoever Snarly Voice is, he may have left a calling card or two." Dorsey let his eyes root around the apartment, not touching, just looked, jotted little notes, and called Capt. Elmo's attention to a few things.

The apartment, despite the neighborhood was nicely decorated, with modern and clean furniture, decorator items on tables and shelves, some original paintings, rock posters, and "This was not where Starr conducted most of her business," Dorsey said. The bedroom was all girly-girl and frilly, and the closet contained two different styles of clothing; that which would be worn late at night on Franklyn Street, and that, which would be worn at a Shriner's convention.

"The lady had a touch of class, Serious. Worked the hard streets and worked the conventions, and knew the difference. One thing I know about Starr Baby," he said, as he came back into the living room, "she was not into any kind of drugs. Whatever this turns out to be, it isn't related to narcotics."

He was down on his knees near the body, looked at everything, touched nothing. "No shell casings, Serious. Our shooter's either nasty neat or uses a revolver. Powder burns pretty obvious, so he was standing right here," and he pointed at his own boots, "when she answered the phone, and punched her ticket. She was into a lot of crap," he said, just talking, more for his own benefit than Captain Elmo's or the uniform's, "but I wonder what would have caused this? Not drugs, not Starr Baby, but shakedown? Maybe so, but not political ransom.

"Starr was into something I was told to stay out of, the shooter said. Have there been other hookers wasted in the last few days? Have we got a whore war underway? I better get back to my computer, Serious. Keep me up to date and I'll do the same." Dorsey was out the door and back to his apartment, with one stop for a large pizza and twelve-pack to ease the pain. "We have one dead that we know, and I'm supposed to stay out of something that I don't know about. This sumbitch, meaning me, is off to a good start on this case," he mumbled, almost breaking the key off in the apartment door.

"Case? What case? Nobody's hired my ass, nobody's flung cash money on my open palm, I ain't got no case, so what the hell am I doing?" The big guy would fight a tank if the price was right, had worked for some serious sleaze-balls in the past, had a set of ethics that only Sol Dorsey understood, and despised working for free. "But," and a big crooked grin softened his bright green eyes, "This is, after all, Starr Baby."

Up and down Franklyn Street, a more than seedy side of the city, saloons were interspersed with tattoo parlors and pawnshops, and that's where the delightful girls of the night, offering pleasures and parties, worked. Each and every one of those soiled doves looked at Simon Sol Dorsey as a friend.

~ ~ ~

Dorsey spent the next three hours sifting through pages of information, none of which provided an answer to why Starr Baby might have been offed. "No other working girls found dead, no bad guys missing and presumed, and no indication of gang bangers getting tough with each other."

He shut off the coffee, congratulated himself, and took a drive to Franklyn Street, that haven of filth and corruption. *I get most of my business because of this filthy neighborhood.* The working girls giggled like schoolgirls when he patted their cute little bottoms, and he took great delight knowing the tweekers and dealers would dive for cover when he was around.

"Time for a stop at The Bar and a talk with Dusty, I think," he said, parking the Caddy in a Compacts Only space. A single red neon sign proclaiming "Bar" welcomes all from the indignity of the street, with warmth, cheap whiskey and warm beer. Dusty was in his early fifties, skinny as a rail, long stringy strands of gray hair hung down his back, and he usually had at least a three-day growth of facial hair.

On the blotter forms, he was Harold Schumaker, and his rap sheet showed visits to federal and state lock-ups around the country. Dorsey could never prove connections to Chicago, Jersey, or Los Angeles, but was sure the man had organized or syndicate connections. "The slimy little bastard knows too much about too many things not to have connections," he said often. Dorsey was sure that heavy weapons passed through the back rooms of The Bar, that money transfers took place in the card room, and that narcotics shipments were arranged right at the long oaken plank.

"Dusty, my man, how they hanging?"

"Don't want no trouble, Dorsey," is all he got back, along with a pint of ale and a shot of Jack. "If you're here about Starr, I got no information."

Dorsey kept a straight face, but his mind went into overdrive. *How the hell does he know about Starr? And, my skinny little friend, why do you know something about Starr?* "Not looking for trouble Dusty. Seen Starr around? I tried to call earlier." *Let's see you get around this you miserable excuse for a pimp.*

"Starr won't be comin' here, no more. She took the wrong guy for a dope and she ain't around no more. They haven't found her body yet, though, what I heard." He looked up and down the almost empty bar, toward the door leading to the card room in the back, and toward the pool tables, doing a bad imitation of nonchalant.

Dusty was faking wiping dust and grime from a glass when Dorsey's huge left hand struck out, fingers laced tightly around the dude's throat. The bartender found himself flying through the air, bounced solidly against the wall, and flopped around like a cod out of water. Two regulars near the far end of the bar got up and walked out the door, not even glancing Dorsey's way. One of the dudes at the pool table gave a slight shrug, and made his shot. Dusty looked up and found Dorsey standing over him, a forty-five revolver cocked and inches from his nose. Dorsey snarled, "All of it, puke, or die now."

"That's the word on the street, Mr. Dorsey. I don't know nothin'."

"Who passed on this 'word on the street'? Why do you know that Starr is dead? You got five seconds," Dorsey exploded. He aimed the large revolver at Dusty's balls and said, "four, three," and the gun went off, missing that tender little area by an inch or less.

Dusty was screaming for mercy, ready to tell Dorsey anything and everything. "Man, no!" he said, over and over, trying to cover his groin, not even realizing he hadn't actually been shot. He thrashed around in the crusty muck of the saloon's floor and didn't calm down until Dorsey slapped him twice. Dusty caught on fast, started talking fast, and his eyes never left the revolver aimed at his nuts, which were now half-way to his throat.

"George 'The Mole' Francis said guns were brought in from Los Angeles to take care of some problems. He mentioned Starr. That's all I know."

"You said Starr was dead and they hadn't found the body, Dusty. Give it to me straight or die. I got no time for screwing around," and he cocked that huge gun again. Dusty was a quivering husk of skin and bones, writhed around in the muck of the filthy bar, cried for mercy.

"Find The Mole, Dorsey. He'll tell you. He said Starr knew things the L.A. people didn't want known. He said there were others."

Dorsey walked back to the Caddy, serenaded by sirens responding to "shots fired, The Bar, Franklyn Street." *Georgie The Mole gonna die, I do believe, Georgie The Mole gonna die.* He eased the Caddy around the corner before the first unit slid to a stop in front of The Bar. "Christmas just a few days away and I got no joy in my heart right now," he said, heading back to his apartment.

~ ~ ~

George 'The Mole' Francis was a keeper of the flame, destroyer, enforcer, pick a name, for one of the local gangs known as Bayshore. The Bayshore Gang was involved in protection, narcotics, numbers, and money laundering, and backed their play with big guns and tough guys. Some believed that there were connections to Chicago and Los Angeles, maybe even New York and Jersey. But then, weren't there always 'connections?'

The Mole stood less than five feet tall, weighed maybe ninety pounds if he was carrying two guns, had thin black hair that he combed straight back and held in place with grease. He had weasel eyes and thin lips topped with a Hitler moustache.

According to local legend, The Mole had spent time in many federal courtrooms but had never been convicted of anything. He was said to have as many as ten known murderers in his command structure. He was considered one of the most dangerous men in the city. *I'm gonna blow that mole out of his hole, I am, I am,* Dorsey was humming to himself, tearing up the city streets in that beautiful fifty-six Caddy.

"So Georgie and Bayshore may be behind this," Dorsey mused, driving back to the apartment. "Starr's hit might mean a cleansing, might mean wiping out competition, might mean damn near anything. I got nothing but a dead little prosti, a dumb-ass bartender who knows too much, and the name of a gangster. Off to a rousing start here," he stormed, all the way home.

"You know what's worse?" He said this to a stranger after parking the Caddy and heading toward his apartment. "I ain't gonna get paid for this. Starr Baby's killer is gonna fry, I'm the one gonna put him in the pot, and I ain't gonna get paid. Well, just damn me," he snarled, scaring the hell out of the guy.

He got that pot of coffee boiling and had his laptop open and ready when the telephone jangled its greeting. "Dorsey," he bawled.

"Take my head off, why doncha? You don't know me, Dorsey, but I'm calling because I've been told you're about the best in the private investigations field."

"Yeah, I've been told that too," he chuckled. "I'm good at what I do, and because of that, I charge a lot. How can I help you?"

"I think my partner may be involved in something illegal, and if it implicates me, it may cost me my life. We need to meet, because I don't want to say anything more over the telephone."

"My immediate reaction is to say yes," Dorsey said with a smile in his voice and on his craggy face, visions of a paying customer floating through his brain, "but not until I know who you are."

"My name is Raymond Bargetto, you may have heard the name."

"Yes, sir, Senator, I certainly have. Are you familiar with Maglio's Deli on Pacific Avenue? I'll be in there in fifteen minutes. I'm a big guy and I'll be wearing a black leather jacket."

"I know what you look like, Mr. Dorsey. I've seen you in court. I'll be there, alone."

I wonder why he specified that he would be alone? Doesn't matter, this will be a paying job, damn it, he howled, and the smile continued through the process of shutting off the coffee, computer, and lights. *Life is good, sometimes.*

2.

"The broad is dead, Mr. Whistler, so what's your problem?" The Mole was rocking back and forth, thumbs hooked in his belt, coat open far enough that Whistler could easily see the semi-auto tucked in a shoulder holster. "She ain't gonna cause no problem, sweetheart." There are some people that simply feel they have to 'play the part' and George Francis was one of them. He was known to preen some when he passed mirrored windows on the street, and the word flamboyance didn't carry enough impact to describe him.

The Mole dressed as if he might be waiting in the wings for his introduction at a 1930s burlesque show in Sheboygan. Extreme to the extreme with pleated dress shirts and string ties, velour jackets in weird colors and patterns, and always, a cap, worn to almost cover one eye.

Whistler ran the Bayshore gang, took his orders from Rollo Fernandez who headed the Los Angeles arm of the Tijuana Cartel of Mexico. Heroine, cocaine, meth coming north by the ton was Fernandez's responsibility, guns and clean money going south was up to Bayshore and others in the north. Fernandez was believed to take his orders from a man named Lemuel Simpson of Chicago.

"She is causing a problem, asshole," Whistler said. "You mouthed off to that bartender and he mouthed off to Sol Dorsey. And, now, because of your big damn mouth, Dorsey is gonna meet with Bargetto. The fucking killing of the whore was supposed to implicate

Bargetto," he all but screamed at the little gangster. Whistler was putting together the deal of a lifetime, something that even the big boys back east would talk about, he was in a rage.

"You bring Dorsey down on me, Mole, and you'll be bait for the fish. I need Bargetto to make this work and an implication that he might be associated with a known prostitute would be something I could hold over his head. You screwed it up, Mole.

"Get out of here, Francis, and if you're damn smart you'll get out of town before Dorsey finds you. I ought to just shoot your dumb ass myself. You get me involved in this, and you're one dead Mole-ass."

Georgie the Mole, no longer the tough guy, tucked his head and slunk out the door and into the dark of the city's protection. "I gotta kill Dusty," he muttered, "and then Dorsey. Damn, that man was one angry bastard. Maybe I better kill him too."

Whistler got on the phone as soon as Georgie the Mole left. "Jimmy, get over here right now. We got a problem and it's gonna get worse. No, not on the phone, just get your ass over here now." Whistler walked to the large window and looked fourteen floors down to busy streets of the big city. There were well-lit ships moving through the bay, bridges were lit, but he neither saw nor felt any of the gayety of the season.

"Get me a Scotch. Janice, and then make yourself invisible. Jimmy's coming over and you don't need to see him right now. I may have a good job for you, though. You heard of Sol Dorsey?"

"Sure, Gerald, who hasn't? You gonna give him to me?"

"Dumb-ass Mole blew Jimmy's step-daughter away and now Dorsey's on the prowl. Take him out, Janice." She poured Whistler a potent glassful of

Scotch and waltzed out of the room, humming a little tune.

Of the many criminal types that hung around Whistler, Janice Wilson was generally accepted as the most dangerous. Never convicted, she was the accepted shooter in a number of un-solved political deaths in California. She had homes in the city and in Los Angeles and was a known associate of Rollo Fernandez, the head of the Los Angeles branch of the Tijuana Cartel.

~ ~ ~

"Senator Bargetto, I presume," Dorsey smiled when the big man walked up to his table. He stood up and shook hands with the elderly gentleman. "I don't believe we've met before. Sit, please, and tell me your troubles.

"Maglio there," and he pointed to the fat little Italian behind the counter, "is one fine specimen of Italian descent, makes the finest Mexican crab enchiladas in the city. I ordered a platter, and a pitcher of his famous ale as well."

Bargetto had just the hint of a smile on his face, settling into the banquette. "No, Dorsey, we haven't met, but I am aware of your work. Crab enchiladas sound more than enticing, right now. I lost a friend last night, and right now, I fear for my life."

He wore a three-piece black pin-stripe suit with red necktie, a homburg, which Dorsey would love to filch, and highly polished wingtips. The essence of an elderly politician. The senator's eyes swept the room, touching on just about every table and every patron.

"We're safe here, Senator. I know everyone in the joint, three of them are off duty cops, and I've got my eye on the door. Keep talking, and then we'll discuss finances."

"Finances are at the heart of everything, Mr. Dorsey. Everything." Bargetto was nearing seventy, had a full head of steel gray hair that was long and wavy, wore a silver white moustache, and stood a hefty six feet tall. His eyes were cold, Dorsey saw, no smile lines around them either, and the tip ends of his mouth turned down, as in a constant anger.

Dorsey saw a strong chin and jaw line, broad shoulders and deep chest, and just a hint of body fat in the middle. *This man was an athlete when he was younger. He surely isn't a happy man right now.* Dorsey smiled easily, giving the man lots of time to tell his story.

"I have made my money by way of investments," Bargetto said, "and for the most part they have paid off well. I've been described as being ruthless, but that may not tell the whole story. I won't lie, I won't cheat, but I will take advantage of every opportunity that offers itself, I will take advantage of what many call loopholes, and that may be behind the ruthless moniker." He chuckled, slightly, and took a sip of ale.

The man's humor has a finesse to it that I like, Dorsey thought. *His face is very plastic and he wears a frown to cover that delightful humor. I think I like this man.* Senator Bargetto continued.

"There's a large piece of land that has come on the market, and with another man, I am planning on purchasing it and turning it into a large home site development. I'm afraid my choice of a partner may bite me in the ass, to be blunt with it. His business ethics seem to leave him from time to time. There will be issues with permits for the development, for one thing, and I'm about to start my re-election campaign for another.

"I cannot allow myself to become involved in a fraudulent land scheme, Mr. Dorsey, and I'm afraid that's what my partner is leading us into. There, sir, in a nutshell is why I called you."

"I understand your problem, Senator. I do, but I'm not sure where I fit into the picture. It seems more a business-related problem that an attorney would be able to handle, more than a private investigator." *Damn, Dorsey, don't talk yourself out of a paying job.* Dorsey sat back, poured each of them another pint of ale, and watched Bargetto's face, changing from anger to snarl to anger to a slight smile.

"I need a big old pit-bull to find out exactly what's going on with my partner. I need to keep all this as quiet as it is possible. The last thing I need right now are headlines screaming nonsense about my business dealings.

"I've brought a file full of information for you, Dorsey," and he handed a computer disc across the table. "This has everything I think you'll need to come up with whatever is going on. If it's fraud, we'll snuff it out immediately, if it's just working around and through the system, that's fine.

"The main thing, Dorsey, is silence. This must not reach the newspapers. I admit, I like being a senator, I enjoy life in Washington, and I want to be re-elected. Now, back to finances." and he offered a genuine smile with the comment.

"I usually charge what is called a day-rate plus expenses, which would be the case here. I can't put a time frame to this though. My day rate is one thousand per, plus those dratted expenses, and the first three days in advance. I'll try to be as quick as possible, but you also want thoroughness, I'm sure."

"Yes, I do," Senator Bargetto said, writing out a check for three thousand dollars. He included his business card along with the check. "My private phone number is on the back of the card, Mr. Dorsey. You may call me at any time of the day or night, and preferably with good news." Again, Dorsey was surprised with what he considered, a genuine smile.

Bargetto stood and they shook hands. "I'll keep you informed, sir. Have a good evening, and Merry Christmas." He watched the tall, rather dignified gentleman walk out and motioned for Maglio to bring another pitcher of ale. "Better bring some more enchiladas, old man. I don't remember eating today."

I get to pay the rent on time, maybe get those new boots I've been looking at, and getting this situation fixed for the senator will certainly add creds to my dossier. I can still work to find out why Starr Baby was killed. Life is good, he chuckled.

~ ~ ~

"Dorsey said he heard two shots, Doctor. Are you positive there are two wounds? We know where the second bullet went and it didn't go through the vic." Captain Elmo was in the morgue with the county pathologist, Doctor Amy Finley, and she was going over the autopsy on Starr Baby.

"One shot through the head from very close range, and one shot into her back, not so close. Two weapons of differing caliber. I'd suggest two shooters, Serious. The back wound would have been sufficient to kill the girl, but I think it may have come after the headshot."

Elmo was remembering the scene when he and Dorsey discovered Starr Baby's body on the living room floor. He could see her, on her back, kinda scrunched up against the sofa, her head splashed across the scene. "The forensics people at the scene never said a word about a wound to her back. She was almost propped up, her back to the sofa."

"That is strange, Doc. What kind of angle on the shot to her back, based on how we found the body? The front door of the apartment was slightly ajar when we arrived. Could that second shot have been taken from the hallway, maybe by someone who didn't know Starr was already dead?"

"I'll work that up for you, Captain. The killing shot to her head was a nine-millimeter, but the wound to her back was made by a forty-five revolver."

"Nine-mil? You're sure?"

"Yes, why?"

"There was no brass. The guy picked up his brass. He shot Starr, grabbed the phone and said something to Dorsey, then grabbed his brass before leaving, and then, not shutting the door. Interesting.

"Work up various shooting scenarios for me, Doctor, and get them over to my office as soon as you can. I wonder if those shooters were there together or not? Whoever shot the girl in the head took a second shot that went into the sofa. The shooter at the doorway, or wherever he was, must have only shot once.

"Well, get that to me ASAP," he said, leaving quickly for his office. He was back to police headquarters in minutes and picked up two files on the way up to his office. One concerned reports of mob activity increasing in northern California and the other on Starr Baby, one Monica P. Fetterman. *Dorsey's right, she was not even slightly connected to any narcotics dealers. Two different people come to her apartment to kill her on the same day, almost at the same time. Might have been a gunfight if they had arrived at the same time,* he smiled to himself.

He went into the squad room and poured a cup of really stale, really bad coffee and slipped into his office. He picked up the phone and called for his Detective Sergeant to come up, pulled one of his huge black cigars out and lit it, blowing a cloud of EPA forbidden smoke toward the ceiling.

"I might have to cite you on that," Sergeant Jenny Adams said, coming in, "or start wearing an Israeli gas mask."

"Humph," Serious Elmo said, indicating she should sit, and he handed her the file on known mob activity in northern California. "Let's talk."

Adams was a detective sergeant for one very good reason. She was a cop first, last, and always, and had the intelligence to pull it off. A graduate of San Jose State with a degree in criminology and a desire to spend her life as a working detective, Adams was also a tall, well developed woman who spent her off duty hours sharing a small piece of property with a couple of horses and some egg-laying chickens.

"Big boys are rumbling again, eh?" she said, taking the files from Captain Elmo.

3.

Dorsey spent several hours poring over the files Senator Bargetto gave him and started to see a picture of what Bargetto was attempting. "The man has an opportunity to purchase a ranch on rolling hills, six-hundred-forty acres, and wants to build a planned community. See that everyday," he mused. "It's the permits that seem to have a big part in the program."

He was taking notes as fast as he was reading, and talking up a storm, too. "It's really easier to get a permit for a high end, planned and probably gated community than it would be for a high density, low-income community. I wonder which one would bring in the most money for the least outlay?"

Bargetto's partner, James Torrance was a known developer, like the senator, but when Dorsey started digging a little deeper, he found part of Bargetto's problem. "The man doesn't always play by the rules, eh? For a planned community, Oak Woods, the partners would have to promise large sized lots, specific landscaping, parks, and some street maintenance. The lots then would be expensive, creating a high-end community, something which Bargetto is definitely in favor, and so, right now, I don't see the problem."

He got another cup of coffee, poured some good bourbon in, "Nice to have good booze in the house," he snickered, having slipped that big check in his account first thing in the morning. "Mr. Torrance, sir, we need to know a lot more about you. Why would a

United States Senator be afraid of you, and what are you doing to make him afraid?"

He couldn't get it out of his head that Bargetto said he felt his life was in danger. "I don't see that yet. I see plenty of opportunity for underhanded dealing, for criminal activity, but I don't see the level of danger Bargetto thought he saw. I plan to tell the gentleman from Washington that he needs to do more research on potential partners in the future." The chuckles helped him pour just a wee bit more go juice in the coffee. "You be dealin' wit bums, Senatah, Suh."

Dorsey rooted through junk scattered on the kitchen table until he found his cell phone and punched in some numbers.

"Serious, I need some deep background on a guy. Yeah, I got a job, smartass, and a good paying one, too. This dude's name is James Torrance, and he's a land developer, kinda shady. See if you can find out anything, ok?"

"I'll get right on it, Dorsey. Yes, sir, I will. I'll set aside my duties as Detective Captain of this fine metropolitan police department, and get on it right away. By the way, Starr Baby was shot twice, not once. Why don't we have lunch somewhere and I'll tell you all about it."

"Red Neck Randy's House of Chili? See you there, Pal."

Red Neck Randy's House of Chili sat on the edge of a dividing line in the city, a line that said blue blood on one side and red neck on the other, and Randy's joint was filled with representatives from both sides. Rough board walls held signs for every known beer and whiskey ever sold, graffiti filled both bathrooms, and the chili was hot enough to bring steam from the ears of many. Randy Shorter came north from a little town along the Rio Grande, his mother born on one side of the border, his father on the other, his education straight out of the streets of Laredo.

"A tureen of chili, a platter of corn bread, and a pitcher of cold beer, my friend," Dorsey said, his eyes were smarting from the chili-fied air. A big sign hung over the cash register declared Randy's Chili to be straight out of Texas. "You want beans, you go somewhere else."

His hush puppies and French fries were still proudly cooked in lard, "Just like mama did," and the cornbread had chopped jalapeño peppers sprinkled about. If you were able to ignore the smell of the ocean or the sound of the foghorns, you might be tempted to believe you were deep in the heart of Texas. The foot stompin' music helped.

Serious Elmo joined Dorsey in a few, ordered the same, and the two got straight down to business, both blew their noses often. "Damn fine, Randy. Damn fine," Elmo said, feeling the perspiration build on his forehead. "Dorsey likes his cornbread, but how about a platter of hush-puppies also, eh?"

Elmo squared up at the table and got serious right away. "How are you mixed up with this Torrance feller? He's not in your class, Sol?" Dorsey and Elmo started working together when Elmo was still a uniformed officer, and Sol Dorsey had already decided that he would be an investigator but never a cop. There was an easy rapport between them.

"He has a partner, Serious, a highly respected partner who is afraid Torrance is leading him into something fraudulent. Senator Raymond Bargetto to be precise."

Elmo took a quick breath on that one. "Torrance and Bargetto? Whew. Does the name Whistler mean anything to you?"

"I knew his mother," Dorsey shot back.

"Smartass. Gerald Whistler is involved in the Bayshore Gang, and is a known associate of James Torrance. Bargetto's fears may be right on, Sol. Torrance and Whistler were indicted for land fraud in Colorado a few years ago, but the case disappeared when witnesses started turning up dead or very forgetful.

"I have a file on my desk that also tends to indicate that Mr. Whistler and his associates might be influenced some by Chicago rats and Los Angeles snakes. It looks like he is nesting with the mob in some way. Now, you bring Bargetto into the picture, Sol, along with Jimmy Torrance.

"Bargetto didn't do his homework on this one. Here's a file folder on the Torrance-Whistler case from Colorado, and more info from other sources. Whistler has been accused more than once of hiring guns, so keep your ass on guard."

"It's nice to have a paying job, again. Tell me what you found out about Starr. You said she was shot twice?"

"Yeah. I brought the autopsy report, too. Are you sure you only heard two shots? The third one was to her back. And, Sol, different caliber guns. The headshot was nine millimeter, the back shot forty-five. The head shot close up, as you saw, the shot to the sofa up close, and the back shot from a distance. That tells me there had to be two shooters, but I wonder if they were together?"

"No, Serious, I only heard two quick shots and the phone disconnected. That front door of the apartment was open when we got there. You said the back shot came second, so the killer could have left, another killer showed up, found the door ajar, saw Starr, where, on the floor? And shot her anyway?

Interesting. Anything else I need to know while I have you?"

"The Detective Division of the department is going to send you a bill someday," Elmo said, with just a hint of a smile. "Torrance is living in the redwoods south of here, near Santa Cruz, and the property is heavily guarded according to a source down there. That information is in the file as well."

The two large men finished their huge tureens of chili, ate more cornbread and hush puppies, drank another pitcher of cold beer each, and called it a good lunch. "You take care of yourself, Dorsey, and keep me posted. Torrance and Whistler are dangerous people." The detective captain stood up and said, "This land deal is out of my jurisdiction, Dorsey, but Whistler lives here and Starr was murdered here."

"I can feel a lot of computer time in my immediate future, Serious, and then I might just head down the coast. Haven't been in the redwoods for a long time. Lunch is on Senator Bargetto, today," he said, slipping a credit card toward Randy.

"Come by the office, Sol. I want you to meet someone who might help you out some. Sergeant Jenny Adams, originally from Santa Cruz, has copies of the files I just gave you. I think you two will make a good partnership."

"I want to head south tomorrow," Dorsey smiled, "and I need the rest of today to absorb all these files. I'll be in your office in the morning. I've met Sergeant Adams, Serious. She's damn sharp looking with a pretty head full of brains." He was smiling as he slipped behind the wheel of the big Caddy.

Many private detectives don't like working with a woman but the thought has never entered Dorsey's mind. *I've worked with some pretty damn fine women investigators in the past, and some damn fine looking ones, too,* he smiled, watching the holiday crowds, trying his best to hum a Christmas song or two.

~ ~ ~

He parked in front of his apartment and was half way to the front door when he heard screaming tires coming around the corner from Third Street. Three fast shots were taken as the black four-wheel drive Ford pickup whipped down the street. The first shot was through the front of the apartment building, the second through Dorsey's black leather jacket, but not through him, and the third shot went into the apartment building as well. Dorsey was flat on the sidewalk, forty-five in hand but didn't have time to take his shot.

Cops swarmed the neighborhood within minutes, including Detective Captain Ulysses S. Elmo. "Don't think the truck even had plates, Serious. You need to have your men check those front apartments. There are people living in there. And, look at my jacket. Geez. Hey, guess what, I can sell this for lots of money. Can you see the ad? 'Black leather jacket worn by famous PI Sol Dorsey when bad guys shot at him'."

"Just write your report, Dorsey," Elmo said, shaking his head, but with a little boy smile on his mug. He directed a couple of officers to check on the apartments, and got information on shell casings that were found.

"It was a semi-auto, and probably 7.62 ammo. You're lucky old man, this time."

"Professional hit, Serious, and that brings up Bayshore Gang and Gerald Whistler once again. I've heard The Mole mentioned twice, and you brought up Gerald Whistler. Connections, Serious, and before I tangle with my computer I think I better take a little trip down to Franklyn Street and have a talk with

Dusty at The Bar. I'll let you know what I find out."
Whatever's going on must include one hell of a lot of green stuff. First Starr is knocked off and I'm threatened by the gunman, then I'm shot at big time. Lots of bucks involved here.

It took an hour to get the reports written, for evidence to be collected, and for Dorsey to wend his way down toward the docks and Franklyn Street. He swaggered into The Bar, mid-day customers not much different than those found after midnight, most hoping that Dorsey was not in an ugly mood.

The big man noticed that Dusty was not behind the bar, and snickered, thinking that the man was probably still pissing his pants. There were five or six at the bar, a couple playing pool, and one sitting alone at a cocktail table, reading the racing form. Dorsey made a beeline straight for him.

"Been lookin' for you, Georgie," Dorsey said, towering over the little man. "Let's take a ride, shall we?" He grabbed the Mole by his coat collar and jerked him to his feet. "Be back in a short time," he said to the bartender. "Don't worry, if the Mole owes you money I'm not planning to kill him."

4.

The fifty-six Caddy moved through major business sections of the city, store fronts gaudy with the Christmas season, shoppers coated up for winter weather, even the sounds of sleigh-bells ringing, none of which was enjoyed by Georgie the Mole. "Don't you just love this time of year, Georgie?" Dorsey asked passing by one storefront with animated characters that danced and pranced about. "Wanna sing a little song?"

The Mole had heard the stories, often told by those who heard them from those that had heard them, but even so, even if they were half-truths, they frightened him to the bone. Stories of being held in the air by the neck until you passed out, about being hit and stomped until every bone was fractured, about spilling your guts to this man who exemplified terror in criminal minds.

"Just so we're clear on this, Georgie my friend, I'm not a cop, therefore, you have no rights," and he chuckled, waving a Merry Christmas to a jaywalker, who promptly gave Dorsey the finger.

The Mole all at once made a move to open the door of the Caddy and jump, it didn't matter that they were speeding along at more than thirty miles per hour, jump, get away. There was no door handle, and Dorsey's big right fist came screaming around from the steering wheel and smashed the man's already broken nose.

"Electric doors, Mole," Dorsey laughed. "They open when I say so. Another move and you're a dead man, even though I promised that dude I wouldn't kill you," and he laughed some more, smacking Georgie The Mole one more time. All he got back was whimpering. "You sniveling little puke. Big tough guy? That what they say about you?" and that right fist flew around again, splashing blood on the passenger-side window.

North of the city, along the coast, were great sand dunes spread back from the surf line, and Dorsey took his time driving out to the area. Late at night, couples could be found, blankets spread, so they could watch the submarine races and enjoy the privacy. Dorsey parked the Caddy, jerked The Mole out and pushed him deep into cavernous canyons of towering dunes.

"That's far enough," he said, spinning the gangster around and planting a big right fist square to the man's nose, splashing blood over both of them. "Need to have a little chat, Mole. I ask, you answer." He reached out with his right hand and took hold of Georgie's neck, lifted the man high into the air, shutting off any chance for the man to breathe.

"Tell me about Starr Baby," he said, slowly letting the man back down, releasing those five gnarly fingers holding his throat.

The Mole was coughing, tried to catch his breath, and stammered, "I don't know nobody by that name." The left fist came out this time, connected between two blood-shot eyes, and The Mole was flat on his back, watching birds and clouds go 'round and 'round.

"Okay, then, how about the name Torrance? Like in Jimmy Torrance?"

The Mole was flailing around in the deep sand, trying to get his feet under him, wanting to set a new speed record for the running mile, and couldn't. He was on his hands and knees, blood streaming from his nose and mouth, his eyes so swollen he could barely make out the huge man towering over him.

Dorsey pulled him to his feet and slapped him across the side of the head with an open palm. "I believe I said, I ask, you answer. Again, tell me about Jimmy Torrance." Dorsey pulled the forty-five from its shoulder holster and cocked it.

"You have five seconds, Mole. Five," and a short pause, "Four," another short pause, and he fired a shot through The Mole's left foot, sending the man screaming down into the sand, trying to grab his foot.

"Three," said Dorsey, cocking the big gun again.

"Okay, okay, don't shoot me, Mr. Dorsey. Please, I'll tell you anything you want. Please." The Mole was crying like a baby, and sobbed out all the sordid details, probably even added an item or two thinking about the gun in Dorsey's hand, and Dorsey's fist.

Dorsey was back in the Caddy within fifteen minutes, cell phone in hand. "Yeah, 911? Listen, I heard a gunshot and some screaming near the beach, about five miles north of town. Yeah, near the sand dunes. No, my name isn't important," and he hung up. *I love these little throwaway cell phones.* He was making his plans to drive down the coast in the morning, after his meeting with Sergeant Adams. *Maybe I'll ask her to come along and we can spend a few days in the redwoods.* Dorsey was smiling, humming a little Christmas ditty as he drove into the city.

"So Starr Baby discovered something about a shipment of AK rifles and wanted to tell me all about it, and The Mole did what he was paid to do. He didn't say who paid him, and probably doesn't know." He let his mind whirl along for a couple of minutes. "Now, it seems that Torrance, Whistler, Starr Baby, and Senator Bargetto are all mixed up in something.

"I'm right back to the idea of big money," he murmured. "We have a huge potential land fraud case, we have massive amounts of heavy weapons being imported, and we have a darling little prosti dead, all with large dollar signs hanging on everything.

"Okay, The Mole, that's one shooter, I think, if he was telling the truth, now we need to know about the second bad-boy." He was worrying also about the fact that Whistler's name wasn't mentioned by The Mole. Whistler was prominent from Serious Elmo, but The Mole was talking about Fernandez and the Los Angeles connection.

"Okay," he muttered again, setting aside his Christmas humming. "I may have two or three things going on here. Starr is shot by one of The Mole's hired guns because of guns either to or from Fernandez, and then is shot again, and that's where Mole's part of it ends. Is the second shooter connected to Whistler? And where the hell does Torrance and Senator Bargetto come into the picture?"

He played with half a dozen possibilities as he drove back to the city and worked his way through traffic, thinking about driving to the redwoods later the next day. "It'll be good to smell those trees. Mr. Torrance is actually living on the land he and Bargetto are planning on developing, so I will go out of my way to introduce myself.

"Strange, though, that The Mole didn't know anything about the attempted hit on me. There might just be a huge conspiracy behind all this and the land fraud might only be a small part. Lots of criminal activity so far," he laughed, stopping for a large pizza to go, then another stop for a twelve-pack, and finally, back to the apartment and the computer. The house phone was ringing when he walked in.

"Dorsey," he bawled.

"The Mole was found beat-up and shot, north of town, Dorsey," Serious Elmo said. "You wouldn't know anything about that, would you?"

"The Mole, eh? Nope, don't know nothing."

"Don't do this, Sol. It's not proper procedure."

"I'm not a cop, Serious. I have my own rules, my own, Dorsey procedure," he chuckled. "What hospital is the fool in?"

"Mercy General and you stay away from him. Don't make this worse."

"I'm heading south for a few days, remember?"

"Go to hell, Dorsey," Serious snarled and the phone went dead to Dorsey's snickers.

He called Mercy General and ordered flowers for The Mole with a card to read, "Let's get together again some time." He was laughing gently when he opened his computer, found the number and called a motel in the Santa Cruz mountains for a reservation. With hot pizza and cold beer, Dorsey spent the rest of the day and evening on his computer and telephone.

~ ~ ~

"Jimmy, listen carefully. The Mole is shot-up and beat to hell, and it appears that Sol Dorsey is probably to blame." Gerald Whistler's anger could almost be felt at the other end of the phone line. "The Mole knows too much about what we're trying to do, and now Dorsey does too. What happened to the hit we planned? Those were guns that you said don't miss."

"Dorsey just got lucky, Mr. Whistler. The Mole brought those guns up from Los Angeles, but he didn't know about the hit. I planned that one and they just got anxious, is all. Dorsey's a dead man, he just doesn't know it.

"I'm taking The Mole out today. A man's already making the move. Dorsey will get his tomorrow. We need to forget about Dorsey and problems with the Chicago people and work on the Santa Cruz people. They need to feel the warmth, Gerald, need to feel their pockets full of big fat 'C' notes. Once we get those permits, and we get Senator Bargetto's name plastered about as the man behind the project, the money will roll in."

"You keep saying that, Jimmy, and all I see is money rolling out and Sol Dorsey beating the hell out of your big-time criminals. Put together a meeting with our people down in Santa Cruz for tomorrow or the next day, and I want answers. Make it day after tomorrow, and let me know where. I'm tired of hearing about things going wrong. Get my meaning?" he snarled.

"Yes, Gerald, I do. I'll put it together." Torrance was sloppy, Whistler remembered from the fiasco in Colorado, and he knew he had to stay right on top of him. It was a sloppy hit on Dorsey, and the only good thing that Whistler could think of, was that The Mole didn't know anything about it, so couldn't say anything to Dorsey.

Janice will have better luck getting Dorsey than Jimmy could ever think of, he mused, pouring another Scotch, glaring out the windows at the holiday brightness.

~ ~ ~

Dorsey spent hours on the computer and finally set it aside after taking the last slice of pizza down and opening the last can of cold beer. "That man is in serious damn trouble," he muttered, looking over several pages of notes he had taken. He pulled up the house phone and called his client.

"Senator, this is Sol Dorsey," he said to the answer phone. "Please call me as soon as you get this message. I have important information that you need to act on immediately."

He set the receiver back in the cradle, and began pacing around the kitchen. "He hasn't done one thing illegal and right now that man's political career is about to come to a screeching end. If he had just done a small amount of background, he would have known." He was on his third lap of the kitchen when the phone rang.

"Dorsey," he bawled.

"I really like the way you answer the phone, Dorsey," Senator Bargetto laughed. "You said something important has come up?"

Dorsey ran through everything he had learned about the land fraud conspiracy and the two men behind it. "Believe me, Senator, Torrance and Whistler have Los Angeles organized crime connections. I've already been shot at and threatened, I have, lets say, interviewed one of the city's notorious hit men, and I have proof that your name is directly connected to this conspiracy.

"You need to contact your attorney tonight, tomorrow morning latest, and get out of this contract. You must do this immediately, I can't emphasize how important this is."

"I'll call him as soon as I hang up, and thank you. After I cancel my contracts and break off any relationship with these people, then what?"

"There is danger in this, Senator, big danger. They are not going to willingly let all this money get away from them. I would suggest some serious personal safety precautions, sir. I'm going to continue my end of the investigation because I've already gotten so deeply involved. For my own protection, I have to bring these fools down."

"You've already earned your retainer, Mr. Dorsey," the senator said, quietly. "I can't thank you enough for that. I want to see to it that these people are found out and brought to justice, so I will be forwarding a check for ten thousand dollars, Dorsey, for you to continue your work.

"I've never worked with a private investigator before, and I admit I had my doubts about contacting you. You've done a fine job and I want you to be able to continue. Have a Merry Christmas, Dorsey, and keep me informed on what's happening with your investigation."

"Thank you, Senator, I will. Stay safe and have yourself a fine Christmas." There was a smile wide and bright enough to light up Pacific Avenue when Dorsey hung up the telephone. "Liquor cabinet will be filled with some fine Kentucky this winter," he murmured, heading for the shower and a long sleep. The neighbors would testify that Dorsey's shower was four full Christmas carols long.

5.

"You've gotta do something about this coffee, Serious. Even that acid I make is better than this. Oh, yeah, good morning. Is Sergeant Adams going to join us?"

"She'll be here shortly. Sit down and be quiet for a minute," Captain Elmo was even more serious than usual as he stood behind his desk chewing on the stub of a horrible black cigar and holding a cup of coffee as if it was a Marine K-Bar. "Georgie the Mole is dead, Dorsey, and there are lots of questions flying around the department this morning."

"I didn't kill the puke. He was breathing fine the last time I saw him. How'd it happen? I thought you said he was in the hospital?"

"He was," Serious Elmo snarled. "He was in his bed, holding a dozen roses with a slashed throat. Want to know what the card said?"

Dorsey snickered, remembering how much fun it was sending that card. He also recognized the implications of what Elmo was saying. "Okay, Serious, I'll get serious too," he said, taking a swig of hot coffee. "I sent the roses and the card, but I didn't kill the little shit-head, but I'll bet Jimmy Torrance paid the knife man.

"Before you climb down my throat on this, let me tell you all about what I've learned in the last twenty four hours." He opened his leather jacket and pulled some folded papers out, opened them up and handed them to Elmo. "If you were serious about putting Sergeant Adams on this case, she needs to be here now. Within the next thirty hours or so there's going to be a lot of blood spilling, and we're going to be dodging bullets from more than one source, if my observations are right."

Serious Elmo read through Dorsey's notes quickly, picked up the phone and told Adams to come to his office immediately. "You didn't kill The Mole, Dorsey, I know that, but because of you, that is, what he probably told you, he's dead. You better start being the smart guy I've known for years and lay off the smart ass crap." He threw the stub of cigar in a waste can, opened a drawer in his desk, and pulled an equally big and black cigar out.

"You're not gonna light that thing, are you?" Dorsey asked, feigning gagging. He had his hands clinching his neck when Sergeant Jenny Adams waltzed through the office door.

"Oh, God, Captain, don't. Please don't." she said, looking at Serious Elmo, then Dorsey, and aping Dorsey, grabbed her throat and let her eyes go way up inside the lids.

Adams was a tall, very well proportioned woman, dressed in a pants suit that, one, did not hide her delightful little bottom end, and two, allowed well developed breasts to fill the material. Her eyes sparkled through a raft of freckles across her nose and cheeks, and red hair flashed through curls hanging just to her collar.

Elmo chuckled, pulling a wooden match from his desk, striking it across the desktop, and lighting the monster cigar. "You know that's illegal," Adams said.

"Arrest me," Elmo snarled, "but sit down and listen first. Dorsey, knock it off and give us both a run down on what the hell is going on. And, while you're at it, tell me why this department is involved in something taking place two or three counties away from this city."

"You're not involved, Serious, only your resources," Dorsey chortled. Sergeant Adams laughed, caught herself following a glower from Elmo. "Then again," Dorsey said, "because of Starr Baby's murder and the slashing death of The Mole, maybe you are. Anyway, here's why Starr Baby and The Mole are no longer with us."

"Jenny, you're from Santa Cruz, so you might already be slightly aware of what I'm going to say. County Commissioner Amos Sterling, actually the Chairman of the Board of Supervisors, is believed to be the politician that will get the land deal pushed through that Bargetto got himself involved in.

"Bargetto thought he and Jimmy Torrance were going to develop a high end planned community. Torrance is actually planning just the opposite and more than twice the size Bargetto had in mind. Torrance is backed by Gerald Whistler, kingpin of the local branch of the Los Angeles family.

"The permits for such a project would simply not be available. I believe much of the land is in or near the redwoods, which would end any project immediately, but money talks and it has been flowing into Sterling's bank accounts. In Santa Cruz, if you want something done, you have a tripartite to work through. Sterling at the head, then District Attorney Jimmy Lucent, and Sheriff Terrence Bogart.

"The permit process has already started, and under the table, changes to the planned community are being made without anyone's knowledge except those three. The commissioners still think they are talking about a six hundred forty acre limited planned community." Dorsey took a breath, down deep and looked at the two.

"The Bargetto Plan, I'll call it, consists of large lots with expensive homes in a well ordered planned community. The Torrance Plan is twice that size, dense population living in low-income housing. The planning commission and county commission will be discussing the Bargetto Plan, but if they vote approval, they will be approving the Torrance Plan."

Adams and Elmo sat, almost stunned, for a couple of seconds. "How much money is involved in this, Sol?" Elmo asked quietly.

"If the project sold out, it is estimated to be worth hundreds of millions of dollars. Here's how it works. The partnership of county officials, Torrance, and Whistler would sell the lots, then the construction contracts would be handled by the partnership of Torrance and Whistler, and the mortgages would be handled by the partnership of Whistler and his Los Angeles money sharks. At the end of the day, maybe more than a billion dollars, U.S."

"How much of this do the feds know, Sol?" Adams asked. "This is federal from the git-go. Why are we involved?"

"I'm going to say it again, Jenny. You're not, I am. My client is Senator Bargetto and my job is to keep his name out of this. I'm also involved because of Starr Baby's murder. Her legal name is Monica P. Fetterman, her mother is Elsa Fetterman, Jimmy Torrance's ex-wife. Starr Baby is Torrance's stepdaughter. I think she found out about the deals and tried to contact me.

"Between her murder, now The Mole's murder, and the land fraud scheme, we have enough broken law to keep an army of attorney's busy for a decade or more. If the feds aren't aware of what's going on in Santa Cruz County, they will be soon. I'm only interested in keeping Bargetto's name clean and solving a couple of murders."

There was a gentle knock on the door and a uniformed officer stepped in with a fresh pot of coffee. "Somebody smoking in here?" he asked.

After realizing he wasn't going to get an answer he ducked out, Elmo snorted, and Dorsey poured fresh coffee for everyone. Adams caught herself almost blurting out, "he is," and just sat quiet, staring at the wall. Elmo snorted again. "Is it safe to say, Dorsey, that you might have some kind of plan?" Elmo knew Dorsey well enough to know that behind all the smart-ass, behind all the bravado, there was a determined investigator's mind always at work.

"I want you to assign the murder of Starr Baby's investigation to Sergeant Adams, and then ask me to help her as a consultant to the department. We've done this before, Serious, and it's worked well. Bargetto's attorney is already cancelling his contract with the Whistler/Torrance deal, but the senator wants me to help bring down the fraudulent land deal." Dorsey looked over to Jenny Adams, and continued. "You'll have to get out of your uniform, Jenny."

"Well," she said, "There's a line I haven't heard before." She gave him a quick smile, and said, "This isn't a uniform, Mr. Dorsey, and I'd rather keep it on, at least until we get to know each other."

Elmo spit blue smoke clear to the ceiling and Dorsey sat very still, a little boy's grin spread across his mug.

~ ~ ~

Sergeant of Detectives Jennifer Adams was a ten-year veteran of the department, stood a solid five feet eight inches and weighed in at one hundred thirty eight and one half pounds. She studied Tae Kwon Do, other Asian practices, held numerous shooting championships, and in her words, "takes no crap from anyone." She was wearing a smile on her attractive face as she left the office to put paper work together and make plans for a trip to Santa Cruz. She headed quickly to her apartment to pack.

"I don't know if Captain Elmo assigned me to work with Dorsey or the other way around, but this is liable to be the job that gets me those lieutenant's bars. If I live through it," she chuckled, slipping into a pair of jeans with a western snap front shirt and highly polished western boots. She had a nine-millimeter tucked into the middle of her back and a little thirty-two inside her left boot.

What the patrons of Maglio's Deli saw was a stunning reddish-blonde woman dressed in western attire, including a buckskin sport jacket. Her blue eyes blazed with pride and dignity as she looked about for her companions, spotting them at a large banquette for six. "I decided I should wear something, Sol. Is that okay with you?"

"Crap, now I've got two of you to put up with," Serious Elmo snorted, pouring Jenny a pint of ale and making room for her on the leather seat. "The paperwork is going through the channels now," he said. "Jenny, as far as the department is concerned, you are the lead investigator for the cases involving Starr and The Mole. In real time, Sol, this is your baby.

"As you said, what you're looking for are the resources my department can provide, and the gift bag is now open. I will expect police procedures, my dear Mr. Dorsey, as you are now a paid consultant for the department. Do not get us involved in another civil rights violation court case."

Over the years, between Dorsey and Elmo, the department has had to defend at least three civil rights cases, and because of Dorsey, lost two of them, despite the fact the crimes involved were solved, the criminal involved paid for the crime, and peace in the valley was restored.

Dorsey, his arm gently waving Captain Elmo off, said something to the effect of, "okay fine, whatever", and motioned to Maglio for another platter of crab enchiladas. "I wonder how long I'd live if Maglio ever closed this joint?" Dorsey racked back on the leather-covered bench, smiled and looked at Jennifer Adams.

"Nice jacket. I have reservations at the Hi Top Motel near Felton, Jenny, and I think we should head down there today, right after we finish here. My dear Captain Elmo, sir, I booked two rooms, according to current police protocol." He ducked a huge left hand that barely missed the middle of his nose, laughing on the one hand, thinking that he might have gotten lucky. *That would have hurt.*

"Thank you for the comment on my jacket, Sol. When I'm doing my horse work on the weekends, this is how I dress. Most comfortable, and not even a little cop-shop. Are the rooms connected? Sure would make it easier. For work, smart ass," she said before he could say anything.

"As much as I would enjoy your company, I think it's best that we have two vehicles when we're down there. Requisition something that doesn't say police all over it. These guys have already proved that they want me dead, so this is going to be dangerous. We're walking into their home nest, Jenny, so no secrets from each other. Yes, I asked for connecting rooms."

"No problem with that," she said. "I'll bring my own truck, Sol. I drive a Ford F-250, four wheel drive, and it's as red as red can get. It will also climb a telephone pole if it can grab hold."

"I have maps of what Bargetto planned and a vague idea of what Torrance is planning, all the addresses and phone numbers of those involved, and as much of the case files as I could get on disc. So, that out of the way, let's celebrate, make merry, and enjoy the victuals handed out by one fine Sicilian who is a master at Mexican cuisine."

"One more thing, you two," Serious Elmo said. "You won't have any back up down there. Remember what Sol said about the county sheriff. He's one of them, not one of us. You'll be on your own, and I can't send in the cavalry."

~ ~ ~

"According to Andy Castro, that bitch Sergeant Adams is teaming up with Dorsey and they're coming after us, Jimmy," Whistler said. "I want them eliminated. Don't use local guns, bring in some heavies from Los Angeles, and blow those two away. Shark bait, food for crabs, is what I want to hear back from you."

"I got a tail on Dorsey, but didn't know about Adams, Ger," Torrance said. "She's city detective, she can't operate in Santa Cruz County."

"She's working for Dorsey, dummy. Get your head back out in the daylight, and find out where those two are, and eliminate them." Whistler remembered how slow Torrance was on the uptake and let his anger boil over. "It was supposed to be done two days ago. Don't let me down."

Torrance hung up, poured a double of twelve year old, and let a lady called Peaches rub his stiff neck. "Man's got an anger sometimes," he mumbled, looking through his cell phone for a number, punched it in, and waited for an answer.

"Better be important," a voice said. "No calls to this number, remember?"

"I need two experts as fast as they can be delivered. The last two weren't. Same target plus one. Aptos, tomorrow," and the connection was severed.

Aptos was a high-end community between Santa Cruz and Watsonville on the Monterey Bay. Torrance had a five-acre property in heavy timber, well off busy roads. Large black SUVs with tinted windows could be seen arriving and leaving the property regularly, along with vehicles that carried official Santa Cruz County license plates. Torrance made a second call immediately.

"Amos, Jimmy," he said. "I'll be at the ranch in a couple of hours. Let's have cocktails and some rare rib-eyes. Bring Jimmy and Terry."

Amos Sterling, Chairman of the Santa Cruz County Board of Supervisors called District Attorney Jimmy Lucent and Sheriff Terrence Bogart, and passed that information along, sat back and smiled. *I think it's time to put my own plans into action around here. There are too many fingers in this pie to suit me.*

6.

"**I** think I'll take the coast road down instead of the freeway," Dorsey mumbled putting his laptop, briefcase, and single piece of luggage in the trunk of the fifty-six Caddy. "Too cold to put the top down, but still a nice drive." He was humming a little Christmas ditty, thinking of what it would be like to spend the holiday in the Santa Cruz mountains. He made one stop for what he called 'camp victuals', packages of Top Ramen, hot dogs and buns, family size bags of chips, and a twelve pack of Sierra Nevada Pale Ale.

"I like to live the good life," he said, as he slipped the bags into the back seat, belted in, and headed south. He had five hundred horses under the hood, twin four-barrel carbs that pumped gas and air in, and headers that pumped exhaust out. There were electric doors, hood and trunk were opened electrically, and he had brand new independent front suspension along with power steering and power disc brakes. The only things Dorsey took better care of were his guns.

Within just a few minutes he realized he had a tail and called Jenny. "Got a pale blue pickup with me, Jen-babe, I'm on the coast highway, coming up the pass. Where are you?"

"I was gonna take the freeway, but I can switch over real quick. I'll catch up. Know the truck?"

"Nope. Keep me posted," he said. He kept the Caddy close to the speed limit for a few minutes then opened it up for a short spell of five miles or so, watching the pickup in the rearview mirror. The road became a mountain pass leading down to the coast, tall redwoods, ferns, madrone, and little traffic. "Bastard thinks he's a good driver," Dorsey muttered, and nudged the eighty mark on the speedometer through some tricky turns.

"Okay, buddy-boy, time to find out who you are." Dorsey slowed back down to fifty, the pale blue pickup did the same, never getting close enough for Dorsey to identify the driver and his companion. As they approached a tight turn on the two-lane road, Dorsey swung the big Caddy into a power one-eighty, and drove head-on at the pickup.

"I like that new independent front suspension," he smiled, as he forced the pickup off the road and into a ditch. He quickly whipped the Caddy into another complete turn-around, and slid to a stop next to the truck.

He was out of the Caddy, forty-five in hand, walked up to the pickup, now on its side in the ditch. "They will have to climb out and I'll just wait for them, I think." He found his cell, told Jenny what was going down, and opened a bag of chips. He hadn't seen another car on the road for some time. "Or, maybe I'll just call 911 like a good citizen," he chuckled. "Don't dare open a beer, damn it."

Jenny's flame red pickup slid to a stop behind the Caddy and she ran up to Dorsey. "You okay? What's the scene?"

"Your next question should be 'who's on first'," he quipped getting a blank stare back. "No movement from inside, so far. They didn't hit hard enough to get hurt, so I think they are all tangled up in their seatbelts, kicking and smacking each other. Want a chip?"

She took a couple and munched them down. "Are you going to do anything? It would be nice to know who they are."

"Hired punks is who they are, and bad drivers, and dumb. Let's continue on, and in ten-minutes or so I'll call 911 and report a drunk driver in a pale blue pickup."

Jenny Adams just shook her head, jumped back in her pickup and followed Dorsey back on the road to Santa Cruz. "I think this is going to be one long learning experience," she chuckled, double clutched into fourth gear and let the cold air blow in from the open window.

One of the men in the ditched pick-up was unconscious, having driven his head into the windshield because of no seat belt. The other was trying to get himself unbuckled, did, and fell across his knocked out partner. He found his cell phone, and made one call.

"Janice, the bastard got away. We're on our side in a ditch on the road to the coast." All he got back was nasty words and exclamations indicating he would not work for her again.

~ ~ ~

Amos Sterling was king of the county in his estimation, but maybe a little less in the thoughts of some others in the county, including Jim Racine, editor of the *Eagle Star Press*. Racine hired two bodyguards following threats that included possible bombings, arson, and murder. Sheriff Terrence Bogart, after reading the sheet of paper the threats had been pasted onto, chuckled, saying something about kids today and just some punks having fun.

"You consider a murder and bomb threat just some kids having fun? You're not going to investigate this?"

"Oh, Jim," the sheriff said, "Take it easy. Maybe you just riled somebody with your inflammatory editorials is all. I wouldn't worry too much."

Two days later Racine's garage burned to the ground, and the fire department arson boys called it just that. "No, it wasn't arson," Sheriff Bogart told the firefighter. "Looks to me like Racine put some hot ashes in the garage near a gas can. He should know better."

"The fire was started with gasoline, Sheriff," firefighter Robert Simmonds said, "but it started outside. This is arson, Sheriff."

Bogart refused to investigate the fire, and two days after that, Racine's dog was mutilated and left on the editor's porch. The sheriff called it childish pranks. Racine hired the two bodyguards from the National Guard unit Racine is attached to. Both saw duty in Iraq and Afghanistan.

"No, Captain Racine, there's nothing in the regulations about you hiring us. We're not active duty now." Sergeant Jack Swafford had served two tours in Iraq and two more in Afghanistan, had medals hanging all over his chest when he dressed up, and was looking forward to helping his friend and guard platoon leader. "Bogart and Sterling think they own this county, Jim, and I know they can play mighty rough. Who are you asking to be with me on this?"

They were at Racine's cabin in the redwoods near Felton, a small former logging village north of Santa Cruz. The cabin was built from redwood logs more than a century ago and featured a covered veranda that encircled the cabin, giving the building the effect of being rather large.

"El Charo himself," Racine said, pouring each of them a little bourbon in cups of steaming coffee. "Master Sergeant Tomas 'El Charo' Gutierrez will be charming us with his presence shortly. The two of you should scare the bejeesus out of just about anyone even thinking of doing something stupid."

Dust was flying as a horrible old pickup, bent and twisted, smoking and belching, slid to a stop in Racine's driveway. "El Charo has arrived," the tall, wide, heavy Gutierrez said jumping from the truck, waving a grocery bag around. He was followed out of the pickup by a long-legged, scroungy looking black mongrel dog with a long tail that had never once been known to not be wagging furiously.

"I have offerings from the gods," El Charo said stepping onto the porch. "Steaks from one of my own beeves, wine from my neighbor's vineyard, and sourdough biscuits from Maria's oven. Am I welcome?"

"You do know how to make an entrance," Racine said, laughing and fending off the dog's tail.

~ ~ ~

Dorsey led the vehicles into the parking lot of the Hi-Top Motel in Felton and within the hour the two were settled in their adjoining rooms. The Hi-Top was built back in the 50s and has fared well despite the hundreds of thousands of tourists that flock to the redwoods and Santa Cruz's famous white sands and cold Pacific Ocean waves every year. The rooms reflect the old days, with spacious rooms, well-appointed furniture, and clean bathrooms.

"Let's use my room as the computer and office room since I only brought enough clothes and personal effects for a few days," Dorsey grumbled. "Three filled-to-the-brim suitcases? I hope at least one has guns in it."

"A girl must always have her stuff," she smiled back at him. "I sleep with my guns, Dorsey." Was that a threat, he wondered, watching her try to get settled.

"Setting aside our little personal-effects differences, I brought a list of people that I know here in the area, that just might be able to help us. The first person we have to contact is Jim Racine. He's the editor of the *Eagle Star Review*, and is a relentless enemy of Sterling and company."

"Senator Bargetto didn't want the press involved in this," Dorsey said, "but I think that's already gone by the boards. If we maintain that we are investigating the murder of Starr Baby and The Mole, we might keep his name out of print."

"Racine will see right through that, Dorsey," she said. "He knows me and my family, and I'm sure he's heard of you, hot-shot. Maybe with others we can do some pretending, but not with Racine. Do we have a plan?"

"That's our first order of business, Jenny, since we haven't sat down together since this started. This is Christmas week and that usually means government and some businesses will be working short staffed. That might be to our benefit. Let's plan on meeting this Racine feller first, then I want to see the property that is behind all this."

"While you're doing that," Jenny said, "I'll get as much paperwork as I can from the planning commission and other agencies, and see if I can get a reading on what people are being told and what they might be thinking, as far as the project goes.

"Do you want to make contact with Torrance or any of the county officials?"

"I want us to scope them out first, but yes, I think we'll have to have direct contact. Too many questions, too many laws being broken, too deep a conspiracy to not have direct contact. The more I think about all this, I feel there's more to it than this huge conspiracy."

"Well, you have the DA, the sheriff, and the chairman of the county commission involved in a conspiracy that could net somewhere near a billion dollars, you said. Jeez, Sol, you think there's more?"

He laughed, popping two cans of beer and handing her one. "Greed breeds greed, dear girl, and with this kind of money involved, greed becomes the driving force. Think about this for a minute. With Whistler comes the Los Angeles family, and then Torrance brings the Santa Cruz element to the table, and the pie slices get just a bit smaller and smaller as more and more need to be compensated.

"At some point someone in that long chain is going to want more than just his slice of pie. That's how most conspiracies end, my good Sergeant Adams, with selfish fighting eating it up from within."

"My God, I'm spending the weekend with a philosopher," she feigned a swoon, and polished off a beer. "I also know you're right. After we talk with Racine let's find Torrance. That would be in line with our murder investigation. I'll call Racine right now."

"It's getting late, but go ahead and call and we can meet him first thing in the morning. I'm so hungry I'm having delusions," he said, popping another two beers for them. "I can almost smell a hardwood grilled steak, three inches thick and three pounds heavy, covered in mushrooms and garlic, with a quart of mountain aged red wine so hearty it pours slow."

"That sounds like dinner for six, Dorsey," she said, slipping into her room to call Racine. Dorsey stepped out of the room to give the surroundings a good look, mostly to see if there might be a good steak house next door or a pizza parlor, or at the least a convenience store stocked with beer. "What kind of podunk area did I bring us to?" he muttered slipping back into the room.

"Racine lives about a mile from here, Dorsey," Jenny said coming in from her room, "and he would like us to come down to his place now, if we can. He has a couple of people with him he wants us to meet."

"Hope he has food and beer," Dorsey said. "Better wear a heavy coat. I just stepped out and it's cold out there, and it feels like more rain coming."

7.

"**D**id you authorize tails on Dorsey?" Whistler screamed into the telephone.

"No," Jimmy Torrance said. "I have two people coming here from Los Angeles, should be here late tonight. According to Sterling, Dorsey is sure to call on Jim Racine and we'll pick up the trail from there. Did something happen?"

"Yeah, two fools with enough illegal guns to put them away for life were following Dorsey and he ran 'em off the road and into a ditch. They called me for bail, Jimmy. The dumb bastards called me for Bail!" he screamed. "Now, that Captain Elmo has me pegged as a gun-runner. All I see is amateurs, Torrance, kids playing games. The hit on Monica was fouled, The Mole tells all and is dead, the hit on Dorsey misses, and now this.

"Count the dollars, Torrance. How many dollars are we looking at? I better start seeing some professionalism around this job."

"Those weren't my people, Gerald, it wasn't my play. I don't know anything about this. Did you get names? Something we can follow up on?"

"I sent the names and incident report to you by e-mail, Jimmy. If this wasn't you, I wonder who else is after Dorsey. Maybe they'll get lucky," he laughed, "and kill him before we get a chance. See you tomorrow," and he hung up.

Whistler seemed to have forgotten that he suggested in strong language that Janice Wilson take care of The Mole and Dorsey. Wilson normally did her own work, seldom hired anyone, but did put two men on Dorsey's tail. They were to simply tail and keep her informed. She used a fine combat knife she had taken from a Columbian drug runner to kill The Mole.

"Your job was to just keep track of Dorsey so I could get to him, she screamed at the two young men, extricated from their pick-up and now extricated from jail cells, for the moment. "Stupid punks," she spit, pulling at a silenced semi-auto, pumping three shots into the chests of each man. "Tony, take these little boys ten miles or so off shore, weight 'em down some and dump 'em. "Stupid punks," she snarled again.

"When you get back, find Dorsey and call me. Got that, Tony?" He was quick to say yes and got body bags out and opened. At least he would be safe on his boat, he mused. "I have to go down south for a few days, and I don't want to hear about another failure. You find him and you be the professional I thought I hired."

~ ~ ~

Torrance walked into the large living room of his ranch house north of Aptos, poured a glass of whiskey and thought about what Whistler said. "Count the money, he said, and that's all I've been doing since discovering this little bonanza." He walked to a small office just off the main room and picked up a sheaf of papers from his fax machine, sat at his large walnut desk and started paging through the notes.

"Damn," he said, slamming a single sheet of paper down on the desk. He slammed his fist onto the desk three more times, standing up and pacing about the room. "According to Jimmy Lucent, that contract was air-tight. He's the district attorney, he should know these things. Bargetto can't just cancel our deal. No, no, no," he said.

Torrance picked up the phone and tried to call Lucent but the office was closed, and he tried the private line, and got voice mail. "Just call me, Jimmy, it's important," he said, hanging up the phone. *The sheriff wouldn't know a contract from an apple and Sterling would go off half-cocked about deals and permits and water and crap. Bargetto can't back out, half the project is his land, that's what made it so good.* Torrance paced completely around the ranch house, his mind going a million miles an hour and not coming up with answers. *Starr Baby was supposed to compromise Bargetto so he couldn't back out and got killed, and Bargetto's name alone would be worth hundreds of millions of dollars. Damn,* he thought, his mind tumbling all around the land project.

"I don't want to call Whistler, but I gotta," he muttered, heading back to his little office. He stopped at the liquor cabinet on the way and poured a very healthy glass of bourbon before making the call. He could almost feel the tension leave his body when Whistler didn't answer the phone and he got the answer machine instead.

"Gerald," he said, "I just got a screwed up e-mail from Bargetto's attorney. When you get a minute you might want to call him and clarify what he was trying to say. I'm meeting with Santa Cruz people tonight, Los Angeles people should be here tomorrow," and he hung up, wiping sweat from his brow.

While he was on the phone Sterling and Lucent arrived and as they poured their own drinks said the sheriff wasn't too far behind them. Torrance nodded and simply handed the letter from Bargetto's attorney to Lucent. "We need an explanation, Jimmy," is all he said.

Lucent was hard-boiled in his attitude toward his elected position and it's built in power base and didn't take kindly to having his legal opinions questioned. Judges found themselves in serious political jeopardy when they ruled against the gentleman, and more than one man had found himself in prison on trumped up evidence and witness tampering. As he read the missive his brows furrowed and his mouth quivered with anger.

"He won't get away with this," Lucent snarled. "I'll see to it that he will never be re-elected, I'll destroy him before I let him get away with this."

"That's fine, Jimmy," Torrance said, quietly, his anger halfway under control. "Make your threats and get it out of your system, and then you can tell us what is really going to happen. There is enough money involved for each of us to own a South Pacific Island and live like tropical kings, Jimmy. I don't want to lose that.

"Now, get yourself put together and tell us exactly what that letter means. Mr. Whistler is going to be contacting Bargetto's attorney first thing in the morning and it's safe to assume there may be changes on the way."

"What's going on, Torrance?" Sterling asked. "Let me see that." He took the fax from Lucent and read it quickly. "You said that was an unbreakable contract, Lucent. You better make this right," he snarled, sweat beading on his forehead. Sterling's anger equaled his arrogance, and he squared his shoulders, let his chin jut forward, and Torrance was sure he was looking at Mousseline strutting around Rome during World War Two.

"We have votes coming up from the planning commission and from taxing committees, all of whom will want to know that we have contracted guarantees from Senator Bargetto. You make this right," Sterling barked, handing the fax back to the district attorney.

~ ~ ~

"It's chilly here in the mountains," Jenny Adams said as she slipped into the Caddy for the short ride to Jim Racine's Felton cabin. "Do you know that it will be Christmas in just three days? Why are we chasing bad guys at Christmas?"

"Bad guys don't give a damn about Christmas. What are you getting me?" Dorsey asked, firing up the five hundred horses he had tucked under the hood of that fifty-six. "Maybe we should decorate the motel rooms, or put up a tree."

"Oh, boy, do you have the spirit," she scowled. "Turn right and it'll be a large log cabin with a big veranda porch all the way around. I want diamonds and chocolate, and not necessarily in that order. You're getting a lump of coal."

That brought a guffaw from Dorsey and he spotted the cabin and pulled in next to a horrible old pickup that had more dings and dents than areas without them. "Look at that wreck. Racine must be rolling in dough, eh?" When he got out of the car he was almost mauled by a scruffy dog with a massive tail. "As big as you are, dog, I'm glad you know how to wag your tail in greeting. Jeez," he growled, helping Jenny out of the car.

Two huge men were standing on the porch as Dorsey and Adams came up the short walkway. "Which one of those bruisers is Racine?" Dorsey asked, sizing the two up. The one on the left, a Mexican dressed in full western cowboy gear stood well over six feet and was heavy in the chest and shoulders, while the other, equally as tall, was simply heavy from his feet to the top of his head.

The tall Mexican cowboy was giving Jenny, the tall, well-developed cowgirl a full looking over, including a generous welcoming smile. She heard

Dorsey's question and was in turn busy giving this wide-eyed cowboy an equally long look.

Before Jenny could answer, Jim Racine appeared between the two heavies, smiling a welcome. "Hi, Jenny, it's been way too long since you visited." He hugged her and shoved a big hand toward Dorsey. "You must be Sol Dorsey, hello and welcome to my little abode, I'm Jim Racine."

The two men shook hands and Racine led the way into the cabin. "These two fine gentlemen have graced me with their size and strength, along with their desire to clean up this little county of ours. Sol, Jenny, meet Jack Swafford and Tomas Gutierrez." The men shook hands all around, each sizing the other, making decisions on how they would react toward the other, should the occasion happen. It would be the gentlemanly thing to do, whether in an editor's abode or your neighborhood saloon.

Racine suggested they gather around the large rock fireplace that was blazing on a chilly early evening. "What brings you back home, Jenny?" Racine asked after offering cold beer around. "We don't get to see you that often."

Dorsey answered for her. "Our desire to clean up this little county of yours."

Jenny laughed, but was deadly serious when she continued. "We're investigating a couple of murders that took place in the city but probably originated down here, and in the process, we hope to squelch a land fraud conspiracy that may be behind the whole thing. Nice to see you, too, Jim," she laughed.

"So, you're a sergeant," Gutierrez said with a smile. "I am too. You're a cop sergeant and I'm a National Guard sergeant. Us sergeants should stick together." The smile was large, open, and as friendly as any smile Jenny Adams could remember getting.

"I've always believed that," she answered. Dorsey scowled, but tried not to let her see it.

They had two more bottles of good home brew. "You make this?" Dorsey asked, taking a long draught. "I should learn how to do this. It's good."

Dorsey went into detail on the conspiracy and Racine listened in awe. "I've questioned this from day one and not gotten one single decent answer. Let me show you something, Mr. Dorsey," he said as he walked to a desk in the corner of the large room. He returned with the letters about his brutally murdered dog and burned out garage. "This is what you'll be up against. Between Sterling, Lucent, and that fool Bogart, no one is safe in this county if they question any of the three."

Dorsey took his time reading the threats and the sheriff's reply to them and handed them to Jenny to read. He looked at Racine, then the two big men, and smiled before saying, "so you two are protection then. I think that's a smart move, Racine, very smart." Dorsey looked at the big Mexican and slowly shook his head back and forth.

"What kind of a damn fool would it be to go up against you?" he chuckled. "I heard Jim call you Charo, is that a nick name?"

"No," he said in a quiet voice, and with no discernable accent. "It means cowboy in Spanish. My family came to this country in the seventeen hundreds to settle a Spanish land grant. I still live on what's left of it. The Spanish horsemen are called vaqueros and the Spanish and Mexican cowboys are Charos. My wonderful friend Jim Racine started calling me El Charo when I was pretty young. We served in Desert Storm together and scared the hell out of the Iraq soldier boys with our wild-west approach to frontal assault."

Swafford was laughing hard when he said, "Saddam had wanted posters on the two of them and I spent a great deal time keeping them out of the jails everywhere we went. These little turds here in Santa Cruz don't know what they're up against."

Jenny shook her head, agreeing, and adding, "And with Sol Dorsey along for the ride, this county will never be the same."

"I think those half-beeves you brought over, Charo, are about ready. Let's eat," Racine said, "and Dorsey you and Jenny can tell us your plans and your idea of a frontal assault."

Great bowls of beans and chili, loaves of sourdough rolls, and enough grilled beef to feed Patton's Third Army filled a massive table in the kitchen-dining room and the group settled in. Cold beer was available in quantity. "This is my way of life," Dorsey said. "I may never leave, Jim. I may just set up camp in your front yard."

"You'd be welcome, Dorsey." Racine got contemplative for a couple of minutes, looking first at Dorsey, then over at Jenny, and giving his two bodyguards a good going over as well. "This is a very dangerous time and I've been trying to keep my thoughts going the right way, but I don't know how we're going to bring these people to face the bench."

"Well," Dorsey said, "Jenny is going to spend the next couple of days digging through everything available at the county complex, petitions for land use change, permit applications, land ownership, and county commission decisions and discussions, planning commission agendas, basically, everything that might lead us to the fraud and conspiracy. We know it's there, we have to be able to prove it, and more than likely, the entire case will end up in the hands of federal investigators."

"Our primary concern," Jenny said, "is to bring your county officials to their knees, begging for forgiveness. Secondarily, we have two murders to solve, and this is just one case.

"How in the hell can you guys eat this much? There must have been ten pounds of meat on that platter and a gallon of beans."

"My mama always said to clean my plate," El Charo said with a straight face. "What about you, Dorsey? What are you going to be doing while Sergeant Adams is at the court house?"

"I'm going after Torrance, but need to do some site work first. Check out exactly where their development is located, check out Torrance's ranch so I know how to get in and out, and work with Jenny on what she discovers.

"Jim, we're going to be making as little noise as possible, and if you could hold back on your reporting about us until it's over, we'll see to it that you are aware of every single thing we come up with."

"That's a deal Dorsey. I have considerable files, Jenny, that you might find very interesting. I'll give them to you before you leave. I keep them here instead of the office. I've had several break-ins at the plant and I don't want these to get away. I've put everything on disc, so it should be easy for you."

~ ~ ~

"It was hard to leave that fireplace," Dorsey said as the two returned to their motel with a large valise filled with discs and paper work. "Those two monsters should be able to keep Racine safe. It's nice to have that kind of backup."

Jenny had a smile on her face remembering the huge Mexican and his "fond farewell, oh sergeant of mine," speech.

"Don't worry, Dorsey. I've got your back," she laughed, getting the door opened for him. "How about we have a nip of your fine bourbon before we hit the hay for the night. We've got some busy days ahead."

"Uh, right away, ma'am," he said, watching her turn down the bed covers and slowly slip out of a western style shirt, unbutton her jeans, and dance lightly into the bathroom for a hot shower. "Right away."

8.

J immy Lucent was pacing about the great room in Jimmy Torrance's ranch home, reading and rereading the letter from Senator Bargetto's lawyer. Amos Sterling poured another full glass of Scotch and stood quietly by the fire watching. "It seems the great legal mind may have slipped a cog or two," he said, not as quietly as one would think. "I wonder what Whistler's friends will think of this, you know, the ones that would get the building contracts, the road construction projects? The home mortgage loans?

"There just might be a little kicking and screaming from the Los Angeles money lenders and mortgage brokers looking to make their piles of green as well. I seem to remember something along these lines being said. Something about superior knowledge of law, something to do with unbreakable contract, or was I listening wrong?

"If you've screwed this up for us I'll cut you into tiny pieces and use each piece as crab bait, bait for bottom feeders, because that's all you would be worth."

The two men had problems in the past, both believing they were to be considered the primary leaders in the county, both with extreme egos and greedy desires for money and power. Torrance stayed near the large picture windows and watched the little emotional dance the two were working toward. "I'll take care of this in the morning, Sterling," is all that Lucent said, scowling again at the now crumpled letter in his hand.

"Here comes the sheriff," Torrance said, walking toward the door to let Bogart in. Lucent and Sterling moved away from the fire to welcome the large man. "Evening, Terry," Torrance said, holding the door open. "Bar's open and the fire's hot."

"Hi, Jimmy, Jimmy, Sterling, sorry I'm late. I just got off the phone with a guy in the city who had some interesting information to pass along. Seems a private investigator named Sol Dorsey is going to be paying us a visit in the next few days. Some dumb ass prostitute was killed and he thinks the perp might be down here. Don't know why I'd be interested?"

Jimmy Torrance wanted to roll his eyes up in wonder, thought what a dumb ass Bogart was, and just smiled. "The young lady that was murdered, Sheriff, was my stepdaughter, and the hit was supposed to reflect on Senator Bargetto. The Mole screwed it up, and now Dorsey has his eyes on us. Believe me, that man is not looking to solve that murder, he's working for Bargetto and he's looking to sink us.

"Our friend the district attorney has also thrown his version of a monkey wrench into our little program." He scowled at both Bogart and Lucent. "Show the sheriff the letter we got from Bargetto."

The sheriff read the letter and handed it back to Lucent. "I thought you said it was unbreakable," Terry Bogart said in all innocence. This time Torrance did let his eyes roll up into his head.

"I want you to see to it that Dorsey doesn't live through his visit to our fine county," Torrance said to Bogart. "I'm very familiar with Dorsey's reputation and our plans are in jeopardy if he lives. I don't want you to scare him, Terry, I want you to kill him. Understood?"

"I'll see what I can do," Bogart said, looking down at the carpet, wringing his hands, edging closer to the open liquor cabinet. "There are a couple of people that I might be able to contact."

"Bullshit!" Torrance stormed. "I have people coming up from Los Angeles, and when they get here, you make damn sure they know exactly where Dorsey is, and you make sure none of your deputies get in their way. I want that man dead, and I mean, dead."

Whistler spent many hours worrying about Torrance and how slow his mind worked, how he often was unable to see a problem even if that problem already bit him in the ass. On the other hand, Torrance spent considerable time wondering just how slow and stupid Sheriff Terrance Bogart really was. *Sterling and Lucent think the world revolves around them and Bogart just stumbles through life.*

Bogart's reputation would have indicated that the killing of a single PI would be a rather simple matter, but reputations sometimes aren't exactly accurate. Bogart was tough as nails with little local small-time hoods in the county, the meth heads, pot smokers, and burglars, and his deputies were known to bust heads just because they could, but the sheriff was not known for his intellectual abilities.

The sheriff was made aware of Sol Dorsey's reputation by Torrance, feared the consequences of what might come from his visit, and had to contemplate working with hired guns to waste him. "You don't think Dorsey can be scared off? I'd be more comfortable with that," Bogart said.

"We are looking at losing hundreds of millions of dollars because of incompetence," Torrance snarled. "Unbreakable contracts that seem to be broken and a sheriff that appears to be a coward. I suppose next I'll have to tell Mr. Whistler that none of the permits we are paying for have been approved. Sterling?"

"The permits are moving through the planning and other committees just like they should, Jimmy. There are no problems there. I know how upset you are, understand perfectly, and feel this may not be the right time for us to start questioning each other." His political background was showing through. "Lucent, are you sure you can't save that contract? We need Bargetto's land and that big name of his to make this work. Think about how nice it would be to have his name attached to our development project, but is that lost? I guess we'll have to ride with what we know until you and Bargetto's lawyers have a talk.

"We do need his land to tie in with what I and Jimmy Torrance have put together. That part of the contract is essential. And, Sheriff, you've been in this from the git-go, you've known the dangers and what needs to be done. This isn't the time to question how we're going to get it done."

"We all have our lives on the line with this deal," Torrance said, nodding agreement with Sterling. "We have been careful to skirt certain issues, and a binding contract with a sitting United States Senator who already has a fine reputation in land development projects is our key." Torrance was wiping perspiration from his face, wanted to scream at Bogart's stupidity, and simply walked over to the bar for one more healthy shot of fine Scotch.

The conversation was ended when Torrance's Chinese cook announced that dinner was ready to be served. "Mr. Hop Su, your timing is once again immaculate. Gentlemen, shall we have supper?"

Hop Su had been with Torrance ever since the man bought the ranch and moved south from the city. He was a graduate of some fine culinary schools and was known in the Santa Cruz County social circles as a fine chef. "Tonight, we have slow grilled tenderloin of pork, new potatoes and peas, and a fresh spinach salad right out of our hot house," Torrance said, patting Hop Su on the shoulder.

~ ~ ~

"I'm most interested in seeing what Torrance's ranch looks like and then a look at what the development property looks like," Dorsey said as he and Jenny Adams sat across from each other at a small diner on the outskirts of Santa Cruz. "Your friend Racine is a tough one, but standing up to professional guns means hiring professional guns and he did the right thing."

"This is already very dangerous, not just for him, but for a lot of people that might accidentally get in the line of fire. I'm sure he's right about hired guns already on the scene." She got a big smile on her rather open and friendly face. "That was a pretty nice hired gun I spent some time with last night. I like large caliber guns," she snickered.

"I've always believed in lots of target practice," Dorsey smiled. "Keeps you sharp." He felt the toe of her boot rubbing gently on his leg. "You either need to knock that off right now, or we will end today's investigative sessions for more target practice."

She was still giggling like a little girl when the waitress brought the coffee pot around. "One more cup," Dorsey said, "and then it's off to work with us. County offices open at eight and I'm supposed to meet with El Charo at eight as well. I'm sure glad that guy is on our side. I also hope he leaves that dog at home."

Adams snickered remembering the dog trying to get in Dorsey's lap, knocking things off tables with his wild tail, Dorsey balancing his beer, and protecting his face from slobber. "There's a good fish restaurant near the main wharf, let's meet there later," Dorsey said. "Keep your cell close. If anything goes down or looks strange, you call. I'll do the same. I'm going to call Serious as soon as I get in the Caddy."

She was still giddy from the night before and would gladly have spent the rest of the day tucked between warm sheets with Dorsey showing off his skills in every way possible. "Never have relations with the person you're supposed to be working with, is something I've believed in from my first day on the job," she said, walking toward her pickup. "What the hell am I doing?" It was said with a smile a mile wide.

She slipped behind the wheel of her big pickup and fired off the engine, letting her mind get back on the job. *I've watched the politics in this county slide downhill for many years. Sterling has been dirty from his first day in office, and Bogart is so dumb he doesn't even know he's a criminal. Jim Racine has been the only voice of reason on this end of Monterey Bay for many years.*

It was a green foreign car of some kind that brought her back to reality when it ran a stop sign and she was able to get the Ford stopped just before impact. "Jackass," she snarled as she restarted the truck and headed to the county complex next to the courthouse. She realized that she better get her head screwed on straight, "and right now. If that had been a hit, I would be one dead little sergeant," she muttered. She kept remembering how Dorsey reminded Racine over and over how dangerous this situation was.

I wonder if that was intentional?

~ ~ ~

"Good morning, Senator, you're up bright and early."

"Now, Dorsey, that's a much better way to answer your phone. I did as you asked and we have cancelled the contract. There were two provisions in the operating deal we signed that let me out. So far you've done far more than I expected. I wanted you to know that."

"Thank you, sir. This isn't over, you know. I'm in Santa Cruz and have discovered just how big this conspiracy is. Massive is an insignificant description. There must be almost a billion dollars riding on this development, and there is ample proof that organized crime, particularly from Los Angeles is involved.

"Is your attorney fully aware of what we've come up with so far?"

"I'm keeping him aware, yes. He's not that familiar with criminal activity, but one of his partners is, and he's on our job as well. Dinkins, my man, says he fully expects me to be contacted by the FBI soon."

"There's no indication of federal probing at this end, Senator," Dorsey said, "but if they aren't aware, they will be soon enough. You're familiar with RICO laws, hell you probably wrote part of them, and I see organized crime at every level in this conspiracy. I'll be making a lot of noise down here starting today, so hang on tight."

"Take care of yourself, Mr. Dorsey, and Merry Christmas to you and your family."

"Thank you, sir, and the same to you." Dorsey clicked off, settled himself a little deeper in the leather seat of the fifty-six Caddy and wished it was summer and he had the top down. "This is beautiful country," he murmured, punching in new numbers on the cell. "I'd love to just ride around through these mountains, top down, radio on with some Detroit blasting out, and cradling a cold beer," he was saying when a voice on the phone interrupted his thoughts.

"What the hell are you talking about?"

"Hey," Dorsey said, waking up from his reverie. "Good morning Serious. Just checking to see if anything is happening on your end." *A pretty girl, tall redwoods and ferns, the Pacific Ocean, cold beer, and I'm supposed to do good work? I need to come down here without an agenda,* he was thinking.

"I do have more information for you. How's Sergeant Adams?"

"Oh, Serious, she is fine. That is, we're doing okay," he caught himself just in time on that one. *I gotta get my head screwed on or somebody will take if off.* "What did you find out?"

"Whistler and Torrance are directly connected to Rollo Fernandez in the Los Angeles organization, and there are hints of a federal investigation into the Santa Cruz deal. Keep your eyes open for that. What do you know? Anything useful for me at this end?"

"The locals are filthy dirty, that is, Sterling, the commissioner, Lucent, the DA, and Bogart, the sheriff. Threats have been made against the local newspaper editor, serious threats to the point of killing his dog and burning his garage down, and Torrance is the local point man for the mob.

"Jenny's going to spend today at the courthouse looking at records and permits and I'm about to head out to give a look-see at the property and see if I can find Torrance. We need to have a little chat."

"Keep me posted and keep your ugly head down," Serious Elmo said, clicking off. Dorsey fired up the five hundred horses and drove out to find El Charo to get this end of the investigation underway. "I really hope he doesn't bring that dog," he chuckled.

9.

Jenny Adams drove through downtown Santa
Cruz letting her mind go back to the years
growing up in this tourist mecca on the north shore of
Monterey Bay. *Fabulous surfing, wonderful climate,
great restaurants and a genuinely eclectic
community,* she was remembering as she pulled into
the courthouse parking lot. *It's a shame it's winter. I'd
love to take one more ride on the Big Dipper.*

The Big Dipper was an ancient wooden roller
coaster on the Santa Cruz Beach Boardwalk, that
every kid that's ever lived in Santa Cruz had ridden as
soon as he or she was old enough to be let on. She
could almost feel the excitement when those old cars
went over the top and hurtled almost straight down at
many miles per hour.

"Well now, look at that," she muttered, dodging a
small green foreign car that first challenged her,
coming head-on, then veered and pulled out of the lot,
tires sending blue smoke into the air. The driver did
what he could to shield his face as he sped away.

"So maybe that wasn't just a dumb-ass running a
stop sign, maybe it was an attempt of some kind." She
quickly jotted the license number down after tucking
her pickup into a visitor's space. "I'll have Captain
Elmo run those plates, but ten to one they're stolen. Is
somebody telling me something or is this a threat of
some kind?"

She was analyzing the two attempts, first, what
seemed like a simple act of running a stop sign, and
the second, what seemed like a direct threat in the

parking lot. "A distinctive vehicle and almost childish acts," she muttered. "If they know who I am, they know I'm armed and dangerous," which brought a little chuckle, "and if they don't know who I am, they will soon enough. This was not the least bit professional," which made her remember Racine saying someone burned his garage down, and his dog had been killed and mutilated.

"I wonder if this was the sheriff's doing?" she thought as she made her way to the planning commission office to get information on current developments. "It isn't something Whistler or Torrance would attempt, and Bogart is as small minded as anyone I know. This would be his style. Whistler would have had guns blazing and I would be dead. Get your ass back on the job, girl."

Jenny Adams was an angry Sergeant of Detectives as she made her way down the hallways of the county building. *I let myself get caught up short twice in the same hour. I'm a better cop than this, I'm a better investigator than this. Wake up, girl, or you're gonna find yourself dead.*

~ ~ ~

Dorsey drove to a shopping center in an area known as Soquel and found El Charo waiting for him, with the dog. "I've got a thousand dollars worth of upholstery in the back seat, Tomas. That dog will rip it right out. Please." Dorsey found himself pleading with the huge man, something Dorsey simply didn't do.

"No, Sol, don't worry. I have his blanket, we'll lay it down, and he'll simply go to sleep. You'll see, it'll be fine." He pulled a faded wool blanket from his rattletrap of a pickup and laid it across the back seat of the Caddy and invited the dog with the monster tail to jump in. As the man said, the dog curled up on the blanket, wagged his tail, and started snoring within a minute.

Dorsey stood stock-still, watching with a wary eye, and finally conceded that Tomas might have been right. "Where are we going and how do we get there?" Dorsey asked after he and Tomas Gutierrez got settled. "I need a good look-see at the property, then I want to see this Torrance ranch. He's been on the edge of decent society for years, but must have gained enough money to get the place, eh?"

"What I've been led to believe is that Amos Sterling backed his loan with a little pressure. I think this land fraud scheme has been in the making for several years."

"Had to be," Dorsey agreed. "Probably Torrance, working with the Los Angeles organization discovered how dirty Sterling could be and made an approach. Small town politicians with big egos have been known to fall hard when large amounts of money are also involved.

"Don't you find it strange that the feds aren't in on this? I've been on this case for a long three days now, maybe four, I lose count, sometimes, and I've been expecting to see a dark suit and plain tie show up at any minute. The feds have to know about this."

"I know Racine has been feeding somebody at the FBI, but if there is a federal investigation underway, nobody seems to know anything about it. Of course, that is the way they would want it," Gutierrez chuckled.

They drove toward Aptos, took a big turn north into gentle rolling hills covered mostly in hardwood and expensive homes. Eventually that thinned into open meadows, lots of trees, but no redwoods. "I thought this development was supposed to be in the redwoods, Tomas. What I see are oaks and scrub brush."

"They'll advertise it as redwood country, but what they're planning couldn't take place in the redwoods no matter how much money they used to buy every politician in the state. You don't mess with the redwoods."

"Don't be obvious, Tomas, maybe adjust your outside mirror, and tell me if you recognize the car about a quarter mile behind us. Been there since we left that shopping center." Dorsey had been cruising slightly below the speed limit, taking in the vista of the property rather than driving as if he was at the Brickyard. "I'm gonna speed this puppy up and let's see what happens."

El Charo used the electric switches to manipulate the rearview mirror on the outside of the passenger door. "Don't recognize it, Dorsey," he said, feeling the big Caddy quickly pick up speed on the two-lane country road.

The following car kept pace with Dorsey and the big man added even more speed. "Looks like we might have to make ourselves friendly and make introductions," Dorsey said, getting a smile and nod from Tomas Gutierrez. "I see a nice wide spot up ahead, Tomas. Hang on tight, I'm gonna do a one-eighty and ram this Caddy right down their throats."

He tromped on the throttle, then whipped the steering wheel and hit the brakes going into a broad-slide, then putting full power back on, driving out of the slide and never leaving the pavement. Within seconds he was back up to sixty and aimed directly at the car that had been following. The driver tried his own brand of a one-eighty and fouled it up, leaving himself parked in the center of the highway.

Dorsey slid the Caddy to a stop and he and Tomas were out of the car, weapons in hand suggesting in loud voices that the two men inside the black SUV should get out and introduce themselves. Dorsey had his forty-five revolver cocked and aimed at the passenger and El Charo was holding a forty-four magnum revolver, also cocked, aimed at the driver.

"One little sneeze and everybody dies," Dorsey snarled. "All I want to see is open hands as you get out of that car." The two men slowly, carefully, stepped out of the SUV, hands open and extended. Dorsey slammed the passenger up against the vehicle and frisked him quickly, removing two small caliber, maybe thirty-two caliber, semi-automatic pistols. "This one shoots peashooters, Tomas. What about your guy?"

"Carrying a thirty-eight special. Strange. Are these fools working for Bogart?" He brought his man around to Dorsey's side of the car and with Dorsey's big revolver ready to blow a head off, frisked the driver head to toe. "That fool is more stupid than you can believe, Dorsey. This guy is a special deputy, not a real deputy, mind you, a guest deputy, and according to the ID, is to be shown all courtesies that a deputy would receive.

"I have a courtesy I would like to show," El Charo said, slamming a huge fist into the man's face, splashing his nose flat, splashing blood in a perfect pattern. "His driver license, oh, wait, there're two, no, three driver licenses here. Well, now, our little conspiracy just grew some, Mr. Dorsey, sir." El Charo had the man's wallet emptied onto the hood of the SUV.

The passenger made a sudden lunge, pushing Dorsey's gun-hand aside and ran toward a four-strand barbed wire fence along the highway. Dorsey waited until he was starting his leap over the fence and shot him in the back, letting him fall across the fence. "See that, Tomas? Even if I didn't kill the son of a bitch, he's all hung up and ready to Bar-B-Que." As he walked toward the fence, that dog with the huge tail, awakened by the gunshot, made two bounds, one from the Caddy, the other brushing past Dorsey, and tried to jerk the body off the fence. It took both Dorsey and Tomas to calm the monster. Getting the man off the fence, Dorsey said something about prior police dog training and El Charo laughed loud.

"He served with me in Iraq. Has two confirmed kills, Dorsey." They spent the next couple of minutes clearing the dead man's pockets.

"Same thing. Several forms of ID with several names. These guys are probably imported from Fernandez in Los Angeles. We also have us a little dilemma now, Mr. Gutierrez, sir. We can't report this to Bogart," Dorsey laughed, "and we can't just walk away. What do we do?"

"I'm glad you're on this, Dorsey," El Charo said. "There is one more thing you need to know about me." He reached inside his black leather jacket and pulled a card case out and flipped it open. "I'm with the California Attorney General's Office of Criminal Investigations. Because of our conversations last night, I am authorized to work with you on this project. You provided a lot of information about Torrance, Whistler, and Rollo Fernandez that we didn't know."

Dorsey gave the card a full look and drew in his breath. "You're more than just with the AG's office, you're the Assistant Director, Criminal Investigations Division? Whew, you sure got me on that, my man."

El Charo had a genuine smile on his face watching Dorsey read the official ID. "So, you're Assistant

Attorney General, criminal investigations. I knew there was something more than National Guard sergeant behind that bulk," Dorsey said, handing him his wallet.

"Well, at least you're not a fed," Dorsey said, but with a smile on his face. "I guess you might have other people in the area? If not, our only recourse at this point is to call the feds. Talk about a rock and hard place. Damn, I do not like working with the FBI."

"I don't either," Tomas said, pulling his cell phone out and punching in a speed dial button. "Horace," he barked, "El Charo. Here are my coordinates," and he punched another button. "Need you here fast." He pulled a set of cuffs and put them on the driver and walked him to where Dorsey had put his buddy's body. "Sit, and if you look crooked you will die." He pushed the man down, called the big dog over, and with two hand motions told the dog to guard the bad guy.

"I've never lost a man when Tails is on guard," he said. Dorsey shook his head in full agreement. Gutierrez walked back to the SUV and opened all the doors. "Chopper'll be here shortly, Dorsey. "Let's see what we find?"

This is sure as hell a big change in why I'm down here. The California AG is investigating and isn't aware of a federal investigation. El Charo must have been expecting something this morning if he has a chopper standing by.

"So, Tomas, when were you going to say anything, and what's with the chopper? You have one standing by at all times?"

Gutierrez gave an off-handed chortle, and then got serious. "After our talk last night and my report to Sacramento, the AG suggested that I bring you up to date at the earliest possible time. This seemed to be the right time.

"I expected something might happen at some point this morning, so I ordered a chopper to stand by. Like you said, Sol, can't call the sheriff and don't want to call the feds. And, my friend, I meant it when I said I'm sure as hell glad to be working with you."

That broke the tension and the two men smiled and got back to business. There wasn't much in the SUV, the registration was phony as hell and the plates surely were stolen. "Hope that whop-whop I hear is a friendly," Dorsey said, scanning the sky around them. A large state of California helicopter with the attorney general's insignia plastered on its side swooped in and landed behind the SUV. Three men, two armed with automatic rifles and the third with a potent semi-automatic pistol stepped from the bird, greeting Tomas with smiles.

Introductions and information spread around, the gentlemen from the helicopter got right down to business. "Tails kill that dude?"

"No," Tomas laughed, "but he does have the other convinced not to jack rabbit on us. The paperwork they carried is on the hood of the SUV, and my guess is they are probably part of the Fernandez organization out of the L.A. area"

One of the AG investigators used a field fingerprint collector and sent prints of both men off for a national check. If they had any type of record it would bounce back quickly. In the meantime, all the data from the weapons was collected, the SUV was dusted and prints taken for analysis, and one man was doing a trace collection.

~ ~ ~

It was two hours before Dorsey and Gutierrez were back in the Caddy, driving toward Aptos and the shopping center where El Charo left his wreck of a pickup. "It's best if the California Attorney General contacts the FBI on this, rather than a field investigator, Dorsey, even though I am a regional head. There'll be feds everywhere within a couple of hours, I think."

"Something told me you were more than just a friend offering protection. Racine is in serious danger, isn't he?"

"Very serious danger. Neither Jim nor Jack Swafford know I'm with the state AG, and nobody else in the county does, either, I hope. We've been looking to take Amos Sterling out for several years, and this project may be the one. Bogart is a fool, only looking to make himself into some kind of southern type sheriff, all ego, no known substance."

"Is Lucent the legal brains behind this?"

"He wants to be, but he isn't capable. You told me driving out here that Senator Bargetto's attorney has cancelled their agreement, so that should give you an idea. It's Sterling who's behind this entire project, and as you have pointed out, has teamed with criminals to get it done. All I have left to do now is get to Racine as fast as I can until the feds make their move."

"My job is done, too," Dorsey said, "as far as the land fraud investigation goes. I still need to figure out why little Starr Baby was killed and who did it. That's what started all this." He was shaking his head, wondering how everything had come to an end so quickly when his cell buzzed. "Dorsey," he bawled.

"Sol, we need to meet A-SAP. Where?"

Dorsey gave Jenny Adams the location of the shopping center where El Charo's truck was parked and said he would be there within half an hour. "Looks like Sergeant Adams has something important to tell us," he said, putting some speed on.

"In your work on this, Tomas, have you found any names that maybe I should know?" Dorsey asked. "I've had one attempted hit from a pick-up and with automatic weapons, and one what I call a very amateurish attempt. Then, this attempted hit this morning, tells me there is a hornet's nest ready to explode."

"Those guys were surely from Los Angeles, but it wasn't exactly professional," he chuckled. "Other than that, the only thing I've run into are Bogart's childish attempts to shut down Racine. What I've been afraid of is Torrance bringing in big guns, simply kill Racine and anyone else getting in the way of their land deal."

"The hit on me," Dorsey said, "was damn professional and damn near got me. Look at this," and he pulled his leather jacket out a bit from his body, showing El Charo the bullet hole. "That's too close for my blood."

"Good thing it wasn't one of those exploding bullets, my friend. That leather would have kicked it off and the right side of your body would have been gone."

10.

"**T**hose are federal plates, Dorsey," El Charo said as they pulled into the shopping center. Two black SUVs with reds and blues flashing had Sergeant Adam's pickup stopped in the middle of the parking lot. She was standing alongside the truck talking with three men and one woman, all in dark blue suits, ties to match, and shiny black shoes.

"Hard to tell they're feds, isn't it?" Dorsey chuckled, swinging the Caddy into a parking spot near the agents. "Are you okay, Jenny?" he asked. "Is this why you called?"

"I'm fine, Sol, and no, it isn't why I called."

"You Dorsey?" the largest of the FBI agents snarled.

"Maybe," Dorsey answered. "Who are you?"

"Don't get smart, Dorsey. Who's that with you?"

"Why don't you ask him?" Dorsey walked right up to Jenny Adams, not the agent, and patted her gently on the shoulder. "Did you contact the boss?"

"Yes, I did," she answered. "He brought me up to date. Good work, you two. Wish I could have been with you."

"That's enough," snarly agent said. "No talk until we interview you."

"No interview until you introduce yourselves. What the hell, no interview until you change your attitude."

Snarly agent was about to say something when two large white SUVs pulled into the parking lot and drove right up to the agents. Four men in dark blue suits with matching ties scrambled out of the vehicles and walked up to the group.

"Tomas, good to see you," a middle aged man, balding and with a pencil moustache said, extending a hand. "I understand everything went well. Good work."

Gutierrez started to say something when snarly agent snarled, "This is a federal crime scene. Who the hell are you?"

The middle-aged gentleman turned from El Charo to the agent and said, "No, Special Agent Whitcomb, this is a California scene, and I'm California State Attorney General Clem Bascomb. I believe I hear your cell phone ringing, and I believe it will be your director on the line. He said to expect your attitude."

Whitcomb turned, pulled his cell and answered it, walking away from the group. He didn't stop until he was a good thirty feed away. "So, Mr. Dorsey," Bascomb said with a smile and extended hand, "I understand you and my number two man work well together. That was quite a scene up the road."

"El Charo can work with me anytime he wants, sir. This is a hell of a mixed up case, and it's my pleasure to turn it all over to you." He wore a grand smile shaking hands with the state's AG. "Can you get Sergeant Adams and me away from the feds? She's been trying to tell me about a problem and won't while they're in our face."

"Why don't the three of you go into Denny's over there and get some coffee. I'll take care of the feds. Don't go anywhere else, though. We still have a lot to talk about."

"Thank you," Dorsey said, taking Jenny by the elbow and aiming her toward the restaurant, Tomas Gutierrez slipped in on her other side, giving her a full smile, and she returning it. The other FBI agents scowled but did not make a move to stop them.

~ ~ ~

"So, first, the little car ran a stop sign, you believe on purpose, then tried to ram you at the court house, and now, followed you to the shopping center. With a million flashing emergency lights filling the air like an el Niño out there, I would believe they are not with us right now, correct?" Dorsey asked after Jenny told her story and they got coffee around.

"I didn't get out of the pickup when I pulled in, but I had my Glock in my hand. They were in the next row over and left as soon as the FBI showed up. What did that one agent mean when he said you'd be in prison for the rest of your life?"

"I blew a guy away, but he was a bad guy, deserved it, I think. Don't you Tomas?"

"Oh, yeah, Sol, he was a bad guy. He needed that shot in the back and the face plant in the barbed wire fence. I'll testify to that, yes sir."

"You two need to not hang around with each other," Jenny Adams said, trying to stifle her laugh. "That one agent was a real prick and the ones with him just stood around with their thumbs up their asses. What's gonna happen now?"

"Besides the fact I have a million questions, we'll let Mr. Bascomb lead the way. Did you get the license number of the car?"

Jenny pulled a pad from her jacket pocket. "You bet I did and passed it on to Captain Elmo to run. Haven't heard back from him." She handed the sheet from the pad to Dorsey. "You are thinking pretty hard about something, Dorsey. Give."

"I have been ever since our little turkey shoot this morning. Stay with me, here. Don't jump in until I've finished." She shook her head okay, so did El Charo, and Dorsey continued. "This whole thing started with Starr Baby. She called me with what must have been a serious problem or some interesting information about something and got blown away by two different gunmen. She is the stepdaughter of Jimmy Torrance and that led us to this Santa Cruz County land development conspiracy.

"What I don't know or understand, yet, is simply this. Since Starr's death, gunmen have taken shots at me before the Torrance investigation. The Mole wasn't aware of the attempted hit. Men have tried to run me off the road, but they aren't connected with our land investigation, that we know of.

"And now, little sergeant of mine, a possible hit that went wrong, maybe twice, and we can't connect it to our investigation. It all trails back to the phone message from Starr, and the gruff voice that said something about taking me out." He sat back in the leather booth and wanted a beer far more than he wanted that coffee in front of him. "What the hell are we looking at?"

"I'd say you have two distinct cases going," Tomas Gutierrez said. "The one with the little prosti and the one with Senator Bargetto. Other than her relationship to Torrance, I don't see a connection."

"That's what's been bothering me so much, that and the fact that two gunmen showed up at Starr's apartment, one was inside and shot her through the head, killing her, and a second showing up later, and shooting her in the back while she was crumpled up on the floor, dead.

"Two gunmen that might not have known each other. That was followed immediately by the attempted hit on me. A semi auto kill shot to the head, a revolver shot to the back and full auto rifle shots at me. Who is related to what and why are they related?"

"If one of the gunmen was there to silence her about Torrance, that would make sense and clear up half the problem," El Charo said. "The other gunman, maybe the hit on you and maybe the attempted something on the highway, and now the maybe attempted something on Jenny, would be a separate case entirely."

"Well, then, Mr. Attorney General Investigator, that means you're as confused as I am," Dorsey said.

Jenny Adams answered her buzzing cell phone as Dorsey sat in the booth looking out the window, watching the play-by-play between the FBI and the California AG. "Thank you, Captain, I've got it. By the way, Dorsey has found a friend, as large if not larger, and equally sarcastic and smartass. I love 'em both." She clicked off her cell, smiling at El Charo and Sol Dorsey.

"Stolen plates on the foreign car. Round that was pulled from the sofa at Starr's apartment matches rounds that were used on a hit involving a shady money launderer who worked for Whistler. Captain Elmo is sending all the information by e-mail. I'll get that printed out for us as soon as we get back to the motel."

"That sounds like the kind of tie-in we might need. Money talks, Jenny, and money launderers have roots into every shady deal in town. If they come up with something from the second shooter that would really help too. As soon as we're through with our interview with the guys from the AG's office, let's get back to the motel and do some serious intel work. There are answers."

"Make sure you get that information to me, as well, Dorsey," El Charo said. "Until either Bascomb or the FBI take this Santa Cruz gang into custody, Jim Racine is in great danger. Jack Swaford is a fine guard, he'll keep Jim safe, but he isn't aware of the entire story.

"I think we're only partially right about you having two cases, but I don't think they're distinct from each other. I think you'll find they are related somehow. One of the shooters at Starr's apartment is related to this investigation, the other and the rolling hit on you, maybe another, but somehow tied in. Maybe just the people, maybe something else.

"A money launderer has to have a reason to have that money to launder," El Charo quipped. "Maybe because of gun sales, maybe because of narcotics sales, maybe your little Starr got in the middle of all that, got scared, and tried to call you. Maybe the money launderer worked for someone connected to this fetid mess down here. How's all that sound?"

"I think Whistler is the connection," Jenny said. "He's got more than just this land fraud conspiracy going, you can bet. He deals in weapons and narcotics, he must have a means of cleaning up his money. He gets his weapons and drugs through Fernandez and company, but who launders all that cash? That's where I'd start," she said.

Dorsey did not have a smile on his face as he watched Bascomb walk across the parking lot toward the restaurant. An FBI agent followed close behind, but at least it wasn't snarly agent. "This won't be fun. Why don't you get out now, Jenny, and head back to the motel. Keep that Glock handy."

She got up, nodded to Bascomb and the agent and headed for her car. The other FBI and AG agents in the parking lot didn't pay her any attention and Dorsey nodded to Tomas as they watched her drive out of the parking lot. "She's plenty tough," Dorsey said. "Looks like we'll be talking for some time, Tomas. The AG pretty straight, is he?"

"Damn straight, Dorsey. He's very good at what he does and he won't take any crap from the feds. This is his case, has been for some time, and ain't no fed getting' any of it."

~ ~ ~

"This is the longest day on record," Dorsey said, walking into the motel room three hours later, carrying a large pizza box in one hand and a twelve pack of cold beer in the other. His eyes lit up when he found Jenny at the motel room desk with an open pizza box holding most of a pizza, and drinking a cold beer. "I could fall in love right now."

"Yeah," she said, "with the pizza or the beer? What was worse, the grilling from Bascomb or the FBI?"

Dorsey popped the cap on a beer, grabbed a slice of pizza, and smiled long and slow before saying anything. "Gutierrez and I filled the AG in on everything that we know, and it was far more than the FBI knew. The fed dude flipped out when we filled Bascomb in on the attempted hit on us this morning, and the dead man. Snarly agent must have just been mouthing off, cuz those pricks didn't know about the attempted hit.

"The Los Angeles connection may be our link, as well, Jenny. I'm going to get some names up to Serious and let him get started on them, and I think it would be best if we head back to the city tomorrow. We can't do anything else down here."

"I feel a drift, Sol," she said. "Everything leads back to Gerald Whistler, doesn't it? The Torrance case is Whistler's, and the Starr murder is Whistler's, and that's the tie. Two crimes looking like one. The hits on you, maybe the first one because Starr tried to call you, maybe the others because of The Mole? Maybe all of them coming from the desk of Gerald Whistler?"

Dorsey smiled his agreement, not being able to say anything with a mouthful of pizza. He finished the beer, opened another, grabbed more pizza, and wrote down three names. "Get these names off to Serious and then, little darlin', let's talk about something other than crime."

"We could talk about fishing," she said, quietly.

"Want me to dangle some bait?"

11.

"Shhh, just listen, no movement," Dorsey whispered, slowly climbing out of bed, slipping the big forty-five from under the pillow, and crept to the motel door. The big man stood very quietly, gun raised to his shoulder. There was a distinct rustling sound, metal-to-metal scraping, and muted voices.

Jenny was just as quiet, nabbing her Glock from under her pillow and slipping up to stand next to Dorsey. He motioned with his hand for her to stand ready, indicated he would jerk open the door and turn on the porch light on the count of three. She was to go first, then he, and take no prisoners.

"One ... two ... three," and he jerked the door open and Jenny, gun first flashed through the opening, knocking a man back several feet. Dorsey was right behind. "Freeze, fucker," he said, jamming the barrel of the revolver into the man's mouth. Jenny spotted a second man trying to hide behind the Caddy and sprinted to cover him with her semi-auto.

"Up, now," she snarled, and motioned the man over toward Dorsey, all at once realizing that she and Dorsey were stark-ass naked. They were howling with laughter, herding the two desperados into the motel room.

"I've got them," Dorsey laughed. "Get dressed, then I will. What the hell time is it, anyway?"

"Looks like about three," she said, pulling on a robe, still laughing softly. "That must have been some kind of sight." She held the Glock in the ready position and Dorsey grabbed his pants and shirt. "Would have been better if a couple of drunks had pulled into the parking lot about then," and she couldn't stop her laughter.

Dorsey zipped up, walked over to the first of the two, the one that Sergeant Adams had knocked back when she flew through the door, and punched him in the groin with a powerful underhanded swing. The man puked all over the motel room, falling to the floor in screaming agony. "Who are you and why are you here?" Dorsey asked, very quietly, kneeling down to glare straight into the man's face.

He pulled the forty-five up, cocked it, and started counting backward, "Three ... Two," and man screamed, no, no, no, over and over. The revolver was an inch from the man's right eye when he passed out. "Baby," Dorsey snarled, standing up and looking at the second man. "Well? Do you want to hear the number one?" he asked taking aim at the man's groin.

"We were hired to mess up your car," the man said, literally quaking, his legs, arms, head, all shaking to a different rhythm. Jenny laughed, looking as a large stain appeared on the man's Dockers, just about where Dorsey was pointing. "God, man, don't shoot."

"Who hired you? Fuck with me and you die. Who?" Dorsey indicated that Jenny could slip into the bathroom and get dressed, motioned with the revolver for the man to sit on the floor next to his unconscious partner. "Who, dumb-ass?"

"He'll kill me," the man sobbed. "He'll kill me if I tell you."

"I'll kill you if you don't," Dorsey snarled. "Die now, or die later, your choice."

"What happens if I tell you?" The little puke wanted protection after he admitted that he might have done damage to Dorsey's only real love, that fifty-six Caddy convertible.

"Empty your pockets, nice and slow, really slow, and we'll take it from there on what happens to you. As you pull your pockets empty, tell me who hired you, and I will not ask again. Got it?"

"Yeah," the puke whimpered, reaching for a back pocket, his hands moved as slow as cold honey. Dorsey snatched the wallet and opened it. He chuckled, setting it down on the floor. "Special deputy, my ass," Dorsey said as the man pulled money from his front pockets, and cigarettes and matches from shirt pockets.

"No weapons? Do you know who I am?" Dorsey asked, realizing these two were cheap punks hired because they were so dumb. "Alright, I got your stuff, now who hired you?"

"We do little jobs like this for Mr. Sterling," the man sniveled.

"You burned Racine's garage?" The man nodded yes. "And killed his dog?" Another affirmative nod. "I should just shoot you. Get you out of your misery." Jenny walked back in, dressed. "These bastards are the one's that killed Racine's dog," Dorsey said.

"Kill 'em, Sparky, and let's blow this joint," she said, giving the punk a big smile.

"Naw, too messy," Dorsey shot back. "Keep an eye on them while I call Tomas Gutierrez." He grabbed his cell off the nightstand and punched in a number, walking out the front door of the motel room. *I might shoot the bastards,* he was thinking, waiting for El Charo to answer, looking his Caddy over, stem to stern.

"I got a couple of going-away presents for you, Tomas, if you can come over to the motel room. Bring that dog, too," he laughed.

~ ~ ~

The motel parking lot was filled with official cars of every description following Dorsey's call to Tomas. While he waited for the giant investigator he called Serious Elmo. "Yeah, Serious, I guess it is a little early, but we're having so much fun down here, you know, me and Sergeant Adams, that I thought I'd call and bring you up to date." He held the phone away from his ear until Elmo quit cussing, then continued.

"Jenny and I are heading to the city as soon as this crap this morning is taken care of. A couple of hired punks tried to put some keying work to the Caddy, but it didn't work. Can't call the sheriff on this," he laughed, "so they are going to get head-banged by the state AG's office and the feds. The fear of God is working.

"Did you get the message we sent last night on Tyson, Wilson, and Mason?"

"Yeah, Dorsey, my department is working overtime to get you your information."

"Whoa, now, Mein Capitan, the good sergeant made the request, as per, official police procedure." There was more profanity and loud words spoken before Dorsey continued. "You're not a nice man early in the morning, Serious. We'll see you in a few hours. Bye now."

He smiled at Jenny Adams as an evil thought roamed through his head. "I wonder if this motel has security cameras? We might not want the FBI or the state people to see our little show."

She was horrified at the thought and despite the early hour, marched directly to the motel office, hearing gales of laughter from Sol Dorsey with each step. Her head was all but spinning as she looked this way and that, three times over, trying to spot cameras, using unseemly language, aimed at Dorsey, aimed at motel management, aimed at anything and everything.

She was pounding on the manager's door when Tomas Gutierrez drove into the parking lot followed by two other official vehicles, one at least from the FBI. It was several minutes before Adams read the notice on the door that said the manager could be reached at this number. "Oh, damn," she muttered, fearing the worst and slowly made her way back to the motel room.

Dorsey gave her a wry look and grin when she came back in, and she immediately averted his eyes. *He's really enjoying this,* she thought, wondering how on earth she would ever be able to get even. "Manager doesn't stay here," is all she said.

"Make out a written report on what happened, Sergeant Adams and give it to AG Investigator Gutierrez," one of the FBI agents said, almost politely. "Well coordinate our efforts with them, and won't hold you and Dorsey up from returning to the city. We know how to contact you if we need more information." Neither one said a word abut security cameras.

Dorsey finished writing his report and gave it to Tomas, and started packing for the trip home. "I don't think you'll get much more than I did from these two punks, Tomas. They're just hired muscle, but it is one more cog in the wheel that will run down our Mr. Sterling. We'll be out of here shortly, so keep us posted, okay?"

"Thanks for those other names, Dorsey. I don't know how they'll fit, but somehow everything seems to be tied to Whistler, even if this ends up being three or more individual cases. Whistler is the fulcrum."

"How did Racine take the news that you will be putting the Santa Cruz gang under arrest? Probably made his day."

"It took a hell of load off his shoulders. No more looking behind him every other step, no more fear of attack, and all of his editorial screaming finally paying off. He's a happy man right now, and will be happier when I tell him that the men who killed his dog are in chains.

"Do you have specific plans when you get back?"

"Just some down and dirty investigating, Tomas. There're people that have had me in their sights and I need to find them before their aim gets better. See you soon, compadre. Stay safe and have a merry Christmas."

~ ~ ~

"I saw you on the phone before we left, Jenny. Who were you talking to?" Dorsey had a wide smile as he asked the question, knowing full well she had tried to contact the motel manager.

"There are no security cameras at the motel, Sol." She simply ended the conversation. Dorsey's Caddy was packed and Jenny got her gear together and tucked away in her classy little pickup. "Time to get out of Dodge," she murmured, firing it up.

They were more than an hour on the road and Jenny called Dorsey on her cell. "That would have ended my career, you know, if there had been cameras."

"It would not have ended your career, but you would never have had trouble getting a date," he chuckled.

"Can we find breakfast somewhere? I'm starving. Pizza and beer is not a very wholesome supper, and that's all I've had since those steaks at Jim's house."

"I was thinking pizza and beer for breakfast," he said. "Okay, a real breakfast at the next spot we see."

Dorsey spotted a roadside diner with a couple of big rigs parked in front and pulled in. "You know what they say about truckers and good food. If the food isn't good, they're here because the waitress is cute as hell," he joshed, just getting the evil eye back.

They found a booth in the crowded diner and took in the good smells of real country cooking. "I think I'll just ask for one of each on the menu," Jenny said, finally getting her smile to work. "This smells good. And two pots of coffee," she said as the waitress got them settled.

"Tell me about these three men we'll be looking for, Sol. I don't think I'm familiar with them or their relationship with Whistler. Would one of them have been responsible for that pickup that was following you a couple of days ago?"

"Probably," he said. "This is complicated because the cases are not tied together, only the one man, Whistler, connects anything. Starr Baby was shot in the head at very close range because of something she knew about drugs, money laundering, and gun running, and that's where those three names come into play.

"Starr Baby was also shot in the back from across the living room because of what she knew about Jimmy Torrance and the Santa Cruz land development conspiracy. To make this more complicated, Starr Baby was shot by each of those individuals because she is a known associate of Gerald Whistler."

"One busy little girl," Jenny said. "So, we have the pleasure of setting aside the Torrance and Santa Cruz conspiracy and work on the money laundering gun running case, right?"

It took the waitress three trips to get all the food they had ordered brought to the table. There were platters of biscuits and gravy, fried eggs, ham steaks, mounds of potatoes, some pork chops, and sourdough toast heaped on a platter of its own. "Will there be anything else?" she asked, not believing that two people could possibly eat what was on the table.

"We'll holler if we need anything," Dorsey smiled, those emerald eyes blazing with warmth. "Thank you." He didn't wait for Jenny, just started dishing food onto his plate. "Cameron Tyson will be the first person we need to get hold of when we get back. He runs an import/export business down near the docks. The feds have always believed most of what he imports is guns and most of what he exports is money. I've always believed there were tons of opium, maybe some crack, and meth for sure involved in his business.

"It's possible Starr heard about a shipment or something and tried to get hold of me. Tyson would hire a gun to take her out and then have that same gun come after me. He's filthy rich, owns a winery, is about as arrogant an ass as you'd want to meet."

"I've heard the name," she said, talking around a large piece of ham steak. "He runs girls, too, I think, along with a real slime ball named Wayne Mason."

"That's them. Mason sets things up but doesn't actually get involved. He would know who would be buying dirty money, who would need guns. Mason's slime, Tyson's flat dangerous. The third name would be Janice Wilson. Heard of her?"

"I thought she was in prison," Jenny said. "She shot up a bank and killed several people if I remember."

"You're close. She shot up an office in the financial district, competitors of hers in the stock and bonds business, but she was never convicted. Seems the witnesses kept dying or losing their memories. She's a hard-nosed killer, Jenny."

"So if we start with Tyson, what is it we'll be looking for first? How guns and money tie into Whistler, and what Starr might have known?"

"That little lady, after we finish this meal off, is our agenda. It's my belief that Whistler gets his orders from Fernandez in LA, and buys guns and drugs through Tyson, and probably uses Wilson to keep order. It's our job to prove it," he chuckled.

Dorsey set his fork down for the first time in ten minutes, finished off another cup of coffee, and pulled his cell phone out to call Serious Elmo. "Hope he's in a better mood."

"If you're calling to apologize, it's about time," Serious Elmo said as an answer to the call.

"Good morning, sunshine," Dorsey said. "Glad you're feeling better. Jenny and I are about an hour or so out, having a late breakfast. Got anything on those names we asked about?"

"How do you know Clem Bascomb? He's been burning up the phone lines around here."

"The Attorney General and I have become fast buddies, Serious. His lead investigator was the man we were working with in Santa Cruz. Bascomb knows how to handle the FBI, let me tell you. Tell me about Tyson. I think he will bring Mr. Whistler down, Serious."

"I've got a full file on him, Dorsey, along with your friend Janice Wilson. I can e-mail it to you."

"Yeah, send it to both of us. Jenny's staying with me all the way through this, right?"

"Sure, Dorsey, sure. Anything else the department can help you with? Do you need a jail for your perps, or maybe a couple more investigators? We're here to help, you know."

"Thanks, Serious. I'll keep that in mind," Dorsey chuckled, giving Jenny a wink, even if she wasn't aware of the conversation. "See you soon," and he clicked off. "He's sending files by e-mail to both of us on Tyson and Wilson, so you can bring yourself up to speed on what we'll be looking at."

There's something about the name Cameron P. Tyson that rings a bell, Dorsey, and I can't click into it."

"Think wine, remember?" he said. "Tyson uses one of California's fine wineries as a cover for his operations. Lives in a huge mansion north of the city, surrounded by acres of vineyards. He's got millions, could go straight and be wealthy just because of his wine, but is far more interested in running guns and narcotics."

Many of those who called themselves friends or close acquaintances of Cam Tyson were not aware of his second career of importing and exporting heavy weapons, heavy narcotics, and working hand-in-hand with American organized crime families, Mexican cartels, and Afghanistan poppy growers. They would describe this wonderful winemaker, capable of hosting the finest parties and supporting the arts and sciences, as a fine upstanding citizen.

"I've had my eye on Cameron P. Tyson for a long time," Dorsey said. "His money is incredibly dirty and has to be difficult to launder, and that's the direction I've been going. To find out who launders his money following a hundred million dollar weapons exchange. That means my first stop has to be Wayne Mason."

"It fits now," she said. "Maybe he has a shipment of guns moving in, Starr finds out about it, and he contacts Whistler who sics Janice Wilson on her. It's all starting to make sense now."

They finished their meal, left a generous tip for the waitress and walked to the vehicles. "Let's get together with Captain Elmo as soon as possible, Sol, I know you and he are very close, but he is my superior officer and I want to make sure he understands what we're doing."

"He does, believe me," Dorsey said. "Let's plan on being in his office tomorrow morning at eight. That gives us time to get everything straight in our minds, go over the files, and take a long hot shower. Are you sure there weren't any security cameras?" He saw it coming and ducked the kind of roundhouse right that would have knocked him clear over the hood of the fifty-six Caddy.

12.

*T*he news criers of paper and electrons carried the story of the Santa Cruz land fraud conspiracy, the connection to Senator Bargetto and his role in bringing down the conspirators. Gerald Whistler, Jimmy Torrance, and the elected officials from Santa Cruz County all had their pictures splashed across many pages of newsprint and on every television news report. California Attorney General Clem Bascomb was quoted often and his team of investigators were extolled by many.

"Sure glad they mentioned a certain PI and his sergeant side-kick," Dorsey chuckled, reading of the AG's exploits and exemplary investigative abilities. It was six in the very early ayem and Dorsey was nursing another severe hangover after spending several late night hours on Franklyn Street, chasing ideas.

He arrived back in the city late the previous evening, grabbed a double hero at a deli and headed for The Bar. "Well, Dusty, looks like you're losing customers by the score. Most of Whistler's people are either in jail or dead, The Mole can't help you with information, or was it the other way around?"

Dorsey was sure that Dusty was the connection between the city's crime groups and the organized groups in Los Angeles, Chicago, and Jersey. He had come close on more than one occasion to being able to haul him into Serious Elmo's office in chains, only to find the slippery little gent running free.

"It's time for you to be straight with me, pimp, cuz if you screw with me one more time, it will be your last. Give me a double shot of Jack and a cold beer and answer some questions." Dusty was visibly shaken, almost spilled some fine whiskey trying to get it in a nervous glass, and would not go eye to eye with Dorsey.

"I have a great need to talk to Cameron P. Tyson, Dusty," Dorsey said, taking a healthy slug of Jack, "and I'd like to do that much sooner than later. Where has he been hanging out, and who has he been hanging out with?" Dusty had to be the connecting point between Tyson and his money people, was probably who set up Torrance and Whistler with Los Angeles for the Santa Cruz land fraud scheme. *It's all starting to come together, to actually make sense.*

Dorsey's mind was a run-away freight train right now and he didn't want to slow it down. He was sure that Starr Baby found out about a weapons deal and died, was sure that Dusty knew the killer or killers, in this instance, and was going to get Tyson this time. *This is funny when you look at it. Tyson has a multi-million dollar weapons deal going down and I get in the middle accidentally and bring down a huge land fraud deal, make the state's AG look good, and I still have a chance to nail Tyson.* He almost chuckled right in the middle of putting the Dorsey glare on Dusty.

Was it the money laundering or was it a shipment of guns that brought down the lovely Starr Baby? With two shooters coming to her apartment within moments of each other, Dorsey might be happy saying it was each, but his mind was going off in a different direction. *Torrance must have had her killed because of the Santa Cruz project, and Tyson had her done in because she knew about the weapons shipment. Wayne Mason would have known about the weapons and how to manipulate all that money through a laundry.*

"I'm only going to ask once, there won't be any count-downs. Where would I find Wayne Mason? Don't screw with me."

Dusty took a quick glance at the door along the back wall of the saloon, which led to the card room, and Dorsey got up, finished the whiskey, and beer in hand strode toward the back room. He held the beer in his left hand, had his right hand gently fondling that big forty-five revolver, and pushed his way into the card room.

There were three tables in the back room with room for five people at each table. Two were in play this early evening and Dorsey spotted Wayne Mason at one of the tables. Mason tried to avert his eyes and duck his head but knew he was seen immediately. All Dorsey did was nod his head at the man and motion toward the door. Mason folded his hand, picked up his money and followed Dorsey back into the saloon.

"What do you want, Dorsey?" Mason tried to snarl. He stood about five ten, weighed close to two hundred very fat pounds, had jowly cheeks and thinning hair. His beady little brown eyes never slowed down, always looked at everything except who it was speaking to him. He was wearing a dark brown suit in dire need of a pressing, an open neck white shirt, and Dorsey noted the man hadn't shaved in at least two days.

"Your ass, fat man," Dorsey smiled. "That's what I want. But before I slice you and dice you and serve you up to the poe-leese, I want Tyson. You spend a lot of time running his guns and cleaning up his money, and I need to chat with the man." Dorsey pushed Mason into a filthy settee along the back wall and sat down across from him.

On the surface, Mason was small-time in the world of gangsters and criminals, but when any of the big boys got caught up in a scheme his name was sure to get bandied about. He helped those that dealt in guns, helped those that laundered money, and helped those that needed help in getting rid of someone or something. He didn't do the deed, he helped get it done, thus was never convicted of doing a dirty deed.

He looked like he hadn't slept in more than a day and Dorsey wondered if the news coming up from Santa Cruz had anything to do with that. A scheme that might have brought close to a billion dollars must have involved even those lowest on the criminal totem pole. *I wonder how much this sleaze-ball knew about that conspiracy? It's time that I found out just what he does know.* He knew it was only in the papers today, so how much would Mason really know?

"We have lots to talk about, you and me, Mason. We have dead people all over this Golden State, we have many of your known associates locked up and spilling their tummies to the feds and the state attorney general. So, fat man, give."

Dorsey's big right hand flashed out of nowhere, wide open, fingers splayed, and slapped Mason hard enough that every head at the bar turned to see what was broken. Mason was known along the west coast as being able to procure just about anything anyone might want, heavy drugs like heroin, heavy guns like AKs, and big money at high rates of interest. He backed many of those that dealt in such commodities, including Cameron P. Tyson.

"Where is Cameron P. Tyson, Mason?"

Mason was nursing an ear that wouldn't stop ringing, an eye that continued to bleed, and an ego that was demolished. He whimpered something about 'down south,' and Dorsey doubled up his fist, but didn't strike. Mason cringed, whimpered some more, and started talking.

"He's in Los Angeles with Rollo Fernandez. He and Fernandez will be back in town day after tomorrow because of the Whistler problem. Don't hit me, Dorsey, I ain't lying."

Dorsey didn't say anything but the thought went through his mind, *he does know about the Whistler problem. I just got back from watching the feds take down the Santa Cruz elected officials, and he already knows this? Will Whistler make a run for it?* Dorsey pulled his cell out and left a message with Captain Elmo that Whistler's people already know about the takedown in the south, they better pick up Whistler now.

"Thank you for that, Mr. Mason," he said, scowling hard at the fat man. Dorsey knew that as soon as he left, Mason would contact Tyson, and that would end any possibility of getting the bastard. He was worried too, that Dusty had learned more than Dorsey would have wanted. *I'm simply going to have to shoot Dusty, and real soon.*

Dorsey was still chuckling when he said, "Let's take a ride, Mason, there's a place I know that you will find most comfortable." He jerked the fat man to his feet and marched him out of the bar and slammed him into the Caddy. Half an hour later he pulled into the area of the sand dunes north of the city.

He didn't bash Mason, simply put cuffs on him with his hands behind his back, used half a roll of duct tape around his ankles, and taped his mouth too. "Just lay back and have a nice nap, Wayne baby, and I'll come get you later," and Dorsey headed back to Franklyn Street and a visit to the Palace Club.

"Hey, Shorty, how they hangin'? A little Jack, some cold beer, and a friendly talk, my friend. I heard you took out Sullivan in the fourth. Good show. You'll be ranked soon if you keep that up."

"Yeah, he was mush, Dorsey. Heard you were out of town, also heard you did The Mole."

"Not me, I think Whistler had him on a short leash and had to cut the ties. Spread the word for me that I'm in need of a long conversation with Cameron Tyson, will you?"

"I can do that, Sol. Whistler's been hanging around Tyson and Mason, putting together something with the Los Angeles group headed by Fernandez. You know Fernandez?"

"Heard he thinks he's a bad-ass, but never met him. Tyson must be putting together guns for him, I'd bet. Fernandez is tied into a couple of Mexican cartels, and they always need guns."

"No, not this time, Dorsey. Something going on up here that Tyson is running. Whistler wants a piece of it, Mason wants a piece of it, but it's really hush-hush. There's gotta be a lot of money involved, whatever the hell it is."

Dorsey's mind again went into overdrive as he put two and two together. Like Mason, Dorsey doubted that Shorty could know about the Santa Cruz scheme falling apart, and he had more information about Tyson and Whistler. He had a million questions ready to be asked.

Dorsey and Shorty McGuire went back many years and never screwed with each other. Dorsey held McGuire in high regard since they boxed. Shorty, active as a middleweight and Dorsey coached light heavy, and still fought an amateur bout from time to time. "I'm working for a couple of people right now, Shorty, and have bucks to burn if you want to do some work for me."

"Doing some training, doing some bar work to keep the rent paid, Sol, and that's about it right now.

Tell me what you need and I'll do what I can. I try to keep my ears open around here."

"I know, that's why I'm coming to you. Try to find out what Tyson is planning, or who he's trying to bring in. Any names or ideas will help. Whatever it is, several people are already dead so I don't have to tell you that it will be dangerous." Dorsey left several hundred dollars with McGuire and headed back to the apartment and computer time. A stop for pizza and beer completed the day.

~ ~ ~

"I've got one stop before I meet you at Captain Elmo's office," Dorsey said. "I might have picked up some info last night that will help us. Get a good night's sleep?" Jenny Adams sounded a little rough around the edges when he called her.

"I'll see you at the office," is all she said, clicking off.

"Okay fine," Dorsey mumbled, as he headed toward the door. "Tomorrow's Christmas," he muttered, "I need to stop at the gun shop and get myself a little gifty. Well, I can do that later." Before he got to the door the house phone rang.

"Dorsey," he bawled, getting some deep chuckles back. "Well, good morning Senator," he said. "You're up early."

"I'm in Washington, so it's a little later. It's you that's up early," he chuckled again. "I just wanted to tell you again how much I appreciated the way you handled this touchy situation I found myself in. You got me out of the deal, set it up so it looked like I rang the bell on those bastards, and kept my name clean. You earned every dime I paid you, Mr. Dorsey, but just between us, I hope I never have to call on you again."

Dorsey found himself laughing despite the hangover. "I'm glad things turned out right for you, Senator. You'll always be at the top of my list, sir. Have a Merry Christmas."

He clicked off with a smile, shut down the stove and headed out the door. Before he piled into the Caddy for a quick trip out to the sand dunes and another chat with Wayne Mason, he gave the street a good long look. *No damn pickups roaring down on me this morning, putting another hole in my good jacket*, he half snarled, half chuckled.

He was still humming Christmas songs when he found the fat man sleeping like a baby in the sand. He slapped him awake, jerked the tape from his mouth and un-cuffed him. "So, Mr. Mason, they tell me that your friend Tyson is working up some kind of deal and you're part of it." He cut away the tape holding Mason's feet together, and jerked him to his feet.

"The way I see it, you're gonna lose if you don't tell me, and you're gonna lose if you do. Give me a hint and I might let you live another day, fat man," and the open handed slap could have been heard many miles at sea. Dorsey opened his leather jacket and pulled the forty-five out, cocked it, and aimed it between Mason's eyes. "We're just inches apart, fat man. Answer me now, and I won't ask again."

Mason was shaking like a leaf, every ounce of over-weight was attempting to jiggle its little dance, he had sweat pouring, he wanted to sob, scream, run, and instead, stood frozen in place, looking down the barrel of a revolver that looked more like an artillery piece. When you look into the working end of a revolver you can see the working ends of the bullets looking back at you.

"All I know," he said, stuttering, quaking, "is it's big money and it has something to do with one of the banks. That's all I know. Janice Wilson is supposed to meet with Tyson and Fernandez tomorrow at Tyson's warehouse on Custom's Circle, down at the docks." Mason was shaking all over, terrified of Dorsey, crying and blubbering, but spilling everything he knew.

"Thanks, Wayne, old buddy," Dorsey said, and punched him gently on the shoulder. He tucked the revolver back in its leather, picked up some of the duct tape, and smiled a goodbye to the fat man. "Have a nice walk back to town."

Dorsey headed back to the Caddy listening to pitiful pleas from Mason about leaving him to walk all the way back. Dorsey turned after a few steps. "You say one word of this to Tyson and you're dead, Mason."

It was a quick drive back to the city and Dorsey was mulling what Mason said about Janice Wilson meeting up with Tyson and Fernandez. " Wilson is Whistler's current snuggle, and one of the deadliest women I know. She's got four notches on her pistol, if they still do that, and those are the one's we know of. I think it would be wise to believe she is one of the Starr Baby shooters.

"This time it's something to do with big time banking. Whew." He was cruising along with traffic when he remembered that Wilson was also known as a CPA and had done time for banking and stock fraud. "Mason is a money man," Dorsey was thinking, "and Wilson is a licensed CPA, and Tyson, Fernandez, and Whistler are working on some kind of activity dealing with a financial institution. All of this from a simple missed phone call.

"I better find out where Janice Wilson is and who she's dealing for."

~ ~ ~

It was five minutes to eight when Dorsey popped into Serious Elmo's office. "Good morning all. Beautiful sunrise this morning, eh? Did you get my message about Whistler?"

"Yeah and you were just a little bit late. The feds were on their way to pick him up when they were ambushed by a run-away truck and Mr. Whistler made his escape. There was no synchronizing between the agents in Santa Cruz and this office here. According to what I just heard, the AG's office was letting the feds handle this end.

"By the way, you two, good job. Glad you're back safe. That out of the way, where do we stand right now?" Serious Elmo was back to full-bore serious.

"I think I know why Starr Baby was shot, and you can bet it's complicated," Dorsey said. "Is there a coffee pot anywhere near? Man, my head hurts." He was looking at Jenny who seemed to be staring at the floor. "What's wrong?"

"Your boots and pant legs are covered in sand, Dorsey. What'd you do get drunk and spend the night at the beach?"

"I better not find somebody at the hospital complaining about spending time with you at the beach, Dorsey," Captain Elmo snarled. He picked up the phone and asked the duty officer to bring a pot of coffee and some cups to his office. "And plan on staying with us in the office for a while." He was glaring at Dorsey the entire time.

"I think our man Whistler is working with Cameron Tyson on something big and Starr found out about it." He ignored both Jenny and Elmo, and continued, with just a hint of little-boy grin on his mug. "Right now, Tyson is in Los Angeles meeting with Rollo Fernandez and the two are expected back here sometime tomorrow. It appears that Janice Wilson, Whistler's girl Friday is with them.

"All I know right now, is that it has something to do with banks or financial institutions, probably here in the city. Starr must have got wind of it through Torrance, her stepfather, or someone, and tried to tell me. All this time, Jenny, we thought it had to do with weapons, but I think it has to do with this new scheme I've heard about.

"With Whistler dodging the feds and out of town, everything may be changing, but I wouldn't bet a lot on that."

There was a light tap on the door and an officer came in with coffee and cups. "Anything else, Captain?" he asked setting the pot on the desk.

"Find a chair and sit with us for a while, Potter. Sergeant Adams, you know Detective Potter," Elmo said, getting a nod and smile from Jenny Adams. "Sol, say hello to our newest officer on the squad, Detective Potter, your new member of the team," he smiled. Dorsey said hello, the two nodded, and Elmo continued again.

Dorsey saw a young man, almost bookish in one respect, but big and strong. Potter stood above the six foot marker and weighed in at a well-toned one ninety. The name didn't say so, but Dorsey was willing to bet money the man's background originated somewhere in the Mediterranean.

"Potter joined us following a stint with the financial investigations division of the district attorney's office. He's an extraordinary investigator, but because he lacks the distinction of a law degree, they chucked him. I for one am delighted by that."

"Why don't you have a law degree?" Dorsey asked.

"Would you want to be an attorney?" he answered, getting guffaws from everyone. "Actually, my mother contracted cancer last year and I am the only living relative she has. I had to leave law school to care for her, and only worked sporadically for the DA.

"When Mom passed, three months ago, the DA said I needed to finish law school if I intended to continue my employment there. Because of Mom's medical bills I couldn't afford to go back and they fired my ass."

"Nice," Dorsey snarled, "really nice. So, your background is financial investigation? This current case seems to be heading in that direction, but it's made several detours along the way, so far. We've gone from attempts to influence a U.S. Senator to land fraud to attempted murder to the operating of security cameras."

Jenny Adams sat bolt upright at that, gasped, and watched Dorsey bend over in hysterical laughter. "You bastard," she screamed at him, and with a doubled up fist went for him. Potter grabbed her before she could do any serious damage, Captain Elmo stood up and said, with serious emphasis, "Quiet."

Peace and quiet were slow to return to the office, and Elmo asked, "What the hell was that all about?"

"Just a little inside joke," Dorsey said.

"Want to let us in on the joke?" Elmo asked.

"No, he doesn't!" Sergeant Adams exploded. "He most certainly does not." Anger was way beyond the boiling point and Elmo saw there was no humor in Adams' reaction.

"Okay, then," the Captain said, "we've had our little fun, let's get to work. No more bullshit, Dorsey. Tell us what you know so far, and Sergeant Adams, you have a report to make as well. Dorsey, you start."

For one of the few times in his life, Dorsey seemed to realize he may have overstepped, and in a muted, almost whisper, he looked at Jenny and said, "I'm sorry." She just glared at the big man, but slowly softened, and after several seconds, nodded her acceptance, even gave him the slightest smile. She still had visions of Dorsey bolting out the motel door, heavy revolver in hand and stark ass naked. And she had memories of why he was stark ass naked, and smiled just a bit more.

"Here's all I know, right now," Dorsey said, and spent several minutes outlining what he knew about the people that seemed to be working toward some kind of financial conspiracy. "I think we'll find that Cameron Tyson will be making a move to take over a financial institution of some kind in order for his import/export business to hide its money transactions."

"I understand Tyson and Mason," Potter said, "but how does Janice Wilson fit into this package? What I know of her, she's a killer, not a financial wizard."

"A killer, yes," Adams said, "and Whistler's live-in. She's actually who tied Sterling and the Santa Cruz bunch into Torrance and Whistler, and brought the idea of using Senator Bargetto as the foil. It's not generally known, but Wilson is also a CPA, and uses her skills with numbers manipulation and money transactions that might otherwise be considered illegal.

"She's incredibly dangerous, and very smart." She reached into a leather satchel she had with her and handed Potter a large file folder. "This is what Dorsey and I did in Santa Cruz. Bring yourself up to date on that, and you might have a better understanding of how this all ties together."

"I still don't see the tie," Captain Elmo said. "There is a tie between what happened in Santa Cruz and what's happening here? And a tie from all of that to the Starr murder?"

"Here's what Jenny and I think is what's going down, Serious," Dorsey said. "There was going to be tons of money flowing through that housing project, with contracts for earth moving, street building, homes built, there was going to be tons of money flowing because of mortgage contracts and high interest loans, and even more money flowing through the fingers of many attorneys. All of these contracts and deals are with their own people that they control.

"This current situation is part two. Understand, Serious, this is still conjecture, but I'm pretty sure of what I'm saying. They believe they need a financial institution of their own, one that didn't ask too many questions, one that could hide various transactions, and one that already has somewhat of a good reputation. Janice Wilson brought Whistler to Tyson, and then got Torrance and Santa Cruz officials in, and all of that was added to the Los Angeles element, Rollo Fernandez. The word conspiracy doesn't begin to explain all this.

"It's that last part that I believe Starr wanted to tell me about. Why two shooters? We may never know that. Why the comment from one of them about taking me out is up in the air right now, as well. A dumb-ass shooter just felt he had to say something."

"Is all of that in your report, too, Jenny?" Elmo asked.

"Every word, Captain," she said. "Dorsey and I were pretty busy down there, and we had some good help from the California AG's office. That Tomas Gutierrez is one hell of an investigator."

"Here's what we're doing then," Elmo said. "This is now my case, Sergeant Adams you have the lead, Potter you're the attached investigator, and in civvies from now on, and Dorsey, you remain as our consultant, meaning you're my immediate assistant. Any questions? Good," he said with a smile, not giving anyone a chance to ask one. "We will meet for our first brainstorming session in one hour at Maglio's on Pacific Avenue, no questions until the gavel falls," he smiled, standing, using his hands and arms to shoo everyone out of his office.

"Except you two," he snarled, meaning only Potter was to leave. "Go change clothes, Potter," he said. When Potter left, Elmo looked back and forth at Dorsey and Adams. "Okay, who's gonna spill it?"

Dorsey smiled but didn't say a word and Jenny Adams scowled and didn't say a word. "I assume then, that whatever this is, is embarrassing to one or both of you, and maybe should remain a private affair? Am I right?"

"It's very private, Serious. I was wrong in bringing it up," Dorsey said, quietly, looking down at his still sandy boots.

Elmo looked at Adams who nodded, and also looked down at the floor. "Very well, then," Elmo said, "let's just let it fade away somewhere, shall we? See you two at Maglio's."

13.

"**I** t's still a good plan," Rollo Fernandez said, staring into light blue eyes blazing with anger. Fernandez was raised in East L.A., came up through the gangs, but with one big difference. He was incredibly smart, had a business degree from UCLA, and learned early where the real money came from. He wormed his way into the Tijuana cartel and is now the west coast head of that organization.

He tied his Los Angeles syndicate of gangs into the Chicago, the Jersey, and Miami, syndicates, and thrives. It was his planning that got the Santa Cruz land proposition moving. "Every single person involved in the Santa Cruz land deal has been arrested? It was a good plan, Janice, right from the start. Torrance was the weak link, eh?" he said.

"Everyone," Janice Wilson said, "except for Gerald Whistler, and nobody seems to know where he is. The people we have working on the bank deal are still around, but I don't think there's going to be a bank deal.

"I agree, the bank is a good idea, it would work well for us, but the plan has nowhere to go now. If we don't have a development project, we don't need a bank, Rollo," she said.

Fernandez was only thinking from the standpoint of having a way to launder Mexican cartel money from drugs and guns, one of the reasons he and Cameron Tyson had gotten together in the first place. Tyson had an ability to buy heavy weapons from many sources around the world, was able to deliver them with ease. Heavy weapons and things like Afghan poppy juice and Columbian cocaine, mix well.

The fact was, Fernandez understood, Tyson made as much or more money from his winery as he did from gun running, and it was simply pleasure to the man to call himself an import/export businessman. "Is he safe, Janice? He's so much in the news, what with wine releases, public functions constantly, people in and out of that mansion of his. Can we deal with him?"

The land development project had come later. "We get that bank under our control, Tyson can move thousands of guns for us and we can distribute tons of heavy narcotics. Clean money opens whole new markets," he said. "Yet, I find myself worried. Whistler and Torrance let us down bad, Janice. Can we move forward?"

Fernandez was about to get upset when Wilson didn't respond to what he was saying, then noticed she was paying attention to her cell phone. Finally, she said, "We now have ourselves another big fucking problem. It seems that Sol Dorsey, that PI up north beat the crap out of Wayne Mason, and he's ready to drop out of the program. He says he didn't tell Dorsey anything, but I wouldn't bet on it.

"I say, it's time to fold our cards on this deal, Rollo. The whole damn world is caving in around our ears. If Mason said anything, they'll come looking for us. Hell, man, you and I are the only ones left walking the streets. Maybe it's vacation time south of the border."

"I'm beginning to agree, and I think I need to make a quick visit with mi compadres in Tijuana. They need to know what's happening and I sure as hell don't dare try to just call them."

She tried to snicker and it didn't work. They were meeting in Fernandez's palatial mansion in the hills east of San Diego, a starkly white Spanish colonial building, two stories tall with red tile roof, beautiful covered balcony that surrounded three sides of the building. Many of the upstairs rooms had immediate access to the balcony.

A covered patio in the back also featured a full Olympic size swimming pool, there were tended gardens, and BBQ facilities that would impress a Texas land baron. One had to look carefully to see the many cameras spaced about the grounds, and it took a quick eye to spot the armed men that moved quietly about.

The Fernandez group handled most of the drugs moving north into the eleven western states and handled most of the heavy weapons moving south into Mexico, Central America, and South America. As unusual as it sounds, it's easier to move guns south than to bring them into Mexico by ship or airplane from other countries. Meth, heroine, and cocaine were the major products moving north while AK47s were the weapon of choice moving south. Most of those were of Chinese origin.

During the Second World War, the Japanese distributed tons of opium into China from their operations in Korea. Many believe the North Korean government today is back in the opium business. It has been suggested more than once that North Korea picked up on the slack that took place during various wars and intrusions in Afghanistan.

When Fernandez talked about having lots of money to launder, he was talking about hundreds of millions of dollars. With that money and what they were counting on from the land development project, the concept of owning a bank made real-time sense.

"Let's get together with Tyson and figure out what we can do," she said. She walked to a full bar and poured a half glass of tequila and downed it in two swallows, felt the warmth flood her body immediately, and poured another for sipping. "As it stands right now, Rollo, you and I should not be under any investigations. We weren't a part of any of the planning on that land speculation project, and neither was Tyson."

"You're right about Tyson, and I wonder just how much of that project he knows anything about. He's managed to evade most investigations dealing with his import/export activities, but he does like to talk too much, and that higher-than-thou attitude pisses most of my people off," Fernandez added.

Wilson paced around the large room, letting her heels click solidly on the tile floor, scowling at the floor, walls, and Fernandez too. "That's why I'm confused about that detective going after Mason. His name shouldn't have come up in the land deal. Why would Mason even know anything about what we're thinking unless someone inside talked about it."

She stopped her pacing and glared at Fernandez. "It means that either Whistler brought Mason into some part of his deal or Tyson bragged a bit during a money transaction. Damn stupid people."

"I think maybe you should go back north, Janice," Fernandez said. "If Mason or Jimmy Torrance started talking, Dorsey will come after us like a damn wolf smelling blood. Go back to the city, if you can find Mason, kill the bastard, and if Torrance is out on bail, kill that bastard too. How many times did we warn Whistler that Torrance was a weak link?

"In the meantime, I'll find Tyson and set up a meeting for the three of us." He picked up a telephone and called his pilot and made arrangements for Janice

Wilson to fly out that afternoon. "Keep me informed, Jan," he said. "If I find anything, I'll pass it on to you as fast as possible."

~ ~ ~

Captain Elmo, with a little help from Sol Dorsey moved two of Maglio's large tables together for their meeting in the deli. "We're gonna need nourishment, Maglio, my friend," Elmo said. "We're gonna need platter after platter of crab enchiladas, and pitchers of your own fine ale." The tables were off in a far corner of the large deli, away from the busy counter area. There were tables beginning to fill, mostly with regulars, and Elmo knew that Maglio would do his best to keep people away from Elmo, Dorsey, and the group.

"I've always liked this place," Jenny Adams said, looking around at all the paraphernalia Maglio had for decorations. "The Japanese glass balls they used on their long nets, all the pictures of the city from a hundred years ago, the ropes, gaffs, fishing equipment. It's like being in a very special museum that serves food and drink," she laughed.

"Look at those wood beams. I bet this place was built in the late eighteen hundreds," she said.

"Actually no," Maglio said. "It was built right after the big quake, probably late that summer. It's been in my family since ought nine."

"How long have you been here, Maglio?" she asked.

"Some of my family came with the gold rush," he smiled, "but I didn't leave Italy until just before the war, when I was a baby, and we went to Argentina, then Mexico, and then here." The deli came after the quake of ought six, survived the depression, even survived every attempt to replace the ancient building with an offensive concrete high rise or two.

"You are still the only Italian I know that makes the best Mexican food in the city," Dorsey piped up.

Maglio grumbled, but did so with a wry smile, understanding that he made good money by letting Elmo and Dorsey do just about anything they wanted to do in his place. "You always gotta park that cop car in front of my place? How about down the street in front of Tony's? Wreck his business, okay?" He'd walk away shaking his head, but smiling when his face was turned from them.

"I want to say something before we get started," Captain Elmo said. "Potter, this is your first time with us, so understand we have an open door policy. If you have something to say, say it. At bull sessions like this, there is no pecking order."

Potter wasn't at his first rodeo, had served in two other police departments before his attempt at being an attorney, and now with Elmo, but he had never run into this kind of situation. The boss just told him there was no boss at these bull sessions. "That's amazing, Captain, but I doubt I'll have much to say or offer."

"We're counting on you to say and offer things, Potter," Jenny Adams said. "You have knowledge of financial institutions and how they work, and we're looking to bring down a possible take-over of a financial institution." The words were strong, but Sergeant Adams said them with a smile and Potter got a hint of a smile from Dorsey as well.

"Here's where we are. Torrance is in jail and Whistler is on the run. Mr. Mason, I just found out, is suffering from exposure after staying overnight on the beach north of town." The comment was made with a glowering stare at Dorsey.

"We don't know for sure where Janice Wilson is, but believe she may be with Rollo Fernandez. There are indications that Whistler, Fernandez, and

Torrance were going to make a financial move on a local banking institution, and of course, we don't know which one. That, my children, is where we are." He sat back looking around the table as Maglio came out of the kitchen with the first of many platters of crab enchiladas.

"Torrance has always wanted to be a big shot in the organization, and I would imagine with the fall of the Santa Cruz development project his name is pretty much out of any plans. I'm sure he's already somebody's target and I have him in quarantine and under suicide watch." Elmo said. "I don't know why, but the feds brought everyone from Santa Cruz up here, and they're in our lock-up. Lawyers are screaming, of course, but it was the FBI's move."

"No it wasn't," Dorsey said. "This is still the state attorney general's case, Serious. Bascomb had no trust in anyone in Santa Cruz and had everyone shipped up here.

"Might be a good time to put pressure on Torrance," Dorsey said. He poured he and Jenny glasses of ale from one pitcher while Elmo poured for Potter and himself. "Torrance is weak, doesn't always think things through and may collapse under pressure."

"I don't want to ask this, Dorsey," Serious Elmo said, "but I guess I have to. Did you get anything solid from Wayne Mason?"

"He knows Tyson and Fernandez were working with Whistler on the bank thing but didn't have any names. He's further down the list than Torrance, I think. He knows something is coming, he knows he'll be involved in some way, and that's it."

"We need to get inside," Jenny Adams said. "Find the Wilson woman and get close. I bet the word is already out to send Mason to the great beyond. That doesn't leave much.

"You said Cameron Tyson is part of this? His name hasn't come up on any of the Santa Cruz land development reports. He's owns a winery and deals in heavy weapons and narcotics, which translates to big money. Maybe they need him on this concept of taking over some kind of bank."

"What do you drive, Potter?" Elmo asked.

"I got a little Honda," he said to Dorsey's great delight.

"My Caddy eats Hondas," Dorsey snickered. "What are you thinking, Serious? Potter looks like a UC undergraduate."

"Mr. Potter actually has a degree in business with a minor in accounting, and might be able to wiggle into the organization as a banker looking for a fast ride, looking to break and bend rules. What do you think, Potter?"

"I'm familiar with banking law, Captain. I just came off the Jackson investigation where we nailed the Jackson Brothers Winery on tax fraud. California has some severe tax laws dealing with alcohol, you know."

It was Dorsey's turn to sit back and survey the table, giving a long look in Potter's direction. "I might have mis-spoke," he said. "That might just work. You'll never pass as a street-smart criminal, but a banker? Yeah, that just might work.

"Start with Mason and work your way toward Janice Wilson or Rollo Fernandez. Don't get too close to Tyson, though. Wilson is the most dangerous, Tyson is the smartest. Just ask him."

"I'm going to work on trying to find our pal Whistler," Dorsey said. "Torrance must have alerted him to the bust in Santa Cruz in time for him to get away. Has the FBI ever coordinated anything?"

"I want to work with you on that, Sol," Jenny Adams said. "I've had Whistler in my sights for some time. Also, we have to remember that Starr Baby was shot by two different gunmen, and was the stepdaughter of Jimmy Torrance. She may have heard about Santa Cruz or may have heard about the banking scheme." She shook her head, looking around the table.

"Or both," Dorsey said. "How about you and I have a nice chat with Mr. Torrance, Jenny, and see what we can pry out of the gentleman."

"Police procedure, Dorsey," is all Captain Elmo said, quietly, pouring a glass of fine ale, made on site by Maglio himself. "Police procedure," he smiled. Jenny chuckled, remembering the sight of Dorsey running out of the motel room, stark-ass naked, wielding a forty-five at one scared little punk.

I love police procedure, she smiled to herself.

~ ~ ~

Adams changed out of her western duds, back into a charcoal pants suit, a pink blouse, and pastel blue scarf, and with Dorsey, walked into an interrogation room at police headquarters. "Mr. Torrance," she said, "I'm Detective Sergeant Adams, and this is investigator Dorsey. Can I get you a cup of coffee or a soft drink?"

"I don't want nothing from you. All I want is out of this flea trap. What the hell is Dorsey doing here? He's a two-bit PI, not a cop."

"He's my partner, Jimmy, and will help me with my interrogation. You do know how to interrogate a witness, don't you, Mr. Dorsey?" Torrance's eyes widened and his brows shot to the top of his forehead. *I still don't understand this fool. He must be just as slow as everyone has said. He's been arrested and jailed, and hasn't said one time that he wants an attorney.*

"Oh, no, Dorsey. You can't do that," Torrance screamed, as Dorsey slowly flexed the long fingers on both hands, staring at Torrance, not saying a word. "You can't let him do that. I'll sue, I swear to God, I'll sue."

"Relax, Jimmy," Adams said, quietly. "We're just going to have a nice little discussion about land fraud and banking and other illegal situations that you've found yourself attached to. Mr. Dorsey is here to help me get to the bottom of this terrible situation. I'll ask some questions, and you, sir, will answer them.

"Isn't that the way we want to handle this, Dorsey?" she asked, so sweetly it was all Dorsey could do to hold back the chuckles.

"That's right, Sergeant. You ask the questions, Torrance answers them. I'll just sit here and listen for those answers. It's important for Mr. Torrance to tell the truth," he said, the flexing of the fingers didn't stop for a second. It flashed through Adam's mind that Torrance was too frightened to remember that all he had to do was say he wouldn't answer any questions without his attorney being present. You can't really put a price on fear and intimidation.

~ ~ ~

The Cessna three hundred series airplane settled down onto the tarmac before five that afternoon and a car was waiting as Janice Wilson stepped out into winter cold. "Hi, Janice," the voice called from inside the large sedan. "Get in, we have lots to talk about."

"Well, now, Gerald Whistler, you're supposed to be on the run. This is a nice surprise." To herself she said, *And it will make it a little easier to take you out if it comes to that.* At Rollo Fernandez' suggestion,

Wilson had been living with Whistler as the Santa Cruz project worked its way closer to becoming reality.

"The organization needs to know that their money is being used wisely, Janice. There are weaknesses in this plan," he said. "No, that's not right, the plan itself is fine, very good, it's some of the people. Make sure Whistler keeps on top of everything." Those thoughts returned as she got into the Mercedes. *He didn't do what he was supposed to do and the entire project is down the fucking drain. You're gonna die, Mr. Whistler.*

She settled into the back of the sedan with Whistler, kept her hand near enough to her purse that she could shoot her little thirty-two snub nose into the man. "Fernandez has been worried about you, Gerald, since Torrance has been taken into custody and Mason has been questioned by Simon Sol Dorsey. Where have you been?"

He smiled, understanding that Fernandez had probably sent her north to kill him, and was prepared in turn to kill her. "I was with Jimmy Torrance just a half hour before Bascomb's people and the feds took him down. There was no alert, and it's just pure luck that I wasn't there.

"I didn't even know about the hit," he chuckled, "until I got to Tyson's place. Cam told me about the collapse of the Santa Cruz deal. Tyson told me you were flying in when he talked with Fernandez. He wants to see you now. Most of the planning for stage two in our deal has to be thrown out, as you can imagine."

Janice Wilson slipped her hand into her purse as he was talking and had a firm grip on the little semi-auto's handle, her finger near the trigger. "If this car varies so much as half a block off the route to Tyson's,

Gerald, you're a dead man. What brought the Santa Cruz deal down?"

"I'm not fool enough to mess with you, Janice," he smiled to her. "Tyson will bring you up to date, but it appears that Mason knew a lot about the Santa Cruz deal, and he wasn't supposed to. I think Torrance is probably to blame on that. Dorsey persuaded Mason to spill everything and then teamed up with the state's Attorney General investigators."

Fernandez told me Dorsey beat the hell out of Mason after the feds took down Torrance and the county officials. Whistler is either lying to me or doesn't know his ass from dirt.

Whistler never tied The Mole to what happened in Santa Cruz, never seemed to put together The Mole's problems with Dorsey. He was acting as if everything that happened in Santa Cruz was almost by accident. *I see why our plan failed. Fernandez wants to blame Torrance, but I have to believe that Whistler is just as slow and stupid as Jimmy Torrance.* Janice had no doubt now that he had to die.

"By now, I'm sure the entire plan has been disclosed," he said. "One rap to Torrance's fat head and he will tell the world what it wants to know. Tyson seems to think there is still an opportunity to get something out of all this. When the Santa Cruz thing went down, it meant that we lost an opportunity to look at close to a billion dollars."

It took about an hour to reach the Tyson mansion in the rolling foothills north of the city. In the brochures, it's simply called 'wine country'. Mile after mile of grape fields covered those hills, with scattered winery taste rooms advertising their wares. It would have been a pleasant drive if not for what was being discussed.

Janice Wilson didn't let go of the pistol until the car came to a halt in front of Tyson's large mansion. "You're safe now, Gerald, but I don't see how it's possible to save any part of our plan. To have that bank in our possession is what would make the Santa Cruz plan work. Without Santa Cruz, what the hell do we need with a bank?"

The front door of the mansion swung open and Cameron Tyson stepped onto the broad porch with a welcoming smile. "Hello, Janice. Rollo told me you were coming. I understand that he will also be joining us, but not until tomorrow. Come in, come in." He was the Earl, the landed gentry, in tan slacks and silk shirt, wearing a smoking jacket, his steel gray hair, nicely waved, with every hair in place, welcoming the peons.

Janice said something about not knowing that Fernandez was planning on coming north. "He decided to after we talked earlier. He's making a fast trip to Mexico and then coming here."

"You seem to be in good spirits considering how much money we just lost and how many people are now gone." Wilson's background was high finance but her expertize was murder. "With no land to sell, no roads to build, no homes to build, and no mortgages to be offered, why is there a smile on your face?"

"Maybe I'm more optimist than pessimist, Janice." He gestured to Whistler, and said, "Gerald, get us some drinks, will you, and let's move out into the garden and be comfortable. We have lost the opportunity to have that kind of money rolling in, but it isn't like we actually lost any. That would be the worst, if we already had it coming in and then lost it."

The day before Christmas in most areas would mean winter, when the word is used in California's wine country, winter is just a word. The sky was clear and bright, the temperature hung in the pleasant zone, there wasn't the slightest breeze, so an afternoon in a garden patio with business partners was not out of line.

"That comment doesn't exactly bring smiles of joy, Cam," she said.

Tyson was in his mid fifties, tanned and trim, and in apparent good health. Just off the elegant garden patio were tennis courts that must have had heavy use. He was a proud man who spoke of himself too often. His demeanor would be described as arrogant in most circles. He enjoyed flaunting his wealth, and Fernandez was sure that would lead to eventual problems for the organization.

They settled at a glass topped garden table surrounded by a couple of acres of winter browned grass, hundreds of rose bushes and other ornamental plants, all suffered from the cooler temperatures, and many hardwood and decorative trees stood naked to the eye, not a leaf in sight. In the near distance stood acre after acre of wine vineyards. Whistler brought the entire bar-cart out and poured drinks for them.

"Goode and Sons makes most of its money from home mortgages and small business loans, which fit into our plans well," Tyson said after everyone was seated and had a cocktail. "All we need do is to find other land that we can use as well as we were going to down south."

"We spent a long time and lots of money and effort to turn those Santa Cruz officials in order to make that plan work," Wilson said. "You make it sound far too simple, Cam. It would take years to create something as sweet as we had, and what do we do in the meantime, run a damn bank? Let's just rob the bank."

"I'm pretty much in agreement with Janice on this, Tyson," Whistler said. "It cost a lot of money setting that deal up, it took years to put it in place, and I don't think we could walk into another situation that sweet again. I think it's time to just walk away from what's turned out to be a bad situation."

Janice Wilson gave Whistler a look, as if to say, let the man talk. In her own mind she knew she was out of the deal. Her obligations had been mostly fulfilled, she worked for Fernandez not Whistler or Tyson. She knew Torrance would spill his guts and she knew she had to kill Whistler. What to do with Tyson? She decided that she would let Fernandez make that decision.

"No!" Tyson said, slamming his fist onto the glass tabletop. "My plan to take over that bank is precise, it's a good plan, it will work."

"I agree fully," Wilson said, quietly. "It's simply a fact that without the land project, we don't need a bank." Her eyes narrowed and her face was grim when she continued. "You better get this straight, Tyson, we don't have a land project, ergo we don't need a bank.

"There is something else that needs to be discussed, and it's far more important than taking over a bank. Jimmy Torrance is in custody and he's a weak man. He isn't capable of thinking a situation through, and I would be willing to bet that everything we've ever thought about is known by the feds." She didn't bother to even discuss Santa Cruz County Supervisor Amos Sterling, Santa Cruz County District Attorney Jimmy Lucent, or the dumb-ass sheriff, Terry Bogart.

She sat back in her chair and sipped her cocktail. "Remember, Cam, it was Torrance, trying to set something up with that prostitute stepdaughter of his that got Dorsey involved in this. She was supposed to compromise Senator Bargetto, but Torrance let her know too much, and she ran to Dorsey."

"Yeah," Whistler snarled, "and that damned Dorsey took Mason for a little ride into the sand dunes along the coast and beat the crap out of the man and is sure to know all about the bank deal. Instead of doing something, we need to pull our heads in and stay out of sight for a long time. We have things in motion that need to keep going, drugs already in the pipeline, and gun deals that have been made but not delivered yet.

"Hopefully, Mason didn't know about most of them, but you can bet Dorsey, that new state AG, and the FBI are snooping. This is a dangerous time for all of us."

Tyson didn't want to believe that. He was of the sort that, once a plan was made it should be carried out, regardless. He didn't see the danger of trying to move forward when the enemy already had a copy of your plan and was ready to attack. He was already putting thoughts together on what to do if Whistler, Wilson, and Fernandez pulled out.

I could use a bank's resources for my import/export business, to finance gun and drug projects. My plan is a good one and I'm not going to just put it aside because of some implied threat from a private investigator. He seemed to have forgotten the implied threat from Clem Bascomb and the FBI. *Besides, I'm the owner of one of this state's better wineries, why shouldn't I own a bank. It would feel good to be introduced as the owner of Goode and Sons S&L.*

"Let's wait until Fernandez gets here before we make any decisions," Tyson said. "I think you're putting too much credence to what one man, like Dorsey, could be a threat to us. After all, remember, we owned the sheriff and district attorney in Santa Cruz County."

"Our problems started, Tyson, when Senator Bargetto went to Dorsey, and they have snowballed into the complete failure of our project. The Mole is dead, Mason is a bloody bruise talking up a storm, Torrance and all the Santa Cruz officials that we owned are in custody, probably singing like filthy magpies." Wilson was angry at Tyson's attitude, and was speaking with considerable emphasis.

"This is a serious threat to all of us, you included. It can't be shrugged off," Wilson said.

~ ~ ~

"What do you think, Sol?" Jenny Adams asked as the two settled down for supper at Red Neck Randy's House of Chili. "He never did ask for an attorney, and he was supposed to be the lead man on the scheme? He's a dork," she said.

"Very slow," Dorsey said. "Or he was leading us down the garden path. Do you buy what he was talking about? I'm pretty skeptical about this bank deal. If they had pulled it off, the bunch of them would have been rolling in more money than even the Fed can produce."

"He was so scared of you and those long fingers of yours that I believe what he told us. What I don't believe is that the plan will continue. Without the development project they don't need a bank. I do believe that Fernandez is behind the project, and he never mentioned Chicago, but where Fernandez goes, Chicago goes."

They ate huge bowls of chili, a mound of corn bread, sweat gallons in the process, and came to the conclusion that it would be best if they found and did away with Tyson, Whistler, Wilson, and Fernandez at the soonest.

"That's our plan, then," Dorsey quipped. "We'll just wipe out the entire Chicago organization, maybe that would be your project, and I'll take on Los Angeles and all the Mexican gangs. We'll just wipe 'em out."

"I can't wait to explain our plan to Captain Elmo," Jenny Adams laughed, slipping into the leather seat in the fifty-six Caddy. "Your place on mine," she asked, that coy smile dancing across her face.

She asked that they make one stop on the way to her place in the hills east of the town, where she picked up a twelve pack. "I don't keep beer at the ranch," she said. Dorsey followed her directions into the rolling hills, where oaks and other trees dotted large open pastures. The sun was down and the stars were brilliant out of the city lights.

Many of the small ranches and hobby farms were decorated for the season. "I wish we lived in country where there really was winter," she said. "Hitch a horse or two to a sled and ride through these mountains over a blanket of pure white snow."

"You can have that," Dorsey said, swinging the Caddy into her driveway. "I wish we had the Phoenix winter and the Santa Cruz summer, that's what I want."

~ ~ ~

"You really can't spend the rest of the night?" she asked a couple of hours later, nestled in his arms under silk sheets and a quilted comforter. "I promise I won't make you run into the parking lot naked."

They laughed long over that. "I gotta get down to The Palace Club and see Shorty McGuire. He's going to set up some appointments for Potter, and I gotta get him up to speed on what we're doing. Next time you gotta show me your horses and things."

"You didn't like what I did show you?" she teased, watching him get dressed. "You remember what a target you are, Dorsey. I want a lot more of you and I want it all in one piece."

He gave her a long kiss, almost decided that Shorty could wait, and finally headed out for the drive to Franklyn Street and the Palace Club. He enjoyed thoughts of Jenny Adams and hummed half a dozen Christmas carols as he drove down out of the hills and back to the city.

He was on a long stretch of open road when he saw headlights coming up on him very fast. "Where the hell did they come from?" he muttered, pushing hard on the accelerator. The Caddy leaped forward, but he was only cruising at about forty-five and the closing car behind him had to be going close to sixty. The big black SUV with heavily tinted windows was along side in seconds, forcing Dorsey off the road and into a sidelong slide.

He fought the slide, did everything he could to keep from going into the drainage ditch alongside the road. It took some time, but with power steering, he had the monster car under control and coming to a panic stop before slamming into the SUV. He had his forty-five out and was climbing out of the Caddy when one of the large gorillas from the SUV slammed the door back into Dorsey's face.

The man slammed the door into Dorsey three more times, then jerked the almost unconscious detective out of the car. Dorsey was hit twice in the groin, felt himself falling onto the gravel, felt more blows coming to his kidneys, and then to his head. He wasn't able to get his feet under him, the terrible blows knocking the very life from him, he tried to grab and only felt air, tried to get his balance back, and couldn't.

All at once, and for no reason, the two men left him and drove off. It took a couple of minutes to realize that another vehicle had pulled up and somebody was trying to talk to him. "My God, man, what happened?" the voice said.

"Call nine-one-one," is all Dorsey got out before he passed out.

~ ~ ~

He came out of the deep fog of never-never land and found himself looking into the beautiful eyes of an angel. "If I'm dead, I hope all the angels look like you," he said through swollen and split lips. She couldn't see his brilliant green eyes, sure as hell didn't think the face she saw was very handsome, but liked what he said. "Where am I?"

"You're in St. Mary's, Mr. Dorsey. Don't try to talk, you've been seriously injured." She stood back a step and another face came into view.

"I like the first angel better," Dorsey said, trying to chuckle, and cringing in pain instead. "Oh, shit, that hurts."

"Tell me all about it, Sol," Captain Elmo said. "Did you get a look? Who, what, where, all that crap."

"How bad is it?" Dorsey asked.

"Nothing broken, you wimp," Serious Elmo said. "You'll be out of here in the next hour or so. Now, talk."

"Two guys in a big black SUV came up behind me at warp five, ran my ass off the road, and whupped my butt. Never saw either one before, I'm sure. Never said a word. Didn't see any plates that I can remember. They must have followed me and Jenny out to her place and just waited for me to leave."

He stopped suddenly. "No, don't tell me. They didn't hurt Jenny."

"No, Sol, she's safe. Another pair went after her and she nailed both, like the good cop she is. They have been turned over to the Attorney General's people. This lovely angel, as you called her, is going to get your ass cleaned up and then you're coming down to the office with me.

"I don't suppose you got things set up with Shorty McGuire yet?" he asked. "You can call him from the office." Elmo walked out of the room punching buttons on his cell phone. "He's fine," is all he said to Jenny Adams, waiting for them at the office.

14.

*I*t was a fight but Dorsey finally convinced the doctors that he was in good enough shape to leave the hospital. He questioned his actions when he tried to get into Elmo's official car. "Damn, those guys managed to bruise or crack every single rib," he said, easing down into the seat.

"I bet your kidneys don't feel very good either," Serious Elmo chuckled. "How the hell did you let those guys run you off the road? Where did you have your mind, Dorsey? Maybe thinking about a little chick-a-dee with long legs and bright smile?"

"Go to hell, Serious. Those bastards came up on me at well over eighty. Must have been parked off to the side, out of sight, and waited for me to go by and came fast without lights. I know that's how I've done it in the past.

"What have you found out about the others? You said Jenny shot two guys? She's good, Serious, real good."

"Don't I know that," he said. "They had a lot f guns several forms of ID, were driving a stolen car, and we're working their prints through the system right now. I want to know why, Dorsey. The big conspiracy is closed, the big boys are behind bars, so why are four guys in two vehicles looking to take you and Adams out?"

"It all relates back to what we think we know, Serious," Dorsey groaned as Captain Elmo aimed the Crown Vic at every pothole in the city. "It's the second part of the operation that's still going on. Weapons and narcotics are still being moved, money is still being transferred, and that possible take over of a financial institution is still being planned.

"Most of what we're seeing is probably coming our way because of Fernandez and company. They have a lot to protect and our operation has put a lot of their operation in jeopardy. I'm sure we'll face more threats as we get closer to shutting Tyson down. Just like always, oh mighty Captain of mine, it relates to money.

"While we're on the subject of money, where is my Caddy? And, please don't tell me it was destroyed."

"It was towed to impound, Sol, so you'll have to have it towed to whatever shop you want. Just cosmetic damage, I think."

Elmo parked at police headquarters and walked to his office. "I want to call Shorty McGuire, Serious, and then I'll be up," Dorsey said, standing on the sidewalk outside the old government structure that was built just after the quake in ought six. He spent about ten minutes on the phone and headed upstairs.

~ ~ ~

"Jenny," he said, limping into Elmo's office. "Thank God you're okay. Looks like you took care of your bad guys. Wish I could say the same for mine. How do you feel?" He couldn't get it all out fast enough, and would have started a barroom brawl if someone had suggested he had some feelings about the sergeant.

"I'm fine, Sol, just fine. Geez, pal, you really look like hell. They did a job on you, hunh? Wish I'd been there to give you some backup."

Before Dorsey could say anything, Elmo got right down to business. "We have four men, two now dead, thanks to Sergeant Adams, and two still on the prowl, and we don't have any idea who they are or who put them on your butts. Why don't we have any response on the dead guys prints?"

"The report's on your desk, Captain," Jenny Adams said. "Came in about ten minutes ago. Both men are known associates of Fernandez and the Tijuana cartel, with long records. I imagine the two that hit Dorsey are already halfway to TJ right now. Fernandez will get them out of the country as fast as he can."

"I've got Potter set up to meet with Shorty in about half an hour, Serious, so maybe we'll get some answers coming our way. With the Santa Cruz caper falling down around their ears, those that are left will be fighting for their life. There is still lots for them to lose, and they still have lots of guns.

"I need a vehicle, Serious. I'm to pick up Potter and deliver him to the lovely Franklyn Street and let him swim through the muck and mire of our fair little town."

Elmo reached in his pocket and tossed the keys to his official car to Dorsey. "Don't wreck it, Dorsey," he chuckled. "Let's make sure we all stay very close in contact. Too many bad guys looking to take us out before we take them out."

~ ~ ~

"Stick with me on this, Potter," Dorsey said, driving the young detective to meet Shorty McGuire. "You need creds, and this guy you're about to meet will get you in the door. He will work you through the filthy streets of ugly around here and get you an introduction to Cameron Tyson."

"Are you sure you're okay, Dorsey?" the young detective asked, slipping into the front seat of the big Crown Vic. "You really do look like hell, you know. Have they been able to ID the two guys Sergeant Adams shot?"

"All of what happened just proves what we've been saying to you about this case, Potter," Dorsey said, grimacing from a pothole bounce to the ribs. "Even though the Santa Cruz conspiracy is down and dead, there are huge amounts of money floating around and people kill over things like that. The two that Sergeant Adams took out are known Fernandez men with Tijuana connections.

"You'll go to the Palace Club and meet Shorty McGuire. He should be bartending, but for sure, he will be there waiting for you. He knows what you look like and you know what he looks like, so just walk right up and say hi.

"He's expecting you and knows our entire plan, so don't hold anything back from him. I'm going to let you off near the docks, so you'll have about a three or four block walk to Shorty's place. You're a disgraced banker, you have good tastes and you're for hire by disreputable financial institutions.

"Make sure you only meet with Tyson. You'll find many financial wizards down there, and most of them can't buy their own whiskey but will always have a deal ready for a sucker."

Potter was a hefty fellow, strong shoulders and chest, narrow waist and hips, sported a new haircut that said conservative banker, and wore a dark blue suit, blue striped tie, and carried a London Fog raincoat over his arm. "You will really look out of place on Franklyn Street, so use those eyes of yours. Keep them mean and don't take any shit from anyone. What are you carrying?"

"I've got a Colt nine-millimeter semi-auto, Dorsey. I'll be fine and will keep in contact with you, as we discussed." He smiled at the big PI and held out his hand. "Get yourself well, Dorsey. You really do look like hell." He slipped out of the Vic and walked off down the street, toward the squalid Franklyn Street, home to the city's criminal establishment.

That kid's gonna go far in this business, I think, Dorsey mused. He didn't move the Ford off the parking spot until Potter turned the corner and was out of sight. *No indication of anyone following him or me. That's a good feeling. I let those bastards run right up my ass and look at me now. Maybe I'll have a chance to do some payback,* he almost growled driving through the decorated city. Dorsey was not humming or singing Christmas carols or any ditty. *I do not look like hell*, he said.

Dorsey's telephone time with Shorty McGuire set the detective up for the job. Dorsey had a throwaway cell phone and so did Potter, and all communication between the two would be with those devices, so that even if someone tried to trace who Potter might be talking with, they wouldn't be able to. Dorsey didn't expect to hear from the young detective for at least twenty-four hours, maybe slightly more.

He drove to his apartment and filled the bathtub with hotter than hot water, poured a water tumbler full of fine Kentucky Bourbon, and eased his body into the steaming tub. When it cooled, he filled it one more time, and finally limped into the bedroom and sacked out, that tumbler as empty as the day he filched it.

15.

another day, another dollar is a saying used by some. Sol Dorsey's version is something like, another day another opportunity to eat lots of stuff and drink more beer. The hot bath had done wonders for the man physically and a long non-inebriated sleep had done its job for the man's mental state. He vaguely remembered hearing his cell phone ring a time to two and gladly ignored it.

"Damn me," he said, wandering into his kitchen. "Sun's up, and so am I." It was almost nine he noticed as he got coffee boiling and checked his phone. "Four calls, and three of them from Elmo. Something going on," he muttered, hitting all the right buttons.

"Where's my damn car?" Captain Elmo exploded on the phone. "You were supposed to drop Potter off and bring my car back. Where's my damn car?"

"Golly, you're a grump in the morning. I never said I'd bring it back. I'll bring it right over, soon as I have breakfast and make a couple of runs," he said, a definite smirk on his face. "I had the Caddy towed to MidTowne Classic, so I need to check on that, and I haven't been grocery shopping yet this month."

"You get that car down here now, I mean, right now," Elmo howled and clicked off, not getting to hear the chortles coming from Sol Dorsey.

Dorsey had a cup of coffee and piece of toast, checked his e-mail, looked at the day's headlines, a couple of stories relating to his road episode and Jenny's save, more background on the Santa Cruz

147

affair, and Senator Bargetto announced his intention to run for reelection.

"Looks and feels like a good day," Dorsey murmured, heading out the door, finding the official car, and drove to the police station. "This might be interesting," he chuckled, walking into Elmo's office. Instead, he found the captain, Sergeant Adams, and another man involved in an intense conversation.

"Sit down, Dorsey," Elmo commanded. "This is Tom Davis from the Attorney General's Financial Investigations Division. He just might have some information for us."

"So, you're Simon Sol Dorsey. You didn't exactly make a friend with the FBI in Santa Cruz."

"Maybe I'll come back a little later, Captain. Too early for this kind of shit. The FBI in Santa Cruz were so far behind what Sergeant Adams and I were doing, and what AG Investigator Tomas Gutierrez was doing that it took your own boss to bring them up to date."

He was half way to his feet when Elmo snarled, "Sit down." He was chomping on another black cigar, glared, and said, "Davis, this man is the finest investigator you've ever met. You want to start an interagency war, you do it with someone else." He looked at Dorsey, smiled nicely, and continued.

"I've turned over most of what we know about Tyson's plans for taking over a financial institution, and I copied General Bascomb with the information. Bascomb has asked that we keep Davis informed of our actions regarding Tyson and company. After discussing the case with Inspector Davis, I don't believe he is the right man to work with us.

"This is purely criminal in every aspect, Davis. You are not up to speed on organized crime in Los Angeles, Chicago, Jersey, or Miami. You don't have any inside information about the Mexican cartels, and are unfamiliar with arms dealers and importing narcotics. We'll keep the attorney general apprised of our operation, but you're out of your element here.

"This is not white collar financial double dealing, Davis. This is kick 'em in the balls, shoot 'em in the head, vicious criminal activity, and Simon Sol Dorsey along with my Detective Sergeant Jenny Adams will bring the bad guys down. You go back to Sacramento and shuffle some papers and we'll keep your boss up to date on what we're doing."

Davis was fuming angry when he slammed his way out of the office and stomped down the old wooden stairway and out the front door. "Well done, mein capitan," Dorsey snickered. "Paper pushers unite," he said with a salute.

"That's enough," Elmo said, quietly. "You and Adams need to bring each other up to date and start making some plans. I assume you got Potter squared away with Shorty McGuire."

"No demands for back up, so things must have gone well. We'll only hear something if he needs help or if he's in the door." He looked at Jenny and smiled. "I was run off the road and seriously injured," and he feigned some horrible pain, "and they didn't feed me at the hospital, I was too sick and sore to make dinner last night, and all I've had today is one lousy piece of cold toast.

"I haven't had a beer for sixteen weeks, Jenny. I need help."

"Sounds like an opportunity for some Texas chili to me. You up to it Captain?"

"Meetings all day. Big boys upstairs need some love. They were dead set against us getting involved in this entire affair, now, they're demanding to know how we're doing, and will we continue to get good press. Doncha love it?"

~ ~ ~

Dorsey and Jenny were working their way through a second bowl of Texas chili and a platter of corn cakes when Dorsey's cell went off. "Dorsey," he bawled, scaring the hell out of a family at the next booth over.

"El Charo here," Tomas Gutierrez said. "Interesting way to answer the phone. I might want to try that. Can you talk?"

"Yeah," Dorsey said, a little more quietly. "Good to hear your voice. According to the papers up here, you aren't getting a lot of cooperation from the bad guys."

"That's what we're telling the reporters, Dorsey. There are so many people involved in this conspiracy, so many we probably don't even know of yet, that we don't want to frighten anyone away. This fool Jimmy Torrance gave us something that I'm sure you can use. The feds aren't buying it, but I'll bet you will."

"We talked to him yesterday, Tomas," Dorsey said. "He gave us a few things, but nothing earthshaking."

"When we took Torrance into custody," Tomas continued, "he told the officers who asked about Whistler, that Whistler had left about half an hour before, and was heading to Cameron Tyson's place north of you, there. Two-bits says he's still there, Dorsey."

"Oh, my," Dorsey said, so softly that even Jenny Adams could hardly hear. "That's the best news I've heard this year, Tomas. Thank you. You coming up our way anytime soon?"

"My sister and her husband live there and want me to come up for New Year's, Dorsey. I think we will be able to spend some time together."

"Good. See you then," and he clicked off. He had a grand smile when he turned to Jenny. "Whistler is at

Tyson's and has been since Torrance was taken into custody. The FBI may have known this and didn't value the information or didn't believe the officer that passed it on." He sat still for a moment, just looking at his cell phone. "We spent several hours with Torrance and he never mentioned that. I wonder if we had sand pounded in places we don't discuss at the dinner table or what?"

"He did tell us a few things about Cameron Tyson," she said, "but I don't remember him saying anything about Whistler being at Tyson's. If that's the case, Captain Elmo needs to alert agencies north of here, and we need to make plans to get north of here, too."

Dorsey punched in the numbers on the throwaway and left a rather terse text message for Potter, paid their bill, and he hustled Jenny out the door and into her official car. "This is the best news we could get," he said, driving fast toward the cop shop.

"I don't think it is, at all, Dorsey," Adams said. "Tyson lives well out of our jurisdiction. Elmo can't send in the troops, big boy. Everything would have to be coordinated with that county up north. That's pretty ritzy territory, and Tyson might even be off limits, you know."

~ ~ ~

Dorsey was fuming by the time they walked into Elmo's office. In his mind, Dorsey could picture he and Adams taking down Tyson and capturing Whistler, and now that ugly word, bureaucrat comes into the picture. Wending one's way through jurisdictional bureaucracy would be a nightmare. "This is why I really don't like having to work with you, Serious. I don't have jurisdictions, I have a case and that's it. Why can't Jenny and I go in and then call for help? That's how I've handled tricky situations in the past."

"Because Sergeant Adams isn't a PI, Dorsey. She's a bona fide badge-carrying, sworn officer of this department, that's why. Now calm your sweet ass down and let's see what we can do about this." He called down for a pot of coffee, reached in his desk and pulled one of his monster black cigars out and lit up. He glanced at the two, daring one of them to say something.

"We think Whistler might be at Tyson's, and we don't know where Potter is." He racked back in his chair and slowly got a smile spread across his broad face and reached again for his telephone, punched in a set of numbers and drummed his fingers waiting for someone to answer.

Dorsey and Adams just sat there, also waiting for something to happen, a cloud of doom etched into Dorsey's brow, a look of anticipation spread across Adam's face. "Yeah, Clem, this is Serious and I have a quick question. Did you tell me that you authorized Dorsey to work as a consultant to your office? Is that still on the books?" There was a short pause, "Sorry about that, and I should have checked with you. Yeah, he was a little over the top and tried to get in Dorsey's face. And, so, you still have Dorsey listed as a consultant. Good, here's what's cooking," Elmo said and spent the next five minutes telling the AG about Whistler and Tyson, and the banking take-over.

"Can he use one of my officers even if it's out of my jurisdiction? Yeah, like in Santa Cruz. Thank you, Clem."

"Okay, Dorsey, you're still a consultant for the AG's office and this is still a California Attorney General's case, and Whistler is a wanted man in this case. Sergeant Adams, you have been assigned to work with the Attorney General's consultant, and see, Dorsey, there is no jurisdiction problem. Why do you always try to make things so damn difficult?"

Jenny Adams wanted to laugh and knew she didn't dare, and Dorsey wanted to continue to fume and knew that now, he didn't have anything to fume about. The situation changed with an officer coming in the door with a pot of coffee and cups. "You know that's illegal, Captain," he said.

"Thank you for the coffee and for minding your own damn business," Elmo snarled. The rookie set the coffee down and almost ran from the office. "Time for some serious planning," Serious Elmo said, pouring three cups of boiling coffee, blowing horrible blue-black smoke toward the ceiling. "We'll find out soon enough if that county offers special privileges to certain winemakers."

~ ~ ~

"Would anyone know or recognize you, Mr. Barron?" Shorty asked when detective Potter came into the bar. Elmo and Dorsey decided that Charles Barron would be a good name for a banker gone bad. Shorty McGuire was not aware of Potter's real name but was aware that Potter was a detective.

"I don't think so, Shorty," Mr. Barron said. "I don't do much public work. I had some cards made," he said, handing Shorty several. ""Without blatantly saying it, the cards indicate that I am capable of working around certain federal and state rules and laws dealing with currency and shading or hiding certain types of transactions. Another accountant type would see that instantly."

"Very good, then. Would you prefer I call you Charles or Mr. Barron during conversations. I need to be comfortable and would be with either." Shorty had done this kind of work for Dorsey many times, and no one along Franklyn Street was ever wise to the man.

"New acquaintances would call me Charles or Mr. Barron, but I think an old friend would call me Charlie. Work for you?"

You bet it will, Charlie," Shorty smiled. "Let's take a walk, shall we? We'll visit three people each of whom has connections that would lead to Cameron Tyson. I know you want to make the connection as fast as possible, but I also know that Tyson has been very difficult to reach lately."

"I've been told the most dangerous person we're liable to run into would be Janice Wilson. She holds a degree in business, is a CPA, and is known to work with and for those that launder coin of the realm. If it appears we're looking to get me hired by her, she would give me to Tyson."

"That's our angle, then," Shorty said, and they walked out onto the busy and filthy Franklyn Street. "Circle the Wagons Pawn and Tattoo Parlor, about half a block down the street, will be our first stop. There's a gentleman named Bill Smith, if you can believe that, runs the joint and is usually barely under police radar."

Bells clanged as they walked in the heavy door of the pawnshop. *No little tinkley bells here,* Potter thought, *somebody wants to be aware of that door being opened.* They walked through a maze of display cases filled with watches, rings, necklaces, cameras, and computers. There were weapons, fishing rods, and leather jackets, most showing miles of road rash.

"Hello, Bill," Shorty said to a short, fat, razor shaved bald man of about sixty years. "Got time for a quick sit-down? Have somebody here you might want to know."

Bill Smith had furtive written large in his squinty eyes, eyes that darted back and forth, from Shorty to Potter, to Shorty, to the front door, to Potter, and back to Shorty. "Yeah," he said, still looking around.

"George, watch the counter," he said to the man standing near the front door. "Let's go back here," Smith said, leading the way into a back room also filled with every conceivable item that might be pawned for a buck or more.

George was one burley security type, and he gathered his two hundred plus pounds into a bundle that stood well over six feet, and swaggered to the counter. There wasn't an inch visible that didn't have some tattoo or another drilled in. The outline of a semi-auto showed prominently under a wife-beater shirt, and his engineer's boots could be heard above any din. *I'd bet there's a knife in one and a gun in the other,* Potter noted.

"Bill, I want you to meet a friend of mine, Charlie Barron, a banker and accountant who is looking for some rather specialized work."

"Mr. Smith," Potter said, offering a strong right hand.

Smith didn't respond to the handshake offer, just nodded toward Potter.

Potter pulled a card from his new, engraved leather card-case and handed it across to Smith. Smith was about to give it a quick gaze and put it down, when apparently a few of the words and phrases clicked. He studied the card for another few seconds then suggested that the three sit and chat for a spell.

"I take it you didn't come into my little store looking for a job, Mr. Barron," Smith said. "I don't do the kind of business that your services suggest, so I must assume that you are looking for an introduction.

I have been known to need help at a higher level from time to time, so who are you looking for?"

The man gets right to the point and I'll bet his hand will jump out with palms open and waiting for something to fill them when he connects me, Potter was thinking as he and Shorty took seats on wooden chairs. "Moving money and material in certain ways, Mr. Smith, ways that often can't be detected, is an art, and I'm good at it. Someone else who is a fine artist is Janice Wilson."

Bill Smith wasn't able to stop the catch in his breath or the quick eye movement, and sat back in his worn out rocker behind the cluttered desk. "Whew. That's a name that isn't spoken in this office often. Janice Wilson," he mused, shaking his jowly head back and forth.

"The last I heard, Mr. Barron, Wilson was tied pretty tight to Gerald Whistler, and Whistler has a bit of a problem right now, if you've read the papers. The only person I can think of that might get even a little close to her right now would be Cam Tyson. You know him? He might help."

"I know the name, Mr. Smith. It's because of work that men and women like Tyson do that keeps people like Janice Wilson and me in business. How would I find that gentleman?"

"It might cost a little bit, but I can probably arrange a meeting," Smith said, those eyes ready to flash dollar signs. "I could make that work for a grand, I think."

"That's a little steep, Mr. Smith, but I'm sure a man in your business understands the concept of negotiation. I'll give you two-fifty today and five hundred when I've met Mr. Tyson."

Both men wore smiles and Smith did offer his hand as they stood to leave the office. At the counter,

Potter opened his wallet, the new leather one with the initials CB hammered into the leather, and handed two crisp hundreds and one fifty to Bill Smith. "Thank you, Mr. Barron. The number on your card is where I can reach you?"

"Yes, that is a good number, or you could just give Shorty a buzz. Keep me posted," he said. Smith handed Potter one of his cards and he and Shorty walked back out onto Franklyn Street.

"That was almost too easy, Shorty," Potter said as they ambled down the street. "I'm gonna flag a cab and let my people know what's going on. I'll keep in contact with you as well."

"I'm not sure Smith has that kind of juice to get right to Tyson, but we'll see. Hope that was government money you were flinging around, not Dorsey's."

"It was," Potter smiled and hailed a cab. "Call me if you hear anything," he said, getting in. Shorty nodded he would and the cab headed uptown. "Take me to Macy's, driver," he said, wondering if that money would really net him Cameron Tyson.

There was an expensive deli inside the Macy's building, but across the street was a little Italian deli run by an old family that dated their emigration to California in the 1830s, well before the gold rush. Potter's mother's maiden name was Maria Antonelli, whose sister's husband owned the joint. Cousin Tony Costello greeted Potter when he walked in.

~ ~ ~

Fernandez made his deal in Mexico and was back on board his private jet, heading north at about five hundred miles per hour, telephone in hand. "You just have a car there to pick me up, Cam, and we'll do all our discussing when I get there. I'm sure as hell not talking about anything on one of these friggin' cell phones." He clicked off, still angry at what he thought was revolt in the ranks.

Sitting alongside Fernandez was Lemuel Simpson, recently of Chicago, Miami, and Jersey. "That Santa Cruz deal would have been so sweet, Lem. We would have had every contract, sold every lot twice or three times over, held every mortgage, made every loan. We would have had our own bank, Lem," he said. "Think about that, and it was one fouled up attorney that jinxed it."

"Feds were on it for a long time, Rollo. It wasn't just that district attorney. I don't think Whistler put a very good team together. Torrance wasn't up to it. I told Whistler not to depend on him, and that little shrew, no, Mole, he was pure amateur, all the way. Whistler called his group the Baryshore Gang and the Mole was his triggerman. Bad deal right from the start.

"What's your plan now?" Simpson ran weapons and narcotics, women and Ponzi schemes mostly in the Midwest and up and down the east coast, and worked with Fernandez on some Mexican deals regularly.

When the feds and other agencies talked about Chicago, they were talking about Lem Simpson. He and Fernandez controlled or had close contact with about a third of the criminal organizations nationwide. If your organization needed guns, more dope, clean money, or fresh young girls, you came to Simpson or Fernandez.

"The feds are all over Tyson now, but he can't see it. I want to finish a couple of the deals we have in the works, and pull back into Mexico. My Afghanistan product is moving well, our Chinese and Iranian weapons are moving well, but we got to pull back.

"I can't get that through Tyson's head. That's why I asked you along. He has a lot of respect for you, Simpson, so maybe you can put the fear of God back into the man. He can't see a problem."

"What are you doing about Whistler, Torrance, and the Santa Cruz officials. Can't let this get away from you. They got to go, Rollo."

"I put Janice Wilson on it. Tyson told me Whistler is at his place and Janice is too, so she should have him eliminated by the time we get there, and Torrance has a hearing tomorrow and won't make that. The officials are locked down pretty hard, but she'll get to them."

16.

Potter was in a small booth in the back of the deli concentrating on a platter of chicken and pasta, talking softly on his cell phone. "I'll put off anything this fella Smith comes up with. I'm sure he was far more interested in the money I dangled than actually getting me in." He got the text message from Dorsey as soon as he sat down at Costello's and called Captain Elmo immediately.

"Dorsey and Sergeant Adams are with two or three deputies from up north along with a couple of state AG investigators, so you just lay low until we find out what is really going on. We'll continue to use your throw away phone for text messages, so stay alert." Serious Elmo clicked off and thumped his desk several times before getting up and walking out of his office.

"I should be with Dorsey and Adams," he said to the duty officer, shaking his head. "Any word from anyone yet?"

"Not yet, Captain. Too early I think. They're probably still setting procedure."

"Dorsey isn't much for procedure but he will have to be on this job. He's got three departments to coordinate, and that's exactly why I should be there." Elmo stormed around the duty offices for another few minutes and finally went back to his own upstairs office and lit one of his monster black cigars. *I dare someone to suggest this is illegal,* he snickered, blowing a huge cloud of blue smoke toward the ceiling.

He spent more than half an hour talking to himself, mostly about Dorsey. "If he stays with the program, there won't be any problems, but if he reverts to being Dorsey, God know what will happen up there. My one hope is that Jenny will keep him on course." Dorsey was the finest investigator Elmo had ever worked with, but Dorsey was a private investigator, not a government paid, that is, bureaucratic investigator. "Come on, Sol, do this with proper fucking procedure," he snarled, crushing out what was left of the cigar.

"I can't get it out of my head that until just very recently, Cameron Tyson's name had not been a part of this investigation. He's an import/export guy, what the hell is he doing in a land fraud scheme? It must have to do with this concept of taking over a bank, and that tells me there would be more than just one money type person involved. A big money type person."

Elmo knew that Tyson was a big money person in the syndicates, that he moved tons of narcotics and weapons, dealt with those that launder huge amounts of cash. "Whoever these boys are, they play for keeps," he murmured. "I'm still of a mind that it all originates with Fernandez and the Tijuana bunch, but I also know how strong the Chicago group is.

"The fact that Fernandez had Whistler as his number one man here, gives me something to work on. Like Torrance, Whistler isn't as smart as Fernandez and sure not up to Chicago's Simpson. Did Whistler bring Tyson into this or did Fernandez? Or did Tyson hear about the land conspiracy and ease himself in?"

Captain Elmo called down to his other Sergeant of Detectives, Sal Gonzales. "Get that computer of yours working, Sal. I need to know the lead money people out of Jersey, Miami, Chicago, and Los Angeles, and see if there is any kind of lead back to Cameron P. Tyson. Mark this Muy Importante."

After all the years Serious Elmo had been in a command position he knew how to delegate responsibility, but it was rare for a police commander to work with a private citizen, and then on top of that, put that person in as lead. Elmo was also aware that he was putting his own position in jeopardy if Dorsey screwed things up. It took a lot of personal responsibility to make a decision like that.

~ ~ ~

Fernandez and Simpson were in the back of a large Mercedes sedan, sent by Tyson to pick them up. They were heading into the coastal mountains on the north side of the large bay, for their meeting with the financier. "Apparently Janice Wilson has not eliminated Whistler," Fernandez said. "That fool must be taken care of, along with the rest of his associates. They are the ones responsible for the collapse of our plan. I still can't comprehend just how much money we have lost."

"Because of those contracts, money would have been coming at flood tide for many years, Rollo." Simpson motioned as a question whether Fernandez could trust the driver, and Fernandez indicated no. "We'll make our plans then, when we join Tyson," and the two ended that conversation and went on to safe items.

They were not enjoying a northern California winter's afternoon, with bright sunshine spreading its warmth across rolling hills dotted with giant oak trees and wineries and other farming ventures spread before them. Their conversation was filled with danger and death.

"We must discuss the shipment of guns that are scheduled," Fernandez said. "Tyson is bringing in no less than one hundred Chinese AKs, Simpson, to be transferred to my people in Tijuana. That order has been paid for and I won't be paid until I deliver.

"Money, Simpson, it's always the money, isn't it?"

~ ~ ~

The sedan pulled into the Tyson compound in less than half an hour and was met by Wilson immediately. "Why didn't you kill Whistler?" Fernandez asked as soon as the driver stepped away. "He has to be eliminated."

"Don't get angry, Rollo," she said. "He has clung like flypaper to Tyson. I haven't been able to get him away at all. I sent two men south to Santa Cruz to take care of those people down there, before the feds get them all separated and in more secure confinement. Torrance is in lock-down and nobody can get near him."

"I guess I'm more anxious than angry, Janice," Rollo said with a little smile. "So much money, gone, and I want Whistler dead. What were you saying about Tyson wanting to continue with this bank deal? No, it must end. We must pull in, stay out of sight and sound, finish the deals we have going, and stop for a time."

"He's emphatic, Rollo. Already starting to find people to pull it off."

Lemuel Simpson had been listening and finally jumped in to the discussion. "He's a fool. He'll get no Chicago or east coast help, Fernandez, and I'll tell him so. If he starts making moves, he'll bring the feds down on us, sure as hell. He either pulls back or dies, Rollo, and I mean it. I'm not jeopardizing my operation for him. Or my freedom."

The conversation was taking place near the front portico of the large mansion. If they had looked about they would have seen hundreds of acres of grape vines spread across rolling hills, dotted here and there with ancient oak trees, a few pastures with milk cows grazing, building the milk that makes California cheese world famous, and enjoyed a winter's breath of fresh air and sunshine. They didn't look about.

The three finally walked toward the doors, just as Tyson came out to greet them. "Rollo, welcome, and, ah, Mr. Simpson, so nice to see you again. Come in, come in." Hands were shaken all around and they entered the great room to join Gerald Whistler. "Let's take cocktails in the garden," he said, motioning to Whistler to bring the bar cart out once again.

"Cocktails are fine, the garden is fine," Fernandez spat, "but I want to talk about our situation. This isn't a party, Tyson. Half our operation is either dead or in jail."

~ ~ ~

"Mr. Dorsey, I'm Detective Sergeant Julius Romero. I've been watching the Tyson property since your call earlier. The sheriff said to report to either you or the Attorney General's representative."

"Nice to meet you, Sergeant," Dorsey snarled. "Actually I am the AG's rep also. What have you seen up there, and give us a good idea of the layout." There were at least a half dozen vehicles in a small depression, about half a mile from the Tyson place. Dorsey and Adams came in Adams' red pickup, the AG investigators, four of them, came in a couple of white SUVs, and the sheriff had three deputies in patrol cars, besides Sergeant Romero.

Romero was trying not to stare at the big man in charge of the operation, but it was hard not to notice a seriously black eye, that was also purple and blue, stitches across the nose, and a slight catch when Dorsey bent over the hood of the car. *Somebody didn't like this guy. His partner sure is a looker.*

"The sheriff gave us all photos of those you suspect may be here or may be coming. Whistler, Tyson, and the Wilson woman have been in and out of the building several times today, and a sedan arrived about half an hour ago bringing Rollo Fernandez and another man. I don't have a photo of that other man."

"Probably a bodyguard," Dorsey said.

"No, he doesn't look like one. A little older, not in the best physical condition. Not dressed as a west coast person, either."

"Good. Now tell me you didn't leave the compound to come down here and not have eyes up there," Dorsey said.

"My partner, Detective Lathrop stayed on site, Mr. Dorsey. This isn't my first dance," he snarled, getting a good smile from both Dorsey and Adams.

"That's good. Now, let's all gather around for a few minutes." He motioned to the AG guys and the deputies. "We must expect to be discovered well before we reach the compound. Sergeant Romero here is going to give us the layout of the place, and then we'll get down to the fine grit of a plan. It would be best, when we go in to bring many of those people out alive, but it it's you or them, make it you coming out of there on your own two feet.

"What are we looking at, Romero?"

Romero was very good at his job and produced a county plat map of the property and spread it out on the broad hood of a patrol car. "The main building is surrounded with out buildings and gardens. The vineyards slope off to the east over here," and he pointed out, first on the map, and then pointed across an open field, where the grapes for the good wine are grown.

"We can follow this ravine, through dense brush and old oak trees to within about ten yards of the house, which would put us at what might be called the back porch. The approach should be fairly easy and fairly safe."

"Anybody ever been inside that big old barn?" Dorsey asked, getting heads shaking no all around.

"The county tax appraiser gave me what he uses to determine the taxable value of the place, Dorsey. Here is the first level floor plan, here's the second level, and here's the third," and he laid out the copied carpenter's blue prints of the three floors.

"That's beautiful, Sergeant. Well done," Dorsey said, getting a nice smile back from the man. "That's good," Dorsey said, going over the map and floor plans again. "Okay, here's what I think will work. I wish there were a few more of us, but we'll go with what we have."

Dorsey had his force spread about so they could advance on the large building without being seen. "I hope Tyson doesn't have armed guards wandering around out here," he hissed at Jenny. "Let's circle around so we can cover that garden area and have access to the back door.

"I want two of you people to circle around and join with the deputy in the front and secure that area. That's the only area I can see where escape might be possible. Okay, quiet is the word, no smoking, and always wear protection," and Jenny snorted loud enough for others to chuckle too.

~ ~ ~

Fernandez and Simpson sat next to each other on one side of a large patio table with Tyson and Wilson opposite them. Whistler was not offered a seat and stood slightly behind and to the side of Tyson, away from Wilson. "Every single person connected to the Santa Cruz operation not sitting at this table is either in custody or dead," Fernandez growled, glaring at Gerald Whistler.

"We have lost the opportunity of a lifetime, not to mention more money than could be conceived. Federal agents, agents from the California Attorney General's office, and God knows who else, are ready to pounce on us. The idea of taking over a banking institution is not going to happen."

Tyson straightened up, grim faced, and almost bellowed, "No! The bank is very important to the rest of our operations and we must go through with it."

"Let me be clear on this," Fernandez said, just as quietly as possible. "There will be no funding from my organization nor from any operation in Mexico. I believe you feel the same way, Mr. Simpson?"

"How many people do you have working these grounds, Tyson?" Simpson asked, as Whistler mixed and poured a second round of cocktails. The meeting started out less than friendly, and Simpson made it as plain as daylight that Chicago carried a big stick and would use it. Tyson, arrogant and egotistical, not willing to accept someone else telling him how to run an operation, was angry and vindictive.

"Why would that be any of your concern, Mr. Simpson? Chicago doesn't grow, harvest, or bottle any of my wine. You might fund some of my export/import operations, but you have nothing to say about my winery."

Simpson sat back, took a sip from his new cocktail, and gestured toward the grape vines a hundred yards or so away. "I just saw some people wandering through the grape vines and wondered," he said, almost affably on the one hand, but as a challenge, too. "What kind of security do we have here, Tyson?"

Tyson, still standing, whirled to look at the vineyard, eyes wide in alarm. He raced for the main house, not saying a word to those at the table, ran as fast as he could out the front door, and jumped in the Mercedes sedan, fired it up and drove off the property.

Detective Lathrop fired up his cruiser and gave immediate chase, radioing Dorsey that Tyson was doing the world-famous rabbit dance. "Don't let him get away, Lathrop. He's armed and dangerous, wanted in several jurisdictions. Don't hesitate to use as much force as necessary to apprehend the man."

Lathrop hit the emergency lights and siren, gave Dorsey a big ten-four, and went to full pursuit. "That was very good, Dorsey," Jenny Adams said. "Captain Elmo would be proud of your proper procedure" Dorsey glared and gave her a harrumph back.

"It looks like our people were on the garden veranda there," Romero pointed, "and we must have been seen. Tyson split but the others are simply looking around like they don't know what to do." Romero was watching the garden group through binoculars.

"Let's go now," Dorsey said, motioning his little posse into action. "Holloway, you take your AG people through the back door and sweep that first floor. Romero, take you troops around and through the garden, sweep the garden, then come in and we'll finish the building. Instead of meeting Lathrop, just secure that front door," he said to the final two men.

"Adams, you stick with me, and let's terrorize that veranda. Let's move now," he said, and everyone took off at a high lope. Holloway and two state investigators smashed through the back door into the large kitchen, found it empty, and moved into the main rooms on the first floor.

"Freeze," Holloway shouted at the man who had been driving the Mercedes earlier. The fool turned, pulling a forty-five semi-auto and died from three rounds, one each from the AG people. "Alright, let's sweep the rest of this floor. Stick together and keep your weapons at the ready. It seems these people are willing to try to shoot first. So are we," Holloway said, and the three moved slowly toward what would probably be the library.

Romero's group moved fast through the large garden, not finding anyone. The sweep was quick since most of the plants were in mid-winter dress and it would be hard to find a hiding place. "Let's move toward the veranda," he said. "Remember Dorsey and Adams are also heading there. Don't shoot the good-guys."

Dorsey found that Jenny Adams, besides being damn fine looking, and a wonderful late night companion, was also an Olympic quality sprinter. The big man found himself half a step behind, his ribs screaming their agony. He followed the sergeant as they pounded toward the garden veranda, both with weapons pulled.

Rollo Fernandez spotted Romero's group first, yelled and pointed, drawing a forty-caliber semi-auto. It was Simpson who saw Dorsey and Adams, and pulled a semi-auto of his own. Janice Wilson was shocked that Tyson bugged out on them, and was also watching Whistler, who seemed ready to make a dash as well.

Dorsey vaulted a small hedge that surrounded the garden and Adams smashed through a little ornamental picket gate, both howling, "Freeze, police." Fernandez was about to take a shot at Romero when Dorsey's hulk took him to the ground, face first. Fernandez' pistol flew from his grasp and Dorsey pounded his face into the concrete several times before jumping to his feet.

His ribs hurt more than they had running and he was willing to bet he re-fractured at least one of them tackling the Mexican. He lifted Fernandez to his feet, spun him around and had the cuffs on him. "Sit," he howled, knocking the man onto his back.

Adams had her semi-auto aimed at Simpson when he turned. She fired once, and Simpson went down hard as a nine-millimeter slug tore through his chest. His shot at Adams nicked her in the thigh, and she dropped to the concrete, taking her shot.

In the meantime, Romero and company gained the veranda and the sergeant had his weapon at Janice Wilson's throat, screaming for her to freeze. Whistler started to take a step or two toward the main house when Dorsey's huge left fist all but crushed the side of his head and he crashed into a brick column near the doors to the house.

Handcuffs flew from every belt pouch and found homes on those still alive, and Dorsey herded everyone inside. "Put them on the floor, and keep them separated. Anybody hurt? No? Good," he said, pulling his radio out, then saw Jenny limping. "What happened?"

"Just a nick," she said, settling into one of the large sofas in the room.

"Somebody help her get that bleeding stopped," Dorsey yelled, keying his radio. "Lathrop, Dorsey. What's your status?"

"Man's not a good driver. Three major wrecks so far, Dorsey. This is a very dangerous pursuit."

"Have you made the call for back-up? We need that man, but we don't need to kill civilians."

"We're leaving this county, Dorsey. My back-up can't follow."

Dorsey turned crimson with anger and howled at the top of his lungs for AG Inspector Holloway. "Lathrop, you stay in pursuit and keep us informed."

"Holloway, is that helicopter still available? Answer now, no fucking bureaucratic nonsense, here."

"I'll make the call and put the pilot on our frequency, Dorsey," he said, pulling his cell phone. "You seem to think you have a lot of authority, Dorsey."

"Would you like to hear the request from AG Bascomb, or would you like to make that call and talk to Baxcomb a little later?" Dorsey snapped, ready to shoot the government fool. "That helicopter should have been in the air the minute Lathrop began his pursuit." Jenny Adams fully expected to see Dorsey slug the investigator, and hoped he would not.

Jenny Adams reached out and laid her hand softly on Dorsey's arm. "Easy, big boy, we're gonna be fine."

He looked down at her and gave a beautiful smile, winked, and pulled his radio back up. "Lathrop, Dorsey. You'll have some help by way of a big white helicopter shortly. Keep up the pursuit."

"Roger, that, Dorsey. We're on the north-south freeway, heading toward the city at about ninety=five per. That Mercedes should be able to do well over that but the driver isn't capable of driving that fast."

"Can you give him a little side nudge, spin his ass off the road?"

"Only with back-up. At this speed, I'd wreck too."

"Just stay with him," Dorsey frowned, wishing it were he in his Caddy in pursuit. *Little bastard would already be spinning through the bushes,* Dorsey smiled, putting the radio back in its holster. "Got that chopper?" he snarled to Holloway.

"It's in the air, Dorsey. Pilot will contact Lathrop."

"Thank you," Dorsey said, nudging Adams slightly. "According to General Bascomb, the surrounding counties and the highway patrol were supposed to have been on alert about our plan, Holloway. They should be a part of this pursuit and that helicopter should have been in the air immediately.

"Plan on explaining this in a detailed report." He glared at the investigator, saw that Jenny's leg wound was being attended to, and barked, "Okay, let's sweep this building. Your leg up to it?" She smiled a yes, and he continued. "This floor is clear?" Holloway nodded yes. "Good, let's get the second floor, then the third. Let's see those floor plans one more time, Sergeant Romero."

He left one deputy to keep and eye on the prisoners. "Don't let them get near each other and don't let them speak to each other. If someone comes down those stairs, and you don't recognize 'em, shoot 'em. Let's pair up and take these rooms apart."

The sweep netted two very frightened women, apparently housekeepers with little knowledge of the English language. "Let's see if our tethered darlings have anything on their minds to add to this mess of ours," Dorsey said, leading the pack down to the first floor. "We lost the two big fish, eh? Both Fernandez and whoever that other fool was are dead?"

"No, not both, Dorsey," Romero said. "I pulled some ID on the elderly gentleman. His name is Lemuel Simpson and he has a Chicago address. He's still alive and not likely to die. Name mean anything to you?"

"You bet it does, Sergeant. He's the head of the Chicago organization, and they are tied in with

Fernandez in Los Angeles, and through them, into the Tijuana Cartel. That's a big fish down and out.

"I know I hit Fernandez awfully hard, but he shouldn't be dead."

"He's still out, Dorsey," one of the deputies said, "but he's very much alive. I put in a call for ambulances, and the sheriff is sending units." Dorsey nodded his thanks for the information.

"Jenny, I want you to talk with Whistler," Dorsey said, "and I'll have a chat with Mr. Simpson. Sergeant Romero, how familiar are you with what this caper is all about?"

"We got a very short briefing before meeting up with you, Dorsey. What have you got in mind?"

"The lady in cuffs over there is Janice Wilson, a vicious killer and very bright woman. See if there's anything she would like us to know about banks, Whistler, land developments, and heavy weapons."

"No, Sol," Adams said quickly. "Let me talk to that bitch. Romero, you take Mr. Whistler. Let me squeeze some good stuff from Wilson."

"Proper procedure, Sergeant," Dorsey said, almost chuckling. "Now, Mr. Simpson may have to wait until after he's been attended to. He's out, too."

Sirens were screaming toward the mansion, some were from ambulances, some from police agencies, and all at once, two cars full of FBI agents. Dorsey assigned Holloway to bring the feds up to date and stepped into the great room to find Simpson. The Chicago gangster was being attended to by a couple of EMTs as Dorsey knelt down next to the man.

"Is he able to talk," Dorsey asked.

"He's coming to, Dorsey, but he's badly wounded. He can hear you."

"Looks like long-term prison time, Simpson. Your standards are getting pretty low when you start working with local hoods like Whistler. How much did you lose in the Santa Cruz foul-up?"

"I want a lawyer," is all Simpson said, ending the conversation.

"That's exactly what Whistler said," Romero told Dorsey when he came back in the main great room. Adams indicated that Wilson too, lawyered up.

"We'll let the AG and feds fight over who gets to talk to whose lawyer," Dorsey smiled at them. "We did fine, Holloway is gonna find out the hard way that he won't ever work with me again. I hope that someday we get to work together again, Sergeant Romero. I like a professional."

"It's been a pleasure, Dorsey. Just out of curiosity, what do the other guys look like?"

"I'll let you know when I find them," he said, trying to keep his cool, and hearing some snickers from Jenny Adams. "The crime scene boys, from the AG's office and it looks like FBI types also, will be here for hours, Jenny. Have we heard from Lathrop or the helicopter?"

A deputy who had been monitoring the chase handed Dorsey what looked like a fax, probably sent from Lathrop's patrol unit. Dorsey gave it a quick read and exploded "Lathrop said he was a miserable driver and he eluded pursuit? When Detective Lathrop gets back I want to see him immediately, Sergeant Romero. In the meantime, let's get these people squared away, separately, and the AG and feds can begin their interrogations. I have a call to make."

Jenny Adams joined Sergeant Romero as he moved the prisoners into separate vehicles in front of the mansion. "Dorsey hates proper procedure more than he hates criminals, Julius, and he has been forced to work this operation with three agencies, and now it's those proper procedures that fouled the operation."

"He seems to be good at what he does. I'm with him, though. The Attorney General's own man did not arrange for interagency backup? That's got to really piss him off. Catching these guys napping and then losing the big one because of an agency fuck-up. Whew, I don't want to be in Dorsey's sights." Jenny just smiled at the sergeant, thinking the exact same thing.

~ ~ ~

Dorsey stepped into the large library of the mansion and settled into a leather armchair, cell phone in hand. "This is some kind of place," he muttered, looking at paintings of old California, two walls full of leather bound volumes, and Spanish California period furniture. "Tyson lived well, I do believe," he said, punching in some numbers on his cell.

"General Bascomb, I need some information, or some answers. We lost Cameron Tyson because of a failed pursuit. What happened to the coordination that I was guaranteed? Why weren't the neighboring counties involved or at least ready to help if called on? And, where was the highway patrol?"

There was no hemming or hawing on the other end of the line, just an angry voice giving answer. "I'm afraid the problem will drift right back to my desk, Sol," Clem Bascomb answered. "I put the wrong man on the job. Holloway was supposed to clear the coordination, have people standing by in case of need, and instead, put paperwork in motion that will be answered sometime next week or maybe in two weeks."

"Damn bureaucrat," is all Dorsey said. "We have Fernandez, Whistler, and Wilson from here, and one extra who turns out to be Mr. Biggee from Chicago, Mr. Lemuel Simpson. The feds are screaming because I'm letting your people have at him first."

Bascomb was laughing hard, when he told Dorsey that he was doing a fine job, and clicked off. "Has anybody checked the fridge for cold beer?" Dorsey asked, walking back into the main room of the mansion.

"I just got off the phone with Captain Elmo," Adams said. "He has alerted the area, and for once not only do we have a description of the vehicle in question, the plates are legal. What's our plan now, boss?"

That struck a nerve, and Dorsey just stood stock still looking at Jenny Adams. "Boss, you said," shaking his head. "We captured most of the leaders and ended a huge conspiracy, I just ran an operation involving several jurisdictions, you call me boss, and if there's one thing about me that stands out high above everything else, I hate proper procedure, and I just chewed out the State Attorney General for not following proper God dammit procedure." He wanted to cuss for half an hour, break something expensive, get in a barroom brawl, and instead, looked at Jenny and started laughing. "Boss," he laughed, "My ass."

His genuine laughter was contagious, and Jenny Adams found herself laughing hard right along with him. "I feel sorry for Tyson when we find him, Sol. You'll take all this out on him, I can feel it coming, break every police protocol there is just because you can," and they continued laughing and punching each other in the shoulders. It finally calmed down enough for her to ask once again, what do we do now?

"Bascomb will have his boys go over this place with a microscope, his investigators will be doing the interrogating, the feds will make a fuss over everything, and you and I, Sergeant will do what we can to apprehend Mr. Tyson. Snaring Fernandez, Whistler, Wilson, and Simpson was a coup we can count," he laughed.

Dorsey took a deep breath before continuing. "I wonder what it was that brought Fernandez and Simpson here? What was being planned as a follow-up to the Santa Cruz operation? I want to grab those two and bust heads, Jenny. There had to be depth to the land development plan and it has to have included both the Los Angeles and Chicago organizations. Maybe they were here for an execution," he chuckled. "It was Whistler's ineptness that killed the Santa Cruz deal."

"I never expected Janice Wilson to simply give up, the way she did," Adams said. "Her reputation describes a vicious killer, not a sobby little girly-girl. I was so looking forward to going one on one with her," she laughed, giving Dorsey a hard little punch to the ribs that almost dropped him to the floor.

"She's the one that controls the scene and that makes her a vicious killer, Jenny," he moaned, trying to straighten up. "But, it was you controlling the scene and the woman became a crying little girl who had no control.

"What do we know about our friend Tyson? He lives like a sheik or baron or something, but his real business, this import-export stuff is heavy weapons, narcotics, and international money transactions. So where would a man like that try to hide?" Dorsey was back to being the terrier with the rat in his teeth, shaking the case until the truth fell out. "A nice talk with our friend Wayne Morris and maybe a visit with Dusty at The Bar, may be in our future, Jenny."

"Captain Elmo had me concentrate on Janice Wilson, so I don't really know that much about Tyson, except that he considers himself a gourmet, wants the world to know how much he knows about wine, and owns a small ocean going freighter he converted as a home-away-from home."

"I didn't know that," Dorsey said, getting a smile on his face. "You know where he keeps this little rusty bucket?"

"Yup, I do," she smiled. "It's a small freighter, about a hundred and ten feet, and according to some of the papers I found in Santa Cruz, he ties up in Moss Landing, the old whaling station in Monterey Bay. While it's fitted out for luxury, the holds are used to bring weapons, narcotics, and other illegal goods in and out of this country." She looked hard at Dorsey before continuing. "I don't understand why you don't know that."

"It's the first I've heard of a boat. Airplanes? You bet. Fernandez had a couple, I'm sure Tyson does too, and you gotta bet Simpson does, but a boat? Damn." He started pacing around the intricately laid parquet floor, mumbling, then pulled his cell phone. "Serious needs to know this right away, Jenny, and we've got to get our end of things here cleaned up and get the hell away to Moss Landing."

"I'll get with Holloway while you talk to Captain Elmo. We still need to make sure those AG investigators understand to keep our prisoners separated. That big beautiful investigator in Santa Cruz, El Charo," she laughed, "was a pure professional, but these guys aren't up to speed."

"Damn bureaucrats, desk jockeys, is all they are. Don't worry about the prisoners, Jenny. They were taken away in patrol units, separately.

"Bascomb should have given us field investigators, and instead, and he's already apologized for the error, instead, gave us so-called division heads.

Over weight and over paid," he chuckled, connecting with Elmo.

~ ~ ~

"Okay," he said. "Serious will get on that boat deal right away. Why is Tyson involved in this operation with Whistler and Torrance? I understand Fernandez and Simpson being a big part of the Santa Cruz deal. They would make hundreds of millions, but what would Tyson's part be?"

Jenny Adams looked at Dorsey, felt the pain in her leg, and sat down on one of the large sofas. "You are going somewhere with this, I hope," she said. "I wondered why Whistler ran to Tyson, also. An import/export guy that deals mostly in heavy weapons sure as hell wouldn't be a part of the Santa Cruz land development scheme. Money?"

"No, not to fund the project. That would have been Chicago and Los Angeles," Dorsey said. "There was one huge chunk of money to be made, which leads me to believe there's someone else involved, and Tyson was the middle man between the organizations and the plan. Who would that be?"

"The bank," he murmured. Dorsey pulled out his cell again, hit speed dial, and waited just a second or two for the answer. "I hate to keep bothering you, General Baxcomb, but here's the deal. Tyson is involved in the Santa Cruz conspiracy, but why? None of us here seem to be able to put an answer to that, and I wonder if a full background check on Tyson's money might be in order. We have heard that he was attempting to acquire a banking institution, but that would involve others. Who are they? And, since he's jack rabbited on us, a complete freeze on all his accounts."

Dorsey nodded a couple of times, listened some more, and said, "Thank you, sir. Just one more thing.

Can you assign that monster and his dog to work with us? Very good, sir. Bye again."

"When we get back to the city, I'm gong to put in a call to El Charo. He was the lead AG investigator in Santa Cruz, I'm still an AG consultant, and you, my pretty, now know that he has been assigned to work with us. It's important that we need to know why Tyson is involved in all of this.

"You asked, 'money?' and of course the answer is yes, it's always about the money, but I wonder if this time it isn't about how to handle these hundreds of millions that would be flowing through their greedy little fingers. Let your mind go free, Jenny, and let's figure this out. There are names that we don't know yet, and they are just as dangerous as those we just took down."

"When you had your little conversation with Wayne Mason," she asked, "did he mention any specific bank or even actually say bank? Maybe Tyson has already begun a move in that direction, or made some kind of contact."

"I think that's the first place we have to start," Dorsey said. "Bascomb will uncover some financial names for us, and you, me, and El Charo will then bring down the evil empire. If you want to do some computer time, you might check out Goode and Sons and see if there are any ties back to anyone in our group. Mason threw that name out, tried to retract it, and couldn't. That might be a start.

"We've got a ton of reports to write, which will take up the rest of today," He said, "and then, I'm gonna poke around down on Franklyn Street. Let's plan on meeting in the morning at Elmo's office. You get some rest and take care of that leg. Maybe a little later I could come over and massage it a little, make it feel better."

She smiled, "Let's worry about getting back to the city first, Mr. Dorsey," and they left the mansion, found her Ford pickup, and headed south.

17.

"**I**'ll drop the Mercedes off at some parking garage in town, take a cab, and you make sure I have a car of some kind waiting for me, Dusty. Screw this up and you're dead. Those guys came out of nowhere, and I gotta get to the boat. I heard guns and screaming, I don't know who's alive or dead. You gotta help, Dusty."

"Car'll be waiting for you, Cam. I always keep one or two ready for whoever needs one. Plates are reproductions, done by old man Pettigrew. It'll be behind the building, so come, get the keys, and go right out the back door.

"Are you sure you want to head to your ship? Wouldn't you be better off grabbing a flight on one of Fernandez's planes. He always has one around ready for whoever might need it."

"I'd need a Fernandez okay, and he's either dead or in jail. I need to get to the boat."

"The car will be waiting for you, Cam," Dusty said.

"Good, Dusty," Tyson said, and clicked off. He managed to create a major freeway accident involving more than half a dozen cars and trucks, and got off the highway before the helicopter arrived on the scene. He hoped that would keep the cops busy and off his tail. At a certain level of danger, most police departments call off high-speed chases.

He drove through dozens of high-end developments in the foothills, under a canopy of large mature trees, evading discovery. When he came back onto the freeway, he drove at or near the speed limit into the city.

He drove through one of the richest communities in California, in a very expensive, rather conservative sedan, sharing the road with very expensive, rather conservative sedans. The helicopter crew didn't have a chance in a million spotting that Mercedes. Whether Cameron Tyson was brilliant as a getaway man or just lucky wouldn't be answered.

Tyson parked the big sedan in a lot near the docks, flagged a cab and was inside The Bar, having a quick brandy within half an hour. *They'll find that car, and since it is mine, all they'll find are fingerprints of people they already know. How did I get in this mess?* The brandy calmed him down just a little, but his mind wouldn't slow down.

"If you see Wayne Mason, you tell him for me that he is a dead man. They're all gone, Dusty, the whole damn bunch, and it's all because of his big mouth. You tell anyone you saw me, and you'll be sharing a casket with him. Got that?" he snarled.

Dusty found himself looking at a snared or trapped animal. Tyson's face was red, sweat pouring off, his eyes were wild, and he was ready to bolt at the slightest sound or movement. "The truck's tank is filled, Cam, but you gotta know every cop in California is looking for you. You sure you don't want me to find you someplace safe, right here in the city?"

"I gotta get to the ship. We'll steam well off shore, and head to South America. I thought about one of the airplanes, sure as hell the cops are watching them, and besides, without Fernandez saying something, I wouldn't get one."

"What makes you thing that boat's safe?" Dusty knew Tyson wasn't thinking at all, was sure he would be caught well before he reached Moss Landing. He was also worried that Tyson, like Torrance, would spill his guts with one well-placed fist to the solar plexus. "I can keep you safe right here in the city," Dusty said one more time.

Tyson grabbed the keys from Dusty and hurried out the back door and into a white Ford pickup parked in the back. Tyson was southbound out of the city within minutes, bound for Highway 1, which would take him through Santa Cruz and Watsonville on his way to Moss Landing. "Three hours, four at the most," he muttered, "and I'll be on the boat." He opened his cell phone and punched in some numbers, getting the skipper of Sangria on the line.

"I want that ship moving when my foot hits the deck," he snarled. "Bastards are everywhere and we have to make international waters as fast as it is possible. No questions, just have that ship up and ready when I arrive."

"She'll be ready, Sir," Captain Augusto Ramirez said. "She's always fitted and ready for sea." The California Attorney General's investigator standing behind the skipper nodded, took the phone and turned it off.

"Well done," El Charo said with a smile on his face. "Now, we'll have a quiet wait for your patron, eh amigo?" He directed a team of AG investigators to tear the ship apart for evidence of anything Tyson might be involved in.

"We need names of associates, particularly if they're involved in guns, narcotics, or finance. Have at it, gentlemen," he smiled. "If Tyson doesn't show up within a couple of hours I will leave you and head to the city. Find me some names, guys," he said, walking out on deck with a big dog wagging a huge tail right beside him.

~ ~ ~

It was late in the evening before Dorsey and Adams made it back to Elmo's office and debriefing. Captain Elmo took that opportunity to have some fun with his favorite PI. "Well, it seems that you have learned just how important proper procedure is, eh Dorsey? I'm proud of you."

"Stick it, Serious," Dorsey snarled and Jenny chuckled. He shot her an angry glare, growled something, and plopped down in a cane chair. "I want a barrel of beer, a tanker of food, and less dark humor." Then he smiled and continued. "Tyson is on the loose and the only thing I can say for sure is, it ain't my and Jenny's fault. Damn me, but we had the bunch of 'em, Serious. We just walked right in the door and caught 'em with their skivvies in a wad.

"Were you able to get things in motion fast enough to stop that fool? A boat, of all things."

"What's worse, Dorsey, Sergeant Adams had that in one of her reports, and we didn't catch it. We could have had a watch on the damn thing. I put out a BOLO on Tyson in Monterey County and haven't heard back from them. It's out of our jurisdiction by a thousand miles or more, Dorsey. Well, okay, a hundred miles," he snorted. "Everything belongs to the feds, to Bascomb, and probably real soon, to the Coast Guard.

"I also have a BOLO on the Mercedes around our jurisdiction. I doubt Tyson is stupid enough to stay with that car. What a surprise to come up with Simpson. Every jurisdiction east of the Hudson River has put a hold on the man.

"You two can stand down, get a good night's sleep, and we'll meet here tomorrow morning and wrap this thing up. Good job, both of you. Damn fine police work," Elmo said, reaching into a desk drawer for one of his filthy cigars.

"Has anyone heard from Potter? Is he okay? The last I heard is he was about to make contact with Tyson, but he wasn't at the mansion. We might still be able to use him to get information along Franklyn Street." Dorsey liked the young detective and worried that in all the excitement that he might have walked into a hornet's nest.

"I had him stand down," Elmo said. "He'll be here in the morning. He's known now along Franklyn, so it is possible he could ferret out something. We'll sleep on it."

"You goin' home?" Dorsey asked Adams.

"I know I should, but I also know we're missing something. Got an idea rompin' and stompin' in that pea brain of yours?"

"Everyone's a comedian. I want to take a nice walk up and down Franklyn Street, maybe pop in on Dusty, maybe see if Shorty McGuire knows anything, see what's rumbling.

"I'm also gonna call El Charo and see when he can come up here and start work with us on finding out exactly why Tyson is involved with Whistler and company. We know why he's involved with Fernandez and Simpson, that's guns and drugs, but why with Whistler? That's just really buggin' the hell out of me."

"Franklyn Street's your country, Dorsey. I'm as out of place there as you would be in the ladies' room. I'm gonna buy a box of fine wine, some chocolate, and curl up with my computer. See you in the morning. Don't be dragging a load of beach sand in this time," she laughed, ducking a light cuff to the shoulder.

"Speaking of that, oh Sergeant of mine. How's that leg? Did she even tell you she got shot, Serious?"

"Shot?" he shouted. "What the hell are you talking about? You got shot?" he asked Jenny.

"It's just a nick. The EMT deputy cleaned it up and put some stuff on it. It's fine," she said, rubbing her leg a bit. "A couple of glasses of fine California wine will ease the pain, boys. I learned that from Maglio, you know."

~ ~ ~

It was hard to do, but Tyson was doing his best to stay within the speed limits as he drove south. He spotted a couple of patrol units parked on the side of the highway as he neared Moss Landing, and when he pulled into the little seaside enclave, there were more. "Nothing like being obvious," he snarled to himself, finding a parking lot where he could turn around.

He was back on Highway One in minutes, heading north. "I need to find someplace to hide for a couple of days, let things cool down, then make a run for Brazil. Who the hell can I trust?" he said, again and again. He was a hot potato in Santa Cruz and the city, couldn't go back north of the city, and now, couldn't go south. He finally realized that the only man he could go to for protection was Dusty at The Bar.

Most people thought Whistler was the organization's northern California head, but those in the syndicate knew it was Dusty that spread the orders from Fernandez, and it was Dusty that could make you safe. It was also Dusty who could call in the goons.

Tyson gave just a moment's thought to calling the skipper of his boat and realized there would probably be half a dozen cops on board. "How did those bastards know to come to my winery? How did they know that Fernandez and Whistler would be there? How the hell am I going to get at my money if they even knew about my boat?" He drove along with traffic despite the fact he wanted to go as fast as that little Ford would go. That late winter storm everyone was waiting for came on shore with strong winds and icy rain, making the trip even more somber.

"Whistler's entire operation is gone," he muttered. "The Mole, Mason, Wilson, Jimmy Torrance, everyone, and no more safe houses, either." He was a long four hours getting back to the city where he parked the Ford behind The Bar, after calling Dusty and making sure it was safe.

"You find me a place?" is all he said, slipping in the back door, dripping from the intense rain blowing in the gale. "There were cops all over the boat. Cops all over the highway. I gotta hide, Dusty."

"Yeah, you're more than hot," Dusty said, "and I hope you didn't lead a bunch of cops in here. I been expecting that ape Dorsey to come flyin' through that door any minute. You know Bill Smith?"

"That creepy pawn shop guy? Yeah, I've met him. Never done business with the creep."

"He's got a set of rooms over the Circle the Wagons Pawn Shop. Nothing fancy by a long shot, but there's a kitchen, bedroom, and bath. Smith says you can stay there as long as you want."

"Okay, I'll take it. Get me there, and get me some broad can take care of getting food and cooking it. I can't be seen Dusty. Pick up a throw-away cell phone for me too, so I can keep in touch with my money and stuff."

Tyson had hundreds of thousands of dollars hidden in various off shore accounts from the import-export business, had plenty of available funds from winery accounts and was astute enough to know that every dollar had federal investigator's eyes on it. He had to get enough to fund his way out of the country, and soon.

"You'll be safe, Cam, I'll see to it. I got a few guns sprinkled around the neighborhood, keeping an eye out for Dorsey. That bastard has got to be put down, and hard. If he shows up, he'll be seen, and one of those guys will get him.

"You and me, now, we're gonna take a little walk, so pull your hat down, pretend you're half in the bag, and we got about a block or so to go. It's plenty dark, so keep your head down." They walked out into the raging winter storm, wind howled, and rain splashed their faces. The sidewalk, shiny and wet, glimmered from neon signs that splashed their colors across the spectrum.

~ ~ ~

Dorsey parked the Caddy a discreet two blocks off Franklyn Street and took a long walk through the storm into the foul neighborhood. "Tomorrow's New Year's Eve and I haven't even thought of party," he mused. "Where the hell did Christmas go? I didn't get nothin'," he moaned. "Tomas is supposed to come up. Hope he gets here damn quick." It was cold, with a nasty wind blowing off the bay, not a star in the sky, with clouds so low they hid the tops of the fabled hills of the city.

Storms that blow in from the deep waters of the North Pacific Ocean were cold, losing degree after degree as they flowed around the Gulf of Alaska and bored down on California's rocky north coast. Even the rain had a taste of salt to it, and within just a short time, gutters would flow as small streams. Summer thunderstorms were delightful as they cooled the hot temperatures, but wild winter storms were frightening, seemingly filled with danger and cold, icy death. They would find fishing boats ripped from their docks, stacked on nearby beaches, come morning. Dorsey shivered getting out of his official car for the long walk to The Bar.

"Getting my Caddy back will be my Christmas," he said. "I scream at rookies to watch their back, keep their eyes open, and I get jacked late at night. Damn me," he snarled to himself.

Dorsey had that leather jacket zipped to the top, his battered old fedora pulled down tight, gloved hands deep in his pockets, and watched the neon lights of the city dance and sway through the wet pavement and concrete. A drunk staggered out of one of the many saloons, fell to his right and bounced off a concrete wall, into Dorsey, who tried to push him away.

The drunk turned into a ferocious hunk of two hundred pound mean, first punching Dorsey in the gut, just low enough to have severe effect, then flashing a spring-loaded knife. The blow was fierce, and Dorsey had to struggle to keep his feet under control. The knife swished close enough to his eyes that he felt the air across his face, and he fought, with gloved hands that wouldn't work right, to get at his forty-five, now inside a fully zipped heavy leather jacket.

He danced out of the way of another slashing move by the attacker, got his jacket unzipped, felt the knife across his left arm, cutting the jacket but not going deep enough to find his flesh. "Damn you," Dorsey cussed, his ribs in flames as he swung a heavy right into the man's body, knocking him back but not down.

The man hesitated for half a second and Dorsey drove his right foot into the man's groin, followed by a left hook that straightened him right up. Dorsey finally got that jacket opened and had a grip on that huge revolver. It flashed out of its leather and barked, once, twice, and the man was flung back into the concrete wall, the one he bounced off of at the start of the fight.

He slowly slid down the wall, dropping the knife, his eyes as wide as saucers, but slowly losing the light of life. In a final jerking movement, the big man slumped dead onto the concrete sidewalk, adding his blood to the grime and grit in the gutter. "Damn me, why do I always kill the people that could give me the good intel," he chuckled, moving up against that wall and taking a strong defensive posture.

"Oh, that hurts," he moaned, rubbing his ribs. He leaned up against the wall, getting his breathing under control, wincing with every breath. It took several minutes for the big man to catch his breath, find that he hadn't been cut with that knife, and was seriously pissed that now, for sure, he would have to buy a new jacket.

"A one man attack?" he mused. "I don't think so," and he kneeled down to check for some kind of ID. It wasn't long and he heard the sirens coming up from the local, Twelfth Precinct. "Shots Fired, Franklyn Street", is a common phrase on the phone at the precinct house. Dorsey had his ID out and held high as the first unit slid to a stop.

"Well, Sol Dorsey," the big sergeant said, stepping onto the sidewalk. "Imagine that. Whatta we got, Dorsey?"

"Guy came at me with that switch-blade there, damn near got me, too. Just look at my jacket," he said, holding it up. "I don't think I recognize the fool. Just look what he did to my jacket. Damn, first a bullet hole, now a damn huge old slash.

"You better put in a call to Captain Elmo. This is probably connected to what we're working on. You seen him before?" he asked the sergeant.

"We've spotted half a dozen hired guns up from Los Angeles in the last few days, Dorsey. Bet this is one of them. Sound reasonable?"

"Yup." Dorsey opened the man's coat, Sergeant Hansen alongside, and pulled a wallet from an inside pocket. "That's a nice little thirty-two tucked in his waist, Sarge. He would have had me if he'd used that instead of the knife. Wanted to be quiet, eh? Guess he won't make that mistake again."

"Let's see who he might be," Hansen said, not smiling. He went through the hit man's jacket and pants, pulling his wallet. "Seems he could be any one of these three," he chuckled, pulling three different driver licenses from the wallet. "Different names, different states, same picture. Looks like you may have wiped out half of LA's bad guys, Dorsey, with one shot."

They heard Captain Elmo respond to the call and waited for him and the forensics people to show up. "To hell with it," Dorsey finally said. "Tell the good captain that I'll be at The Bar and he needs to join me when he's through here. "I'll write your report when I've had at least a barrel of cold beer, Hansen," he chuckled, zipping the leather coat up and heading down the street. "I don't think I've had a beer since Christmas," he snarled, "or a pizza." He fought the strong wind, felt the cold rain on his face, and thought of how many ways he might find to kill Dusty when he got to The Bar.

~ ~ ~

"Looks like the place is getting a little class," Dorsey chuckled, taking a seat at the end of the filthy bar, so he could see the whole scene. "When did you start working here?" he asked Harold Stacks, a retired cop from Chicago. "Where's good old Dusty?"

"Started about half an hour ago, Dorsey," Stacks snarled. "Don't want no trouble, Dorsey. Whatcha drinkin'?"

People were being nice when they said Stacks was a retired Chicago cop. His retirement came at the request of several newspaper opinion pieces following a nasty take down of some gang members, with allegations that Stacks may have been acting as a member of a rival gang. It was reported that Stacks was responsible for four of the five deaths during the arrest. No charges would be filed, the chief decided, if Stacks left city employment.

Word on the street was that Stacks made a single phone call to Los Angeles and was on Fernandez' payroll before he had his Chicago Police credentials handed over.

"Had enough trouble today, Stacks, don't need any more." Dorsey had it in the back of his mind that Stacks had been sent to work with Dusty as a representative of the Chicago group. *I wonder what that fool would say if I mention that we arrested Lemuel Simpson earlier today? Bet he'd shit his pants,* he chuckled. "Give me a shot of Jack, better make it a double, and a schooner of ale, and be ready to back that up, too. Been a hell of a day, so far."

That whiskey should ease the pain in my ribs and beer might fill a void in my stomach. Where would Dusty have gone right in the middle of his shift? Where, and maybe more importantly, why and with whom?

Dorsey sat quietly, sipping some Tennessee sour mash and some cold beer, watching the crowd and letting his mind run free. "From the looks of things, nobody wants to be out in this rain. You'll be busy Stacks," he chuckled.

Stacks was probably working security when Dusty was called out, eh? I wonder where that little pimp went? I think I'll just plan on spending some time right here, sippin' and grinnin'. Two men he'd never seen before came in, nodded to Stacks, and went into the card room at the back of the saloon. He watched one of the men reach out and turn the lights on before the door swung closed.

So, there's no game going on, but two guys go in there anyway he was thinking, understanding that there was a not-so-secret way out the back, a means of evading the cops or possible hit on the tables. *I wonder if they're Chicago or Los Angeles? I sure as hell can't ask Stacks,* and he had to chuckle lightly at the thought. *Now would be a good time for Serious Elmo to show up, with a couple of the guys from the precinct.*

The cold rain and high wind was driving more and more people into the saloon giving Dorsey a chance to simply sit and watch. "This case has been going in different directions from day one, with Starr Baby getting shot by two people at different times, and a conspiracy of incredible size simply blowing itself apart, and now, one, apparently lone, conspirator needing to get away. How many people are around to help him, how much of his money can he get his hands on, and what kind of illegal plan were all those people working on at the winery?"

Dorsey realized that he was murmuring, not just contemplating, coughed slightly, downed the beer in front of him and called for another. *So, who killed Starr Baby? My guess is it was a hired gun, probably connected somehow to the Santa Cruz conspiracy was the initial killer and the one who spoke to me. The other shooter? Probably connected somehow to The Mole. Or, Janice Wilson was the second shooter.*

And all of this brings me back to Dusty, who may be trying to help Cameron P. Tyson, who is connected to the Los Angeles syndicate, and probably to Chicago. Where the hell are the feds? Everything we've seen screams for some kind of RICO response from the FBI, there should be ATF people involved, and surely DEA.

The only ones we've run into are local FBI agents making a mess of things. Somebody somewhere hasn't done their job is the only thing I can think of. Looks like old Clem is going to take this one down without federal help.

His thoughts were interrupted when the doors of The Bar were flung open by Serious Elmo and three uniformed officers barging through. The Bar got very quiet, with some patrons doing everything not to be seen, others trying to scoot into some kind of safe zone. Elmo walked straight to Dorsey, nodded and said, "Follow me," and motioned the officers to spread out among the patrons.

"Looking for two strangers, Dorsey."

"Card room," is all Dorsey said, and the door was splintered as two uniforms burst through, service weapons drawn, cocked, and ready for action. "Watch Stacks," Dorsey said, pulling that big forty-five, and aiming it in the general direction of the bartender. "He's one of them."

It took less than three minutes, one shot fired, and two bloody strangers were hauled out of the card room in cuffs. One officer nursed a split lip, and another was bleeding from a bullet wound in his forearm. "This bar is closed," Elmo said loud enough to rattle the bottles. "Everybody out, now. Stacks, not you. Out, damn it, and I mean now," and he swatted at a drunk sitting at the bar.

The uniforms shoved the two prisoners into chairs at a cocktail table and Elmo motioned for Stacks to join them. "Hey, hands off," Stacks howled. "I ain't done nothing, what do you think you're doing?" The unformed officer moved him from behind the bar and shoved him into a chair.

"Shut up and sit nice and quiet and I won't hurt you," the officer said. Stacks used some four-letter words but quieted right down when Captain Elmo took a step toward him.

Dorsey took a look out the front door and found two or three uniformed officers stationed on the sidewalk. "Watch for Dusty. If you see him, grab the little prick and bring him in to us, and anyone who might happen to be with him."

He joined Elmo at the bar just as the Captain of Detectives lit one of those horrible black cigars. "Damn, that's foul," Dorsey said, bringing a big smile to Elmo's face. "You must have learned something after I left," Dorsey said. "What's with these two?"

"Fernandez imported some of his people and I guess Simpson must have brought some in with him. It seems the meeting that took place at Tyson's was supposed to be here in the city tomorrow. These guys are protection.

"That meeting at Tyson's wasn't planned. It just came about, and if you hadn't found out that Whistler was there, we would not have caught those guys." Captain Elmo had a nice smile on his face telling the story to Dorsey. "Now, let's see which one of these upstanding citizens wants to live through the night, shall we?"

Elmo directed the wounded officer to get the hell out of there and get to the hospital, and had the other two take defensive positions and be ready for anything. He walked to the front door and brought two officers in.

"You guys stay in the card room. There's a secret door so stay alert. You want to start the questioning, Sol?"

"Do not say proper procedure, mein capitan, or I'll walk," Dorsey snarled, but couldn't hold it, and grinned as he pulled a chair up opposite one of the gangsters.

18.

D usty ushered Tyson into the Circle the Wagons Pawn Shop and nudged him through the main aisle to the counter. Both men were sopping wet from the short walk up the street. The rain had shards of bitter ice driven by winds breaking the speed limit on that foul street.

"Bill, meet Cam Tyson, your new border. Cam, this is Bill Smith, and you can trust him. Let's see the apartment, Smith," the diminutive man said, the authority stemming from Fernandez and company, not Dusty's size. Smith led the way back out into the storm's fury and onto Franklyn Street. There was a street-side doorway between the pawnshop and the tattoo parlor that Smith unlocked.

The door opened to a steep stairway that led to the second floor. There was a single un-shaded light bulb about half way up, losing its battle against darkness, and a single bannister on the right side.

Smith handed the key to Tyson. "You will want to keep this door locked at all times, Mr. Tyson. There are four small apartments up here," he said, leading the troop up the squeaky stairs. "You'll be the only tenant. The key to yours is on the table by the rocker." Bill Smith, like almost everyone in the city knew the reputation and background of Cameron Tyson, had read numerous news reports of his winery, of his world travels, and stood in awe of the large man.

Smith thought he might also see a way to Tyson's good side, even more than providing him with this safe house. He knew a man who knew his way around money, knew how to hide illicit transactions, and knew how to get hold of that man. *I just need a slight opportunity to be able to talk with Tyson and move into his way and style.*

"I want you with us, Smith, when we go through the rooms," Tyson growled. "There are a number of people that are intent on seeing me out of the picture, right at the moment. This better not be a setup."

"No, sir, no," Smith stammered. "Just follow me," and he continued up the stairs. "Better lock that door, Dusty." At the top of the stairs there was a long hallway with a single light bulb at about the halfway mark. The carpet was old and worn through to the wood beneath in many places, wallpaper hung loose along the walls. There were two doors on each side and Smith walked to the back right and opened that door.

About halfway down the hall, Tyson stopped and started chuckling softly. "These rooms up here, you said there were four. I suppose they normally would be rented at a specific amount of money for, what, a half hour at a time? Am I putting four working girls out of business, Mr. Smith?" And he laughed right out loud.

"You see to it those lovely ladies of the night have other accommodations. Will you do that for me, Mr. Smith?"

"Oh, yes, yes, I will," Smith said, wondering why it was important for the girls to be taken care of. Dusty hadn't said anything about Tyson paying for this safe room he was providing. *Maybe this guy's just a jerk.*

Smith pulled one of his cards from a shirt pocket. "This is my number, Mr. Tyson, and I want you to call me if you need anything. I'll see to it you have food and drink, and anything else."

"That's good, Smith. See if you can round up an excellent international accountant who can access my money," he said, sarcastic as hell. "I have got to get out of this country, and fast."

"There is a telephone in the apartment, and there would be no reason I can think of for any police agency to even know about it. Feel free to use it." Smith had his mind working hard, remembering that he had just met a man named Charles Baron. *I'll get Baron hooked up with Tyson and get the rest of that grand,* he thought with a big smile. *Maybe this Tyson will also slip me a grand.*

The three men walked into a small living room with one window opening onto an alley and a building's blank wall. Tyson surveyed his new home, didn't even try to compare it to the one he fled, and walked into a small bedroom, saw the kitchen just off the living room, and opened the door to the bathroom, finding a toilet, sink, and shower. "All the comforts, eh?" he snarled.

"What the hell?" Dusty said as they heard what sounded like a hundred sirens screaming down Franklyn Street. "I gotta get back to The Bar," and he started out the door.

"Wait for me," Smith said. "Follow us down, Mr. Tyson and lock that door when we're out. I gotta get back to my store. I'll call you as soon as we know what's going on, so you won't worry." Tyson just nodded back to him, reaching under his jacket to make sure his pistol was where it was supposed to be.

~ ~ ~

Tyson's mind was in a turmoil as he found himself in a position never contemplated. There was no organization, there were no people he could contact or depend on. He had a large shipment of guns arriving within days and they would be lost, there was money to be distributed and no one left to distribute, on the one hand, or collect on the other.

I've never been this alone in my life, he finally understood. *My entire life is over with, my winery, my home, all my associates, my money, gone, and I'll be sleeping in a whore's bed tonight, alone.* His arrogance and feelings of superiority had left him with no contacts within either the Los Angeles or Chicago organizations. He distained having relationships with other than the head men, both of whom were now in custody, and knew no one would attempt to come to his rescue.

In Tyson's current state of mind he only thought of getting out of the country and save as much of his money as possible. He seemed to think he could still conduct his business. He was vulnerable and wasn't fully aware just how vulnerable.

~ ~ ~

Dusty dashed onto the street, saw Smith duck into the pawnshop, and started toward The Bar. "Looks like whatever is going on is a block or so away. I got those Los Angeles guns scattered around, so maybe one of 'em found Dorsey." He had a pretty good smile on his face as he walked toward his saloon. "What the hell happened," he wondered, "at Tyson's place? Fernandez, Whistler, and Tyson were supposed to meet here tomorrow, why did they meet at Tyson's today, and with no security?

"Damn fools had me set up security all over the place except where they were. No wonder they got their asses caught."

One minute Dusty was just a means for the Los Angeles organization to keep up with what was going on in the north, and then there was no Los Angeles organization. "It will take months for Tijuana to reorganize, months for Chicago to go through that agonizing period where someone comes out the strong man." Dusty was talking fast as he made his way back to The Bar. "I gotta find out what the hell happened."

The storm was battering the little man about and he got as close to the buildings along the street as possible. He didn't care about the storm, didn't care that Tyson was alone in a filthy little apartment, only cared about what his plans should be. "This city is wide open right now. Whistler and the so-called Bayshore Gang are out of business. This is the chance I've been waiting for. I have contacts because of what I did for Fernandez, for Simpson, and for Whistler." The little pimp was smiling through the storm, making plans for the rest of his life. "I gotta make some calls, get Tijuana on my side first, then have Stacks get me some juice in Chicago. How sweet it is," he kept saying. "So nice."

~ ~ ~

Bill Smith headed straight for his office in the back of the pawnshop and found the card that Baron had left for him, and punched in the numbers. He had a smile on his face just minutes later, following a rather quick conversation with the banker. *Tyson's gonna like this, if Baron can really do what he said he could.* He could only hope that if he was able to help Tyson that he would be repaid with money and maybe a position in the organization. It didn't dawn on the stupid man that since Tyson was hiding in a filthy apartment upstairs there probably wasn't an organization in the first place.

~ ~ ~

Dusty spotted a group of the southland guns standing in an alley and walked up to them. "You know what brought the cavalry out?"

"Heard a shot," one of them said, "and then all the sirens. Sounded like a couple of blocks over. We got people over there."

"It might have been somebody being stupid, or it might be one of your men found Dorsey. Here's what I want you to do, go into my saloon, and if Dorsey is in there, Stacks will give you a nod. Just walk into the card room in the back, next to the hallway, and hang out in there for a few minutes. If Stacks don't signal that Dorsey's there, just come on back here.

"There's a secret door, right behind one of the dealer's chairs you'll see a sign that says 'No Guns', and a hidden button in the middle of the O. Just push it and the door unlocks. After ten minutes or so, be ready to back me up. I'll use the regular back door, the one our deliveries come through.

"Dorsey's a bastard, shoots first, doesn't ask questions, so beware of the man. You're here to protect me and what's left of the organization, and to get rid of Dorsey. Don't let us down," Dusty was talking as if he was running the organization, now that Whistler, Fernandez, and Simpson were in custody.

Dusty was terrified of Dorsey, and was actually shaking as he talked with the hired guns. He watched them saunter down the street and into the bar, and shook even more when they didn't come back out. "That ape is in there, sure as hell. Those two and Stacks should take care of that problem." He was well down the alley and working his way through garbage and other refuse toward the back door of his saloon, and missed seeing Captain Elmo and half a dozen officers come to The Bar.

Dusty also was still a full half block from the back door of the Saloon when the officers splintered the card room door, but he did hear the gunshot. "They're going after Dorsey," he cackled, still picking his way toward the back door. It took him several minutes to get there. He stood very quiet at the delivery door, trying to pick up what was happening inside. There was just that one gunshot, and he had to believe it meant the end of Simon Sol Dorsey.

Then he heard the voices and knew Dorsey had taken his two men out of the picture. Instead of sneaking in the delivery door, he crept up to the secret door that led into the card room and tried to hear what was being said.

~ ~ ~

Dorsey looked around the barroom and then at the group around the table. "One of you fine outstanding officers needs to be in that card room, also. Those two might need some help. There's a secret door that's hard to spot," Dorsey said. "In the no smoking sign, there's a button in the O, but if Dusty or somebody else needs to get in, that's where they would come. Be prepared to shoot whoever comes in that door, because they won't be one of ours."

Elmo said. "Dorsey and I can handle these little cream puffs. "Officer O'Brien, my friend, take Mr. Stacks here behind the bar and have him pour Mr. Dorsey and I a nice cold beer." He smiled, chewing and puffing that black cigar. "And you," he pointed at one of the three men at the table. "Are you the shithead that shot my officer? Are you?"

No answer was forthcoming and Dorsey started toward the guy. "No, Mr. Dorsey, proper procedure first," Serious Elmo smiled.

The back up uniform slipped into the card room just as Dusty slid that secret door open. He spotted them, spun and took off down the alley at warp speed, the three officers on his tail.

"O'Brien, shoot these three if they make a move," Elmo yelled. "Dorsey, out the back, I'll grab men out front and we'll nab that weasel. Go, go," he howled, storming out the front door of The Bar.

He motioned two officers to go inside the saloon, grabbed two more to run with him to that alleyway. "Dusty's trying to run," he said at a full sprint down the slick sidewalk, "and Dorsey's on his tail along with back up." There was an alleyway about the halfway mark of each block that joined perpendicular alleys allowing for garbage pick up and deliveries to the various businesses.

Captain Elmo made the turn into the first alley they came to and ran smack into Dusty, knocking the little fool on his back. Dusty tried to reach inside his coat and Elmo kicked him in the head, knocking the pimp out cold. "Good move, Serious. Did you learn that at the academy?" Dorsey said, coming onto the scene. "I gotta remember that one."

"Stuff it," Elmo said, trying to hold in a smile. "Read this prick his rights when he comes to, and book him," he said to the first officer on the scene. They were walking back to The Bar quickly, more to get out of the storm than anything.

"Take Stacks and the two at The Bar downtown, but just hold them. Make damn sure they're in separate cells and can't talk to each other. O'Brien is inside the saloon, so we'll leave him there until we get some forensics people in there."

Elmo and Dorsey walked in the saloon. "I want this place vacuumed one end to the other when the crime scene boys get here," Elmo said. "Dusty is the contact man for the Fernandez gang and maybe for Simpson's Chicago people as well. There's information in this saloon somewhere that will bring this screwed up mess to an end.

"I'll meet you back at the office, Dorsey. Call Sergeant Adams and have her meet us there. We might find out where Tyson is. It appears that he didn't show up at the boat. You think he might be hiding around this garbage pit somewhere?"

Before he could answer, Elmo's cell buzzed and after looking at the display, motioned Dorsey to hold up. "This is Captain Elmo," he said, "Stand by for just a moment." He motioned Dorsey to follow, and motioned for the uniforms to stay with the group.

Elmo walked into the card room with Dorsey, and put the cell phone on speaker. "You're on speaker, Detective Potter, and I'm with Dorsey. Say again what you just told me."

"Right, Captain. I was in the shower when the phone rang so wasn't able to answer. I got this message when I checked after. The call was from Bill Smith, the owner of the Circle the Wagons Pawn Shop saying that he had Cameron Tyson staying in one of his upstairs apartments. He said Tyson was looking for someone who could help him access some of his offshore money so he could get out of the country.

"He asked if I was capable of doing that? I haven't returned his call knowing you have to make the decision on this. How should I handle this?"

"Wonderful," Dorsey said. "This is even better than what we thought of first. I wonder where that apartment is?"

"Listen to me close, Potter," Elmo said. "Call your man and tell him you don't want to talk too much over the phone. Arrange a meeting with Smith, but don't push hard on meeting Tyson until after you meet with Smith. Be very positive about what you can do for Tyson when you meet with Smith.

"When he tells you where to meet him, call me immediately and Dorsey and I will set up our plan.

Good job, Potter. Damn good job," and he clicked off. "You better call Sergeant Adams, Sol, and get her down here right away. Let's not say anything about this in front of Dusty and those other pukes."

Dorsey had a scowl on his face that would kill a rat as they walked back into the bar area, and pulled his cell out, settling into a chair near Dusty. "Sergeant Adams," he snarled into the phone. "Dorsey here. Need your expertise at The Bar on Franklyn Street. Bring the lead filled gloves and the sparkler. Elmo and I have Dusty and a few Chicago hoods in custody, but they ain't talkin'. Hurry."

Dorsey had a grand smile on his face when he tucked the cell into his pocket. "What's the matter, Dusty? You remember what a sparkler is, don't you? You want to tell him, Stacks?"

"Go to hell, Dorsey."

"Well, just so we all know," Dorsey said, "in some circles a sparkler is called a cattle prod. It's a little electrical toy that's fun to jab at people unwilling to talk."

"We probably won't need that, Dorsey," Elmo said, "but it's good to have it handy just in case." He had a smirk on his face, and used his radio to call for a wagon. "We need to get these guys tucked away, safe and sound.

"Thompson, you will take these gentlemen to the holding cells. Each in a separate cell where they can't communicate. I want you to keep very close watch on our little friend, Dusty. He can be a slippery dude. We're holding them for their own protection, so no booking procedures, no phone calls, and no visitors. The wagon will be here shortly." He gave them all a hard look, and said, "Shoot first, Thompson, don't hesitate."

Elmo turned to Dorsey. "How long will it take Sergeant Adams to get here, Sol?"

"She was already in bed, so half an hour at least. Come over here for a minute," he said, walking back toward the bar. "I didn't want to say this in front of those guys," he whispered. "Circle the Wagons Pawn Shop is about two blocks down the street and there are apartments above the shop that Smith rents out to some of the working girls. One of them would make for a fine safe-house."

"All right," Elmo exclaimed. "As soon as these guys are hustled out of here, we can set up a plan. Tyson will get the surprise of his life, I hope."

"He was pretty surprised when we busted up his little garden party earlier," Dorsey laughed. "I'm sure the word has spread to any other Chicago types that Dusty might have spread around that it's over. They're probably lined up at the airport now, getting tickets to the Windy City."

Serious Elmo had his cell phone in hand giving commands to his department. "I don't want anything on the radio," he said. "Until we have a command post set up, no radio chatter, use cell phones. We'll eventually use a tactical frequency, but not yet. Get the SWAT teams organized and have their commander meet with me here." He looked around the bar, and said, "We'll use The Bar for our CP, so get everything we need down here along with people, and be discreet this time," he snarled.

Dorsey got contemplative for a minute. "Dusty must have had some influence on projects around here, Serious. This is where all the people collected. I found The Mole here, I found Wayne Morris here, apparently Tyson ran here, and we find Chicago gunmen using The Bar for headquarters. Even though Fernandez and Simpson are in custody, it's a bet they won't dime anyone out, but Dusty might, and he just might be in a position to talk about some real higher ups."

"We'll work on that after we get Tyson," Elmo said. "I'll also bet our forensics people will have answers for us, too."

"We've got to get back to thinking like we were before we nabbed Fernandez and company. There's somebody, or group, that is controlling all this money, Serious, and it's probably those bankers that Tyson was working with. We need those names." He sat quiet for a minute, then pulled his cell phone and punched in some numbers.

"Where are you?" he said when the call was answered. "Good, then I'll see you soon. Have you got people looking at Tyson's finances?"

"I have people holding the man's personal accountant, Dorsey," El Charo said. "We have some good information so far, and more sure to come. I'll be with you shortly and we can talk."

19.

"**M**r. Smith, sorry I missed your call. This is Charlie Baron."

"Mr. Baron, thank you for returning my call. As I said in the message, Mr. Tyson is almost desperate to get at his money and get out of the country. I haven't told him about you, yet. I didn't want to until I had a chance to talk to you. Are you capable of getting into off-shore accounts and get money into Mr. Tyson's hands?"

"I'm sure I can, Mr. Smith." *This is the turn of events you just can't anticipate. If I can get to him I can make Captain Elmo aware of where he is, and get a full handle on his finances.* "Are you at the pawnshop? I can come by and you can bring me up to date."

"That would be best, yes, and yes, that's where I am. There are lots of cops in the neighborhood, there has been sporadic gunfire, so be careful. I'm not sure what's going on, but it's at least two blocks away."

"I'll be there in half an hour or less, Mr. Smith. Goodbye." Potter clicked the cell phone off and called Elmo on his regular cell. "Smith is at the pawnshop and I'll be meeting him within the hour, Captain. How do you want me to play this?"

"Nice and slow, Detective, nice and slow," Elmo said. "I'm setting up a net around Smith's block. All those buildings seem to share common walls and the rooflines are similar, so it may take some time to get men and equipment into position. Everyone will be aware of who you are, but even so, try to keep some distance between you and Smith, and you and Tyson if you are able to get into his area."

"Tyson has offshore accounts that he is unable to access, Captain. He apparently thinks that it takes a special person to do that. I would assume that he has a regular accountant on his payroll that took care of such matters." Potter tried to stifle a chuckle.

"What's so funny?" Elmo snarled.

"Well, Captain, if that accountant has discovered that the entire organization is either on the run or in custody, I would bet those accounts have already been accessed and passage has been booked to some exotic land far, far away." Elmo had to chuckle as well, picturing a skinny little accountant with a gleeful look on his face buying tropical clothing for the adventure.

"The AG already has people working on that, Detective, but good thinking."

"Also, Captain, it means that Tyson has been so sure of himself that he doesn't feel it necessary to maintain full control of his resources. He's so arrogant he doesn't believe anyone would have the audacity to take him down. It would make it better if I could wear a bug."

"You're right, it would make it easier, but we'll play it out the way it's dealt. Get down to the pawnshop and try to keep us advised, but be damn careful. These boys play for keeps, Potter. Has Smith already contacted Tyson about you and your abilities?"

"He said he wanted to wait until I got there. I'm sure he wants in on the action."

Elmo snickered his agreement with that, and clicked off. "Potter's a good man," he said to Dorsey. The two then continued getting men and equipment moved into the area. "Along with the pawnshop, there's a tattoo parlor, and the entrance to the apartments is between the two shops. All of the buildings along that stretch of Franklyn Street are two stories with flat roofs, and most of the buildings have common walls," Elmo said, looking at a map provided by the city planning department.

"We'll need men across the street, at both levels and the roof, and men on the adjoining buildings, Serious," Dorsey said. "I wonder which of those apartments Tyson is in? If I was setting him up to keep safe, I'd put him in a rear apartment."

"Yeah, that makes sense. According to this, there are two apartments on each side of a long hallway, so we'll need men in and on the building behind Smith's. I've already called in SWAT Dorsey. We need more men than I have, and we need their expertise. Let's hope Potter can give us that kind of time."

The crime scene squad arrived and started their sweep of the saloon. "I'm sure we fouled the scene some, Derrick," Elmo said as they sealed off the back rooms. "If you can get me names of some local contacts I will buy dinner for your crew, their wives, children, and pets," he said, only half in jest.

"Does the health department know about this place? This garbage pit should have been condemned a long time ago. Bio-hazard from the start." Derrick's reputation among crime scene squads in the Golden State was top notch and Elmo was certain if there were information on Fernandez or Simpson he would find it.

Sergeant Adams arrived at about the same time as SWAT Commander Sandy Summers. "Now there's a sight," Elmo said. "A cowgirl right out of Hollywood and a fully combat ready police lieutenant. Get a picture of that Dorsey."

"You'll never change, Elmo," Summers laughed. "Let's talk."

Summers had been with the department for well over ten years, was nearing forty and had the body and stamina of a twenty-year-old. He was known to swim for miles along the surf line outside the bay and then run in the soft sand to return to his towel. Sun bleached blond hair, cut surfer style, deeply tanned, Summers had the eye of every woman he met every day of the year.

Sergeant Jenny Adams' smile was electric as she said hello. "It's nice to see you again, Lieutenant. Had any hand-to-hand with the sharks off-shore, lately?" Summers just laughed, nodding hello to another beautiful woman.

~ ~ ~

Dorsey and Adams sat down at a table. "What have you done now, Dorsey, to bring out a SWAT team? I can't let you out of my sight for a minute," she snickered.

"We may have Tyson bottled up, and we do have Dusty in custody. Were you able to get any kind of read on what exactly Tyson was up to?"

Jenny opened her notebook and paged through until she found her spot. "Because of the Santa Cruz development scheme, Fernandez and Simpson, at Tyson's recommendation, decided they needed some secure way to handle the huge amount of money that would be flowing. That's how Tyson got involved in the Santa Cruz project, not through Whistler or Torrance.

"As near as I can figure, Tyson managed to come up with a plan to take over the Goode and Sons operation. The bank deals in considerable mortgage notes and real estate loans and would be a good place to hide their operation. I have the names of the board of directors of the S&L and I sent them to Bascomb in Sacramento to see if he could match them with anything from Fernandez, Simpson, Whistler, or Tyson. I'm expecting an answer at any time now."

"Good work, Jenny. Sometime between now and sunrise I expect to see El Charo come flying through that door over there, so we'll have AG help and hopefully he'll have more information on Tyson's finances." Dorsey spent the next ten minutes briefing Jenny on the situation and she brought him up to date as well.

"Let's give that list of bank names to Derrick," Dorsey said.

They walked into the office where Derrick was going through Dusty's files. "Don't you dare touch anything, Dorsey."

"Not on your life, Lieutenant. Want to give you a list of names. These fine gentlemen make up the board of directors of the Goode and Sons bank here in the city. If one or more of them crop up in your files there, you scream for me and Sergeant Adams."

"Will do, Dorsey. You used to be a customer here? You should be dead, you know. The EPA should be notified of this filth."

Dorsey and Adams snared Elmo and brought him up to date on the S&L situation. "So our little murder investigation has blossomed once again," Elmo said. "How many tentacles does this case have?"

"We've done pretty good, Serious," Dorsey said. "We shut down a development scheme and government fraud operation in Santa Cruz, we shut down a winery up north, we've closed one of Franklyn Street's more notorious saloons, and we're about to put a well known savings and loan bank out of business. On top of that, Fernandez and Simpson are out of the picture, the Bayshore Gang is kaput, and we still have no idea on earth who shot Starr Baby."

"You just never quit, do you Dorsey? Either Derrick or the AG boys will match some of those S&L names and we'll shut that project off, and all we have to do now is keep Detective Potter safe and capture Mr. Tyson."

Dorsey's cell phone went off and he checked the incoming. "El Charo, where are you?"

"I'm about fifteen minutes out, Dorsey. Where do I find you and that beautiful sergeant Jenny?"

"There's an all-nighter at Third and Pacific Avenue. We'll meet you there. We have lots to talk about, Tomas."

"You two make damn sure you keep me advised," Elmo said. "If Derrick can tie any of your bank names to Dusty's operation or anything else, I'll let you know. If I need you, don't screw with me, Dorsey."

"There's a time and a place and sometimes I know one from the other, Serious," Dorsey joked, taking Jenny Adams by the hand and the two walked out the door, chuckling.

"Mr. Smith, good evening. That's quite a ruckus a couple of blocks away. Have you heard what's going on?" Potter walked into the pawnshop after getting a full review of what was going on from Captain Elmo. "On top of all that, there's a fire near the docks."

"This section of town gets a little noisy," Smith said. "Glad you got here as fast as you did. It's a different picture we'll be discussing from our earlier meeting, Mr. Baron. I just got off the phone with Mr. Tyson."

"Different in what way, Mr. Smith?"

"When we talked, Tyson was putting together some kind of big deal that has apparently fallen apart. I don't know any of the details." Potter knew those details intimately and was waiting to see how Smith would bring up Tyson's current situation, living in a whore's apartment over the pawn shop, penniless, and needing lots of help.

"Bring me up to speed, Smith. If Tyson is in trouble, needs the kind of help I can bring, then let's move forward."

"I talked with Mr. Tyson after I called you, and he wants to meet with you just as soon as possible. The man's in terrible trouble, Mr. Baron. He is unable to retrieve any of his resources, apparently some are frozen by different agencies and some are in overseas accounts."

"Those resources frozen by law enforcement might just as well be written off, Smith. The accounts that he has overseas might be accessed based on where they are located and what the account type is. Without knowing those two things I wouldn't be able to give an answer.

"It's best that I meet with Tyson so I can get the proper information to get into the accounts." Potter was glad to hear that apparently the attorney general had frozen all the accounts that Tyson might have inside the United States. *I wish I had that information,* he thought, watching Smith pull out his cell phone. *Knowing how those accounts were set up would give me names that could be followed. Getting Tyson taken down will close one big open highway full of heavy weapons, heroine, meth, and cocaine.*

"Thank you, Mr. Tyson. Yes, I'm handing the phone to Mr. Baron now," Smith said, offering his cell phone to Potter.

"This is Charles Baron," he said with considerable authority.

"Mr. Baron, I'm Cameron P. Tyson. Are you familiar with the name?"

"Yes I am. I've read a lot about you and your winery. I believe I may also understand the unhappy situation you've found yourself in. I believe I have the knowledge and background to help you.

"You must also understand that the kind of help I offer simply can't be done over a cell phone. We should do this in person, face to face."

"Yes, I understand that. Have you done any work for Mr. Smith?"

"No, I haven't, but Smith knows about many of the people I have done work for and the kinds of work involved. International finance is intricate, Mr. Tyson, and in some countries there are conflicting laws within provinces. You would have to be right alongside me feeding me personal information in order to access accounts and make transfers.

"Turning various transfers into ready cash at your disposal would take a bit of time, but I assure you, I can get it for you."

"Alright, Baron, put Smith back on the line." Potter handed the cell to Smith with a smile and a positive nod of his head. Smith didn't say anything, just put the phone to his ear. "I'll walk down to the outside door, Smith. Knock twice only. Knock once and I'll shoot, three knocks and I'll shoot. Got it?"

"Yes sir, Mr. Tyson. We'll be there in just a couple of minutes." He put the cell phone back in his pocket and motioned for Potter to follow him. The storm was still raging, a gale blowing in from the deep Pacific Ocean, driving heavy cold rain onto those poor souls having to be in it.

Potter and Smith, bundled against the elements stepped out of the pawnshop and walked the short few feet to the doorway that separated that shop from the tattoo parlor next door. Smith thought he heard Tyson at the door and knocked twice. It was just moments and the door was opened just a crack. Tyson saw Smith and Potter and opened it enough for the two to slip inside. Tyson closed and locked the outside door immediately.

Tyson had a small semi automatic pistol in hand and motioned the two men upstairs. "You lead, Smith. Mr. Baron, nice and slow, you follow. We'll talk when we get to the rooms."

~ ~ ~

"Tomas," Dorsey said as the two men hugged their welcome. "Damn I'm glad to see you."

"Same-oh, same-oh, Dorsey my friend," and he stepped back, turning to Jenny Adams. "And my favorite detective sergeant in the whole world," and he flung his arms around her, lifting her completely off the ground, spinning around once before setting her back on the concrete sidewalk. "Nice weather you have up here."

The three walked into a well-lit twenty-four hour diner, about half filled with late nighters, most half filled with booze and other chemicals. "Grab that big booth back there," Dorsey said as they shook themselves out of soaking wet coats and jackets. "We can talk and get some damn food in us. I swear I haven't eaten a good meal since that steak you burned at Jim Racine's."

They settled in, the waitress was there instantly with a pot of coffee that she just left on the table for them. "Bring me one platter of everything on the menu," Dorsey said, getting a scowl. "Okay, don't get 'em in a wringer, sweetheart. I want ham and eggs, bacon and eggs, and biscuits and gravy, with a side of sausage and eggs. And, my little angel," he smiled, flashing those brilliant emerald eyes at her, "I'm not kidding."

She was writing furiously, not really sure if he was kidding or not. "And you, dearie?" she said, giving Tomas Gutierrez a huge smile, "What would you like, if there's any food left in the kitchen."

"Get me a rib steak, very rare, three eggs, and lots of fries, pretty lady," he cooed, giving her a full Spanish Royal's smile.

"I'll just have toast and coffee," Jenny Adams said, thinking she could snatch fries from Tomas and maybe a slice of bacon from Dorsey.

The waitress was probably about forty-five or so, a bit on the skinny side with short bobbed bottle blonde hair. As she sashayed her way back to the kitchen, dreams of Tomas's smile and Dorsey's eyes danced in her thoughts. "Big tips comin'," she hummed, "Comin' my way tonight."

Dorsey's cell phone buzzed and he saw a text message from Elmo. "Potter's in Tyson's apartment." He put it down on the table and told the other two what it said. "This part of our program could end quickly," he said, "but there's lots more to do. You start, Tomas, then we'll debrief you."

"Clem says again, thank you both for a job well done. We have frozen all the Tyson assets we know of and I have a print out of all the accounts. Those names should be very helpful in wrapping up the Fernandez and Chicago elements of open and abusive crime, my friends," he said.

"Our agents are swarming various banks and other money institutions around the state, and finally, the FBI has caught up and are moving on Chicago and Miami. Tyson was a loner in this, Dorsey. He dealt with anyone that would pay him, and because of that, he doesn't have an organization as such. He has no one to turn to right now, and no money to run with."

"We think he has money in off-shore accounts," Jenny said. "We have an agent with Tyson right now. Tyson wants to access his foreign accounts and do the splitsville on us. We have SWAT units surrounding his hidey-hole, so he should be in custody before we're through with this feast you two ordered.

"Those names though, Tomas, they're going to be the key. We're sure that Tyson, and maybe Fernandez and Simpson were planning to take over that savings and loan, mostly to handle the huge amount of money that would have been flowing out of the Santa Cruz land development plot. That bank plan may have been what the quick meeting was all about at Tyson's winery. We just accidentally found out about it, and spoiled the party."

"Which savings and loan?" is all El Charo asked.

"Goode and Sons," Dorsey said.

"They are all over our list," Tomas said, pulling his cell phone out and hitting a speed dial button. "Susan, my love, my heart's desire, it is I, Tomas Gutierrez with good news for you and yours. It's Goode and Sons. Close 'em down." He turned and smiled at the waitress as she arrived with the first of several loads of breakfast. "We'll be gathering in bankers and other money types for weeks, I think.

"Between what Tyson had in the fire, guns and narcotics, and some shenanigans with the winery, the AG investigators will have enough to get most of them to retirement age by way of court appearances alone.

"By the way, Dorsey, Inspector Holloway has been asked if he would like to participate in California's state worker early retirement plan. He indicated that he had been contemplating such a move for some time, and that now would be just about right."

"Humph," Dorsey said. "One more bureaucrat down and out. What is it that creates such an attitude in some people? A bureaucrat syndrome? Is it in their genes? You're lucky, Tomas. I don't see that problem in the way Clem Bascomb runs his agency."

"It's there, Dorsey, but Bascomb is weeding many of the worst out. It's a form of job protection, I guess, but it really has no place in police work. Bureaucratic nonsense can get people killed or injured." He looked around the table, and continued. "I'm not sure there's a difference between a bureaucrat and a politician, eh, and we know there are politics and politicians in police work."

Even with all the conversation spinning about the table, the two big men were plowing their way through a hefty breakfast bill, and the waitress was even asked for more toast and more fries at least once. She kept the coffee pot on the table filled, and told all her other customers just how much had been ordered. "Gracious," she said, taking a quick sit-down in the kitchen.

"General Bascomb is paying for breakfast," El Charo said, "but you, Mr. Dorsey are leaving the tip." He handed the bill and a state of California credit card to the worn out waitress, and Dorsey handed her a fifty-dollar bill, flashing those wonderful eyes at her. Her eyes fluttered, her smile was bright as dawn, and she swayed toward the cash register.

"I think we can eat in here anytime we want," Jenny smiled, slipping into her London Fog winter coat. "Let's go wrap this program up. No more messages from Captain Elmo?" she asked Dorsey. He just nodded no as they walked back into the raging New Year's Eve storm, it now being well after midnight, and now, the day before a new year.

20.

a s the three men walked into the small living room of the apartment above the pawnshop, Cameron Tyson tucked his semi-auto pistol into a holster on his belt. "Didn't want any surprises," he smiled, motioning for everyone to take a seat. "Smith tells me you may be able to access some of my personal accounts, Mr. Baron. How will we go about this?

"As much as I would like to listen to this, I have to get back to the store," Bill Smith said. "This is a big weekend for pawn shops. I'll lock up."

"No, Smith," Tyson said. "I'll walk you down and lock up. Sit tight, Mr. Baron, I'll be right back."

Potter took the time to look about the apartment, wanted desperately to contact Elmo and knew he didn't dare. "Interesting," he mumbled. "I don't see anything to indicate that Tyson is planning to do some international bookkeeping. Maybe he has everything memorized." He also spent time understanding the layout of the apartment, working on how to keep Tyson from escaping on the one hand, and putting him under arrest on the other.

I could just shoot the SOB, he chuckled, *but the captain would not appreciate that. That locked door and only the one window makes this a bit awkward.*

Tyson returned quickly and sat down on the sofa next to Potter. "So, where to we begin, Mr. Baron."

"I'll need to know which countries you have accounts you want to access, which banks, and the various codes and passwords the banks gave you. The process isn't really difficult, just a bit tedious because of various languages and protocols."

Tyson's face clouded over and he squirmed some in his seat. "I don't have that information, Baron. I would have to get that from my bookkeeper, in Santa Rosa. I'll give him a call."

"I wouldn't do that, Mr. Tyson. The chances are very good that if your accountant hasn't already accessed your accounts and booked passage to Tahiti, the feds have him in custody or under surveillance. I can probably work around most of that problem." He knew it was important to make this process lengthy, keep Tyson tied down, and give Elmo and Dorsey time to storm the castle.

Potter had a notebook and pen out and asked Tyson which bank he should go after first. "The one in the Bahamas probably has the most money, and I will need most of it," Tyson answered, oblivious to his total ignorance of accounting.

"Which bank would that be?" Potter asked, almost softly. *I don't think this man has a clue where his money is.*

"Is there more than one? I didn't know that. What will we do?"

"How about Switzerland, Mr. Cameron. Do you have an account in a Swiss bank? A bank that you know the name of?"

"Well, yes, there's a Swiss account, but Mr. Kemper always took care of all my resources. Rollo Fernandez would know, maybe. He would transfer funds, but I guess that won't help, either."

Potter was working on a plan to allow Elmo access to the apartment, but needed to get word to him without raising any kind of alarm with Tyson. "Maybe we could get lucky," he said. "Let me try to contact your Mr. Kemper. If he's not in custody, he might be able to give me enough to get into one or more of your accounts.

"I'll have to use a bit of subterfuge, Tyson, in case the feds have his phone tapped. Calling on my phone, however, won't give away that it's you calling, or where we are calling from. What's Kemper's number?" Potter had his cell out and on, hit speed dial to Elmo, and tapped in, "I'm in. monitor." And clicked off. Tyson was fumbling around in pockets and finally found what he was looking for.

"Here's the list of numbers I use for him," he said, handing Potter a piece of note paper with three phone numbers scrawled on it. "He would be home, I would think, this time of night," Tyson said.

"If not on a Jumbo Jet or incarcerated, I would think so," Potter mumbled, taking the paper and punching in the numbers. *I'll do everything I can to stay on this line as long as possible and hope that Elmo can zero in on where we are.* Potter watched Tyson closely as he heard the other end of the phone answered. He also caught a distinct second click just before Kemper said hello. *Good, he is under arrest and they are expecting this call.*

"Mr. Kemper, you don't know me, but you need to listen to what I'm about to ask of you. I'm with Cameron Tyson. Are you alone? Are you able to answer some of Mr. Tyson's questions?" Potter held his hand over the phone and asked Tyson, "Would he know your voice?" Tyson shook his head yes.

There was a hesitation from Kemper, which told Potter that the feds or somebody was telling Kemper to say he was alone. He came back on the line, sounded frightened, but said, "Yes, I'm alone. May I speak to Mr. Tyson?"

Potter held the phone out to Tyson and said, "Say just enough so that he knows you're with me. Then I'll get down to business with the man."

"Kemper, this is Tyson. Mr. Baron is a friend and needs some information from you. Please give him anything he asks for."

"Are you okay, Mr. Tyson? I've been worried."

"I'm fine, Kemper. Here's Baron," and he handed the phone back to Potter.

He used my name twice and if this is the AG's people listening, that word will get back to Dorsey right away, Potter knew. "Okay, Kemper, this is Baron. Tyson needs to access some of his accounts in the Bahamas and in Switzerland, and doesn't have the names of the banks, the account numbers, or his codes and passwords to do that.

"I'm ready to write, Kemper. Start with the banks in the Bahamas. Tyson's a lucky man to have someone like you that he can depend on."

"I don't have that information, Mr. Baron. You have reached me at home, and I keep all of that information locked in my safe at the office." It sounded very much like Kemper was reading a script, which surely meant he was in custody and they were waiting for a phone call like this.

"Are there any of the various accounts that you access often enough that you have memorized the information?"

"We use the Bahamas' accounts most often, but all I would be able to do would be to transfer funds to another existing account. I don't know if Mr. Tyson would be able to access anything."

Potter was feeling lucky here, knowing he was keeping the line open, hoping all the forces gathering around could locate where he was. He also was watching Tyson, seeing him get more and more agitated as the conversation dragged on. *He might think he's a big man, but right now, Mr. Cameron P. Tyson, I own you. I hope he does get his balls in a twit. I would love to punch his lights out right now.*

"Okay, Kemper, give me what you can remember, and if you can get to your office, get the rest of the information and call me right back. It's very important that we get Tyson enough money to get out of the country quickly."

"All right, Mr. Baron," and again Potter was sure that Kemper was reading from a script. "I'll get down to the office right away and call you as soon as I get that information put together."

Kemper hung up as Potter was saying goodbye, and the undercover detective looked over at Tyson. "Not much to go on, Tyson, but we can try." Tyson wasn't looking at Potter, seemed to be almost in a dream, an angry, nightmare type of dream.

"Get what you can, Baron. Was he lying to you? Is he planning to take my money and run off with it? How soon can I get my money?"

It never occurred to him that his own accountant would run off with his money until I brought it up. He must live in a cloud somewhere. "Well, let's just see what we can do," Potter said with a smile.

~ ~ ~

Dorsey, Adams, and Gutierrez found their way back to The Bar and Captain Elmo who was in an animated cell phone discussion with someone. "That's what we've been hoping for," he said, waving to Dorsey and gang. "So Potter is with Tyson and you're with Kemper in Santa Rosa, and you have access to Potter's cell." He paused for a minute, listening, then continued.

"Right, Investigator Sanchez, Tyson is in an apartment here in the city, we have the building surrounded. There's no way he can escape, but we want him alive if at all possible. Potter is with him, hopefully still armed, and may be our only way of taking him.

"The apartment is second floor, at the rear of the building. There is a back door, but it was closed off, and Tyson's apartment only has one window, at the back. Keep me posted, Sanchez and I'll do the same for you." He clicked off and looked over at Dorsey.

"About time you got your ass down here," he snarled.

"We've been busy," Dorsey smiled back at Serious Elmo. "Any way to get information into Potter? Don't want to get that boy in some kind of crossfire. What do we know so far?"

Elmo calmed down and spent the next ten minutes bringing Dorsey, Gutierrez, and Adams up to date on what was going down. "By the way, Gutierrez," Captain Elmo said, "It's nice to meet you. What are your people planning?"

"Most of the people I have down here are paper cops, Captain," he said. "I have two men going over those names your crime scene people came up with. Goode and Sons had a branch in Santa Cruz, and interestingly, in Santa Rosa. Tyson's accountant has an office in Santa Rosa."

"I just found that out," Elmo said. "I was talking to one of your investigators, a man named Sanchez, who is with Tyson's accountant right now."

"If there is some way to get word to Potter, I believe he could end this thing immediately," Dorsey said.

"I do too," Jenny Adams said. "Tyson's an arrogant blow-hard, Captain, and while he might be in fair shape, what I saw of Potter, he could take him out in a heart-beat. If we could start a diversion, and if

Potter knew we were going to, he could use it to take Tyson out. It would sure be better than trying to storm that damn building."

"That's why you're a sergeant," El Charo said, aiming those bright eyes and easy smile right at her. "Yeah, that's a good plan. You said," he said to Elmo, "that you were talking with Sanchez at Kemper's office?"

"Actually at his home, but yes, I was talking with Sanchez. What's on your mind?"

"Your man is waiting for information from Kemper, so a call back would be expected. Your man would answer the phone and Sanchez would give him all the info. We could start a big ruckus, catch Tyson's attention, and your man would do the rest."

"I think that's a good plan, Captain," Dorsey said. "I'll get into the pawn shop and make sure that idiot, Smith is out of the picture, and Jenny, you and El Charo take out the tattoo guys, there are two of them."

"Remember what Shorty McGuire and Potter told you about that security dude at the pawn shop, Dorsey," Jenny Adams said. "You take El Charo with you, and I'll take Captain Elmo with me. Once those people are out of the picture, have the SWAT boys start making all kinds of noise, and we'll let Potter finish off Tyson.

"I sure want to do the interrogation of that feller," she said.

She was still pissed that she didn't get to take on Janice Wilson one-on-one, and remembered how Tyson ran out on everyone. "He's afraid of his own shadow, and we'll get all the names of everyone he's ever worked with when I get him hog tied."

Elmo was already on the phone to Santa Rose, passing on the information to Investigator Sanchez. "Very good. Now, once my people have taken out the pawnshop and tattoo parlor, I'll buzz you and you can buss our Mr. Baron. Any problems that you see?" He nodded at the phone, nodded at Dorsey, Adams, and El Charo, and clicked off.

"We have time for a cold beer before the fireworks?" he said. "This would be a good time for us to retire to Maglio's, but I guess that wouldn't work, eh?" and he laughed along with the bunch.

He got serious again and started pacing. "We've been pretty damn lucky so far, and I want it to stay that way." He was watching Adams and Gutierrez slip into flack jackets and check their weapons. "How about you, Dorsey? Better get some Kevlar on."

"You don't have anything that fits, Serious. El Charo has his tailored. I'll be fine. There shouldn't be any gunfire. We'll just walk in, a couple of guys looking to sell a watch and take Smith and his bodyguard out."

"I hope you're right," Elmo said. "Better get going, Sanchez can't call until these jobs are done. Let me get together with Sandy Summers and make sure SWAT will be ready for their part of the show."

Dorsey was thinking about the entire caper, starting out with a phone call from an old prostitute friend in trouble. *This thing just gets a little bigger each time we solve part of it. Senator Bargetto's safe, the Santa Cruz conspiracy is done with, Fernandez and Whistler are out of business, and now we're faced with international banking and the owner of a winery dealing in weapons and drugs on the world scale.*

It's a good thing the California Attorney General is a hotshot, cuz the damn feds would not have stopped the Santa Cruz deal or saved Bargetto's reputation. Now, let's save Potter's ass, put Tyson in irons, and let the paper cops trace out the rest of the criminality run wild.

Dorsey wore just the hint of a smile as he and El Charo made their way up Franklyn Street through rain and hail driven by gale force winds. There was danger in every shadow on a night like this, every doorway could shield an assassin, every car that passed could carry a gunman. The hulking men saw and checked every shadow, every doorway, every passing car.

"According to Shorty, this security dude is pretty damn big, Tomas," Dorsey said. "Probably pumping iron in various prisons over the past twenty. Those guys are usually damn strong but not necessarily fast or agile. We need to make sure Smith can't get at a phone to alert Tyson or anyone else. How do you want to handle it?"

"We're assuming the place is still open, Sol," Gutierrez said. "Have you been inside the store?"

"Yup, many times. Good thinking, there. I'll make the move on Smith, he'll probably be in his office and you take out the gorilla. Let's do our best to keep as quiet as possible."

Adams and Elmo headed for Summers' CP to let him in on the plan and would then take out the tattoo parlor. Summers had his operation in an empty storefront on the block just north of Franklyn Street, with easy access to the pawnshop building.

~ ~ ~

There was very little foot traffic due to the fierce storm blasting in off the coast, and Dorsey was hoping that might mean very few people in the pawnshop. The two big men made the turn into the doors with iron bars, and found the place almost empty. There were two men at the counter, looking at a coin display and Dorsey recognized one of them as being a member of the SWAT unit.

A young couple was looking at rings, and that was about it. The gorilla was standing near the ring couple and Smith was watching the coin guys. "What do you want, Dorsey?" Smith barked, catching the eye of his security man.

"You," is all Dorsey said as he vaulted the counter, landing on the shop owner. El Charo immediately moved on the Gorilla who responded with a switchblade knife about six inches long. From under his jacket, Tomas pulled a short handled quirt and whipped it across the big man's face, drawing blood and a scream.

Gutierrez followed that up with a leap into the air, driving both booted feet into the man's middle, knocking him back into a large display of computers, televisions, and records, all of which tumbled on top of the big security ape. Tomas drove his right fist into the man's bloody face twice, rolled him onto his stomach, ripped his arms behind him, and had cuffs on that fast.

Dorsey had Smith pinned to the floor and cuffed all but instantly, while the two SWAT officers stood with their teeth in the mouths, finally responding with big smiles. "Anything we can help with?" the larger of the two said, laughing and pointing. Dorsey smiled getting Smith to his feet.

"Better get back with Lt. Summers," Dorsey said. "It's starting. You might help my buddy get that giant up onto his feet. Damn he's big." Dorsey walked over to where the couple was standing, terrified that he would attack them.

"It's alright," he said. "All these guys are cops. Looking for a wedding ring?" They nodded a shaky yes, eyes as big as quarters. "These are nice ones. See, the lady's ring had a few diamonds, and man's ring has some heft to it." He took the girl's hand and slipped the ring on and handed the other ring to the young man. "Good. Now, get out of here and stay away. It's going to get very dangerous very soon. Skedaddle now," he said, shooing them off and out the door.

"Mr. Smith isn't going to like that," one of the SWAT officers said.

"Mr. Smith is going to jail soon, so it won't really matter. Harboring a wanted criminal will get him off the streets for some time, I think," Dorsey said, pushing Smith toward the front door where officers were waiting to hustle the men out of the area.

"Do you think Tyson heard any of that racket?" Dorsey asked. "Let's just assume not."

~ ~ ~

Captain Elmo and Sergeant Adams left Summers' CP and fought their way through the storm to the front door of the tattoo parlor. Adams pointed at the door located between the pawnshop and the ink joint. "That leads to the apartment where Tyson and Potter are right now," she said, waiting for Elmo to open the door to the shop.

"Hi. Nasty night to be out walking," the young girl behind the counter said. She looked to be barely twenty and skinny as a rail. She was wearing shorts and a tank top with almost every square inch of skin covered in multi-colored representations of animals, people, symbols, names, and numbers.

"It is," Jenny said. She had looked at drawings of the inside of the store back at The Bar and put it together now. There were two cubicles behind the counter where the work was done. Both had colored cotton sheets as drapes for doors. One was apparently occupied and the other empty. She remembered that off to the side was an office and a small room, probably a bathroom.

Jenny took hold of the girl's wrist, and using the pressure point had her on her knees instantly. Before she could utter a sound, Jenny rolled her onto her stomach, put her knee in the tiny woman's back and whispered, "Quiet as a mouse, now."

Elmo was at the closed curtain in two steps, ripped it open and found a large tattooed man working on a very naked, very well developed young lady. Elmo's nine-millimeter pistol was aimed at the ink artist and he said, "Police, don't make me shoot you." He motioned the naked lady to get out of the room, and told Mr. Artiste to "assume the position, Rembrandt."

Jenny held her weapon on the man while Elmo frisked him of a heavy bladed skinning knife and a little semi-auto pistol. "Typical artist's equipment, I believe," Serious Elmo said, putting the cuffs on the man. Let's go," he said, whirling the guy around and shoving him toward the door. "Come on, sweetie, you too," he said as Jenny got the receptionist on her feet.

"Where'd our naked lady get off to?" Jenny asked.

The receptionist nodded toward the bathroom and Jenny walked over and threw the door open. "Come on, out. You can finish getting buttoned outside. Move it or go to jail with your friends."

Naked lady scampered out the door and Adams and Elmo escorted their prisoners to a couple of cops waiting outside. "Easier than I thought," Elmo said. "Let's get back with Summers, find out how Dorsey did, and get the rest of this operation underway. How many tattoos did that skinny little girl have?"

"How much fun are you going to have with Dorsey talking about finding a naked lady in the tattoo booth?"

21.

Potter knew there was an operation being planned, hoped that Captain Elmo recognized his message, and needed to keep Tyson occupied until the walls exploded with cops. They heard rustling sounds earlier and Potter and Tyson tensed up. "Sounds like Smith is throwing a party down there," Potter quipped. "Have you done business with him before?"

"He's provided some information from time to time but doesn't really have the contacts that I need for the importing. He is able to get the word out once in a while when we find one of our buyers has backed out on a deal."

"If Kemper is able to get to his office and get that information, it might still take me a while to get transactions moving," Potter said getting back onto the program. Getting information was most important, and in a nonthreatening way.

"What exactly is his position, Mr. Tyson? Just in case Kemper's detained somehow, and the feds must be swarming your operations, are there other people we can go to?" Potter could get names of important people in Tyson's organization as a co-conspirator, so to speak, where Tyson might not ever give them out in interrogation.

"I have connections with other organizations, Mr. Baron, but I have always relied on Mr. Kemper to handle my finances. He's the chief financial officer in my winery business, and I depend on him to handle most of my deals with my busy export/import operations."

Tyson was a beaten man, Potter saw, and he wondered just how somebody who gave the impression of being rather smart could be so stupid about his money. "You're saying that the only person in the world that can access your bank accounts is Kemper? As it is, it appears your winery is out of business along with your import/export company, but you have hundreds of thousands, if not millions of dollars that only one man knows how to retrieve? Amazing."

Potter was trying his best to give Tyson the impression that he could be the best friend Tyson has ever had. "Let's see if there is anything I can do, and hope that Kemper is able to get us some of the information we need. Does Kemper have employees, or did you have one of your people work with him?"

"He had two women in his office, one was just the receptionist, but the other, a Ms. Ford, I think. Sally Ford, a real mouse of a woman, but I guess she knew her numbers. I never wanted to work with that woman, just too sure of herself. Nasty temper, too."

"Would she have access to any of the international information? That is, if we can find her?"

"I would guess she might know at least some of the information you would need." Tyson got contemplative for a minute, letting his eyes roam about the dingy little apartment. "There are some men who might be able to help, but I'm not sure how to get hold of them."

"Who would that be? Maybe I could source some contact numbers."

"They are on the board of Goode and Sons, a loan type bank," Tyson said. "We've been working hard to get control of that bank and these two gentlemen have been most willing to help. They have been instrumental in allowing me to transfer some of my various moneys through accounts that cleanse them. They do know my Bermuda accounts, and some in South America."

He wrote the names on a piece of paper and handed it to Potter. *You just kissed about twenty years away, my friend,* Potter said to himself. "Let's hope at least one of the men has a personal telephone listing," Potter said. "Are there any other names you might think of?"

Before Tyson could answer, Potter's cell buzzed and he checked the incoming. "It looks like Mr. Kemper is able to get back to us," he said. That got the briefest smile across Tyson's face.

"Go ahead, answer it," Tyson said, surprising Potter. The detective was sure that Tyson would want to verify that it really was Kemper. Potter held the phone up to his ear and pushed the answer button.

"This is Baron," he said.

"Are we on speaker?" the voice said.

"No, Mr. Kemper, we're fine, just waiting for your call back. Were you able to get to your office?" Potter gave Tyson a nice smile, but knew the voice on the phone was not Kemper's.

"Good, my name is Sanchez, I'm with the AG's office. Captain Elmo is about to unleash a lot of noise, gunfire, banging on doors, sirens, and yelling. Use that anyway you can and that will be followed by the SWAT coming to you in force."

"Thank you, Kemper. Yes, I'm ready, let me have it." Potter looked at Tyson and gave a thumb's up gesture. "I'm going to write down all the info as Kemper gives it to me." He moved a sheet of paper and reached inside his jacket for a pen, lifting his nine-millimeter semi-auto out of its holster, but not bringing it out.

"Okay, Kemper, start reading off those numbers." He made a big display of writing down some numbers and letters, even asking for repeats. Sanchez had hung up when Potter talked about writing down numbers. "Are there any others that will help Mr. Tyson? These are for the accounts in The Bahamas? Good, good, Kemper.

"Be careful now, there are feds all over. We wish you well," and he clicked off, not asking if Tyson wanted to say anything. He wondered just exactly what kind of show Captain Elmo had planned, but kept his hand closed over the pistol, waiting for his chance.

I've got names of the big boys at the bank, and with the attorney general's investigators working on the books, that bank will be out of business soon. Damn, he remembered something he should have done. *I should have brought up Sally Ford's name to Sanchez. Hopefully he knows about her.*

~ ~ ~

"Lieutenant Summers, this is Inspector Sanchez. Detective Potter has given the go-ahead, so start your operation now. Don't hesitate."

"Ten-four, Sanchez," Summers smiled. "It's a go, boys," he said into his radio, "let 'em know we're in town." Into his cell phone he said, "Thank you, Inspector, we'll keep you informed."

There was immediate chaos on the square block surrounding the Circle the Wagons Pawn Shop and Tattoo Parlor, with multiple gunshots, sirens blasting, men running up and down Franklyn Street, and the sound of tires squealing on wet pavement.

"What the hell?" Tyson bellowed, jumping up from the sofa and running toward the front door of the apartment. He had a semi-auto in his hands that fast, his eyes as wide open as they would go. Just as at the mansion, Tyson was ready to run just as fast as his tennis playing legs would take him.

He deserted Fernandez and Simpson, Whistler and Wilson, he would not hesitate to desert Mr. Baron. Only one problem, there was only the one doorway out, and it led down that long stairway and onto Franklyn Street. Tyson left the apartment doorway and raced into the kitchen, no window there, raced into the bedroom, and tried to force the window open. It wouldn't budge.

Potter stood up, had that heavy pistol in hand, but still under his coat, and watched Tyson's panic. Tyson came out of the bedroom at a run, eyes wild with fright, and again raced to the front door and out into the hallway. He spotted the doorway at the opposite end from the stairs and made a run for it. Potter didn't know the door wouldn't open, and moved into the hallway, ready to stop Tyson, with a fist or a bullet, whichever was needed.

The door was bolted shut, and Tyson, leaning hard against the door heard the front door downstairs being splintered by a battering ram. Sweat covered the man's head, as much from fear as exertion, panic flooded the system. Tyson wasn't even aware that Baron/Potter was in the building.

Get hold of yourself, man. There must be a way out, I must get away. I must get my money. With the thought of money came the realization that Potter was in the apartment.

Tyson ran toward Potter, waving the pistol, screaming for help. "You must protect me," he cried. "I'll give you anything, you must protect me."

That gave Potter the edge he needed, and he stepped up to Tyson, grabbed the pistol and wrenched it from the now all but helpless fool, and pulled his own gun. He shoved the barrel into Tyson's mouth and snarled, "You're under arrest, Mr. Tyson," and slammed the man across the side of the head with his own gun. He reached inside his coat and pulled his police ID and badge, and held it high over his head as the first SWAT units raced down the hallway.

Potter had the pleasure of escorting Tyson, reduced to a crying, whimpering, ruined man into the hands of officers on the street below. It was Dorsey who was the first to grab Potter and congratulate him. "That undercover crap is kind of fun, isn't it?" he snarled, giving the young detective a big hug.

"Two-thirds of the detective division of this fine city on the scene, no less than fifty uniformed officers roaming about, and two full SWAT squads in full battle dress, and one junior detective takes the bad guy out." Despite the words, Captain Elmo was smiling as he shook Potter's hand. "Good job, Potter. I guess we'll keep you around for a while. That's the DA's loss."

It was close to ten in the morning before things were somewhat back to normal along Franklyn Street. The storm continued to rage with howling wind driving barrels full of rain and sleet into every face, every crack and crevice in every building.

Elmo called his people together at his CP, once known as The Bar. "We've had a hell of a couple of days and it isn't over, boys and girls. I will expect detailed reports on my desk before four O'clock today, and don't plan on taking tomorrow off."

"It's New Year's tomorrow, Captain," Jenny Adams said.

"I know it is, but the Attorney General wants to wrap this thing up and not lose suspects in the process. According to Detective Potter, Tyson's finances were controlled by this Kemper feller and one other, a woman named Sally Ford. There are millions of dollars floating around out there somewhere and General Bascomb wants them under his control. Potter was able to elicit the names of the big boys at the bank, and they're the ones that have been driving this little problem we've been working on.

"The sooner we get our reports done, the quicker we are finished with our interrogations, and the sooner Bascomb gets all that, the better. Be in my office, eight sharp, tomorrow morning." There was a bit of grumbling but not much as everyone started putting their gear together, finding coats and hats, and thinking about the long reports that would have to be written.

"I don't know about anyone else, but I could handle four full growlers of Maglio's fine ale right now," Dorsey said. "Who's with me?" No one was injured in the stampede that followed.

~ ~ ~

"This meeting is now unofficially called to order," Captain Serious Elmo snarled, looking around the table. There were several pitchers of beer scattered around, with pint schooners in front of Elmo, Dorsey, Adams, Potter, and Gutierrez. Maglio was humming an aria from Verdi, putting together more than one platter of crab enchiladas. "This will have to do as our Christmas and New Year office party, I'm afraid," Elmo chuckled.

"Beats the hell out of tea and scones," Jenny Adams said. "Anyone want to guess who will be taking over the Bayshore Gang? Who will Tijuana pick to take over the Los Angeles operation, and will Jersey now be able to control Chicago?"

"What you just pointed out, dear lady," El Charo quipped, "is what's called job security. I was talking with Sanchez a few minutes ago, and our Mr. Kemper was picked up just in the knick of time. He had already transferred several hundred thousand dollars from Tyson's accounts to a couple that he already had. It seems the little accountant was also stealing from the boss. Sanchez said his bags were packed and his tickets purchased.

"We got him just in time. Anybody understand why there was no security at the Winery?"

"The same reason Tyson didn't know how to access his own money. Stupidity coupled with arrogance. Everything goes to the paper cops and armies of attorneys," Dorsey said.

"I'm not one to get Maudlin, but I do want to take half a second here to say how much I appreciate the fine job you guys did," Serious Elmo said. "We'll never know who the two shooters were at Starr Baby's apartment, but without them, we would never have taken down an international weapons dealer, busted up a huge land fraud conspiracy, taken dirty politicians to the ground, or captured leading syndicate boys.

"And it's all because of stupidity. We always say, follow the money, but the criminal mind makes it a little easier. I'm just going to say, follow stupid, there, he'll lead us to the money."

After all, folks," Dorsey said. "It's what keeps us in business." Even Maglio had to laugh at that one.

Thank you for reading.

Please review this book. Reviews help others find New Pulp Press and inspire us to keep providing these marvelous tales.

If you would like to be put on our email list to receive updates on new releases, contests, and promotions, please go to NewPulpPress.com and sign up.

After such knowledge, what forgiveness?

About the Author

Johnny Gunn the pseudonym of a retired journalist. He says, "I ditched college after the first year by being hired by a radio station as a full time reporter, and the merry-go-round never stopped. I can't say I miss the day-to-day newsroom chaos, but I love allowing my characters to do their thing, not have to report someone else's thing." During his fifty-year career, he published and edited *The Nevada Observer.com*, an internet news magazine; *The Virginia City Legend*, a weekly newspaper; and *The Rhythm of Reno*, a monthly entertainment magazine. Also he was senior editor at *AdNews*, serving the advertising gurus, marketing mavens, and other creative souls in Nevada.

NewPulpPress.com